ALYSOUN

Susanna M. Newstead

A DEAD FALCONER.
AN ABDUCTED WOMAN.
AND A BOAR SPEAR.

ALYSOUN

A SAVERNAKE NOVEL

ISBN-13: 978-84-125953-9-0

M

MadeGlobal Publishing

For more information on
MadeGlobal Publishing, visit our website
www.madeglobal.com

Cover Design: Tai Lago

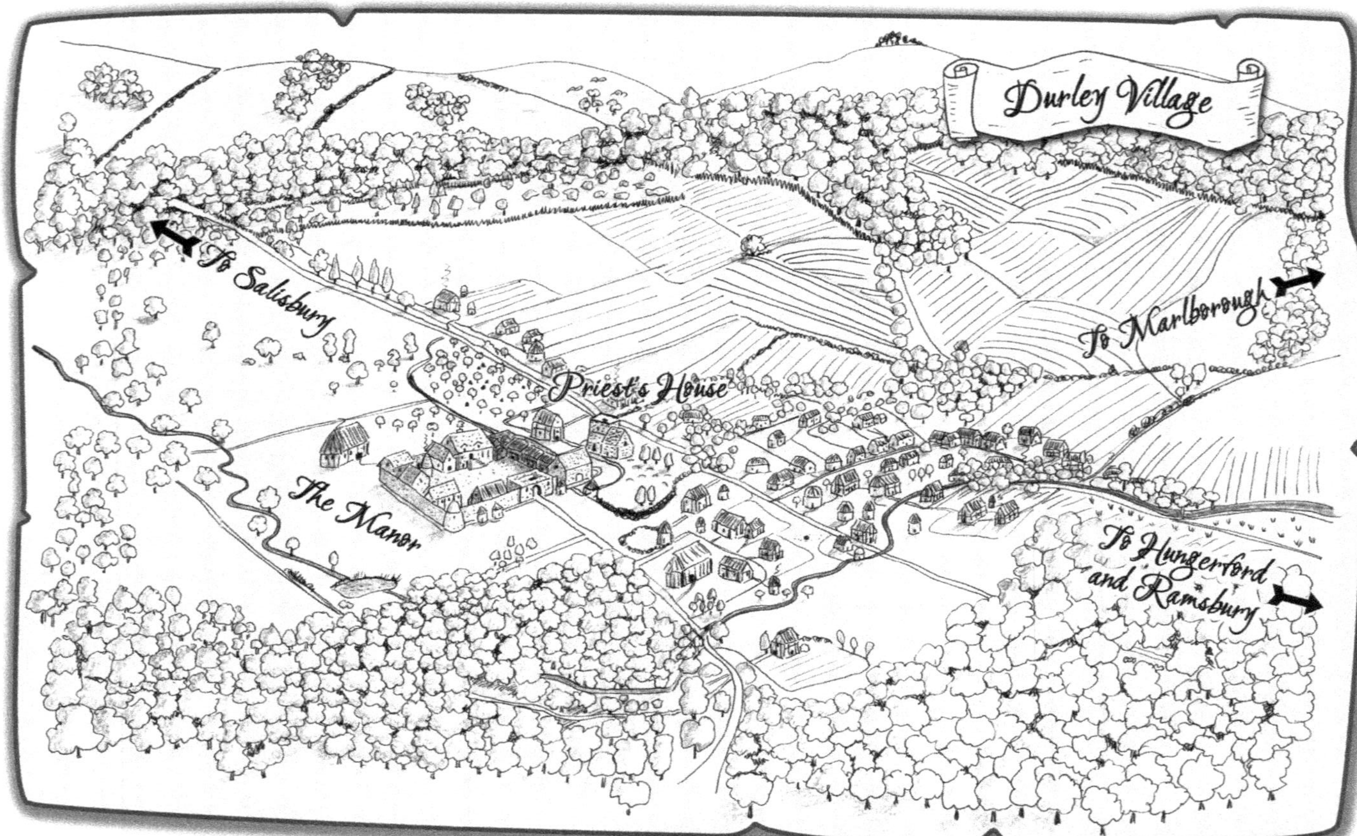
Durley Village
To Salisbury
To Marlborough
Priest's House
The Manor
To Hungerford
and Ramsbury

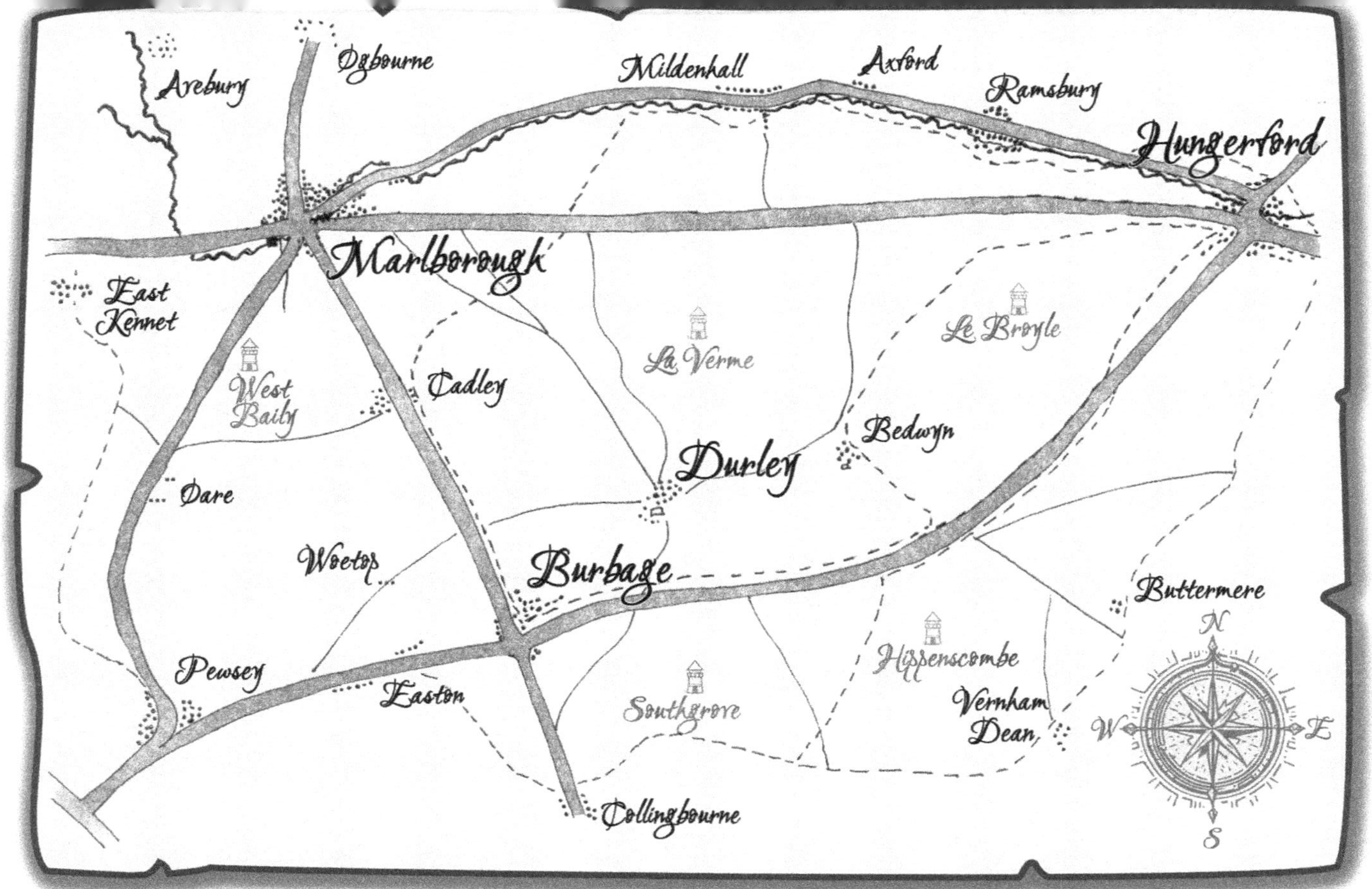
Ogbourne
Arebury
Mildenhall
Axford
Ramsbury
Hungerford
Marlborough
East
Kennet
West
Baily
Cadley
La Verme
Le Broyle
Bedwyn
Durley
Dare
Wootop
Burbage
Buttermere
N
Hippenscombe
Pewsey
Easton
Southgrove
Vernham
Dean
W
E
Collingbourne
S

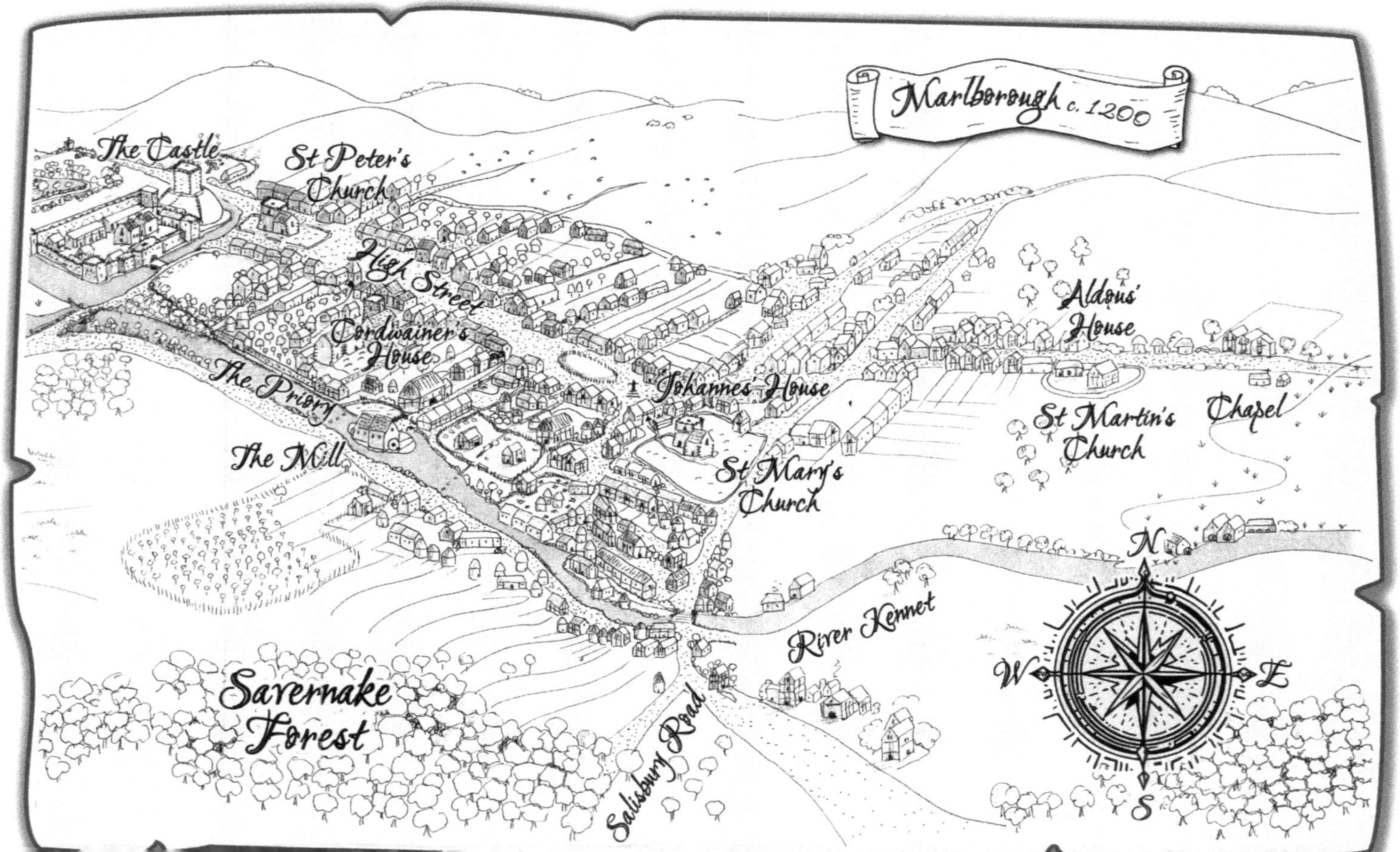
Marlborough c. 1200
The Castle
St Peter's Church
High Street
Cordwainer's House
The Priory
The Mill
Johannes House
St Mary's Church
Aldous' House
St Martin's Church
Chapel
River Kennet
Savernake Forest
Salisbury Road
N
S
W
E

ALYSOUN

Bitweene Merch and Averil,
When spray biginneth to springe,
The litel fowl hath hire wil
On hire leod to singe.
Ich libbe in love-longinge
For semlokest of alle thinge.
Heo may me blisse bringe:
Ich am in hire baundoun.
An hendy hap ich habbe yhent,
Ichoot from hevene it is me sent:
From alle wommen my love is lent,
And light on Alisoun.
On hew hire heer is fair ynough,
Hire browe browne, hire yën blake;
With lossum cheere heo on me lough;
With middel smal and wel ymake.
But heo me wolle to hire take
For to been hire owen make,
Longe to liven ichulle forsake,
And feye fallen adown.
An hendy hap ich habbe yhent,
Ichoot from hevene it is me sent:
From alle wommen my love is lent,
And light on Alisoun.
Nightes when I wende and wake,
Forthy mine wonges waxeth wan:
Levedy, al for thine sake
Longinge is ylent me on.

In world nis noon so witer man
That al hire bountee telle can;
Hire swire is whittere than the swan,
And fairest may in town.
An hendy hap ich habbe yhent,
Ichoot from hevene it is me sent:
From alle wommen my love is lent,
And light on Alisoun.
Ich am for wowing al forwake,
Wery so water in wore.
Lest any reve me my make
Ich habbe y-yerned yore.
Bettere is tholien while sore
Than mournen evermore.
Geinest under gore,
Herkne to my roun:
An hendy hap ich habbe yhent,
Ichoot from hevene it is me sent:
From alle wommen my love is lent,
And light on Alisoun.

13th century English song

ALYSOUN (TRANSLATION)

Between March and April
When the blossom begins to appear,
The small birds take pleasure,
in singing in their own language.
I live in love-longing,
For the fairest of all things,
She brings me such bliss,
I am totally in her power.
Such luck I have received,
I know it is sent to me from Heaven
From all other women my love is removed
And alights on Alison.
Her hair is wonderfully fair,
Her eyebrows are brown, her eyes are black,
With a pleasant expression she smiled at me.
She has a slender and well-formed waist
Unless she wishes to take me to herself,
As her own mate,
I will give up living a long time,
And fall down dead.
Such luck I have received,
I know it is sent to me from Heaven
From all other women my love is removed
And alights on Alison.
At night I toss and turn, awake,
As a result my cheeks turn pale.
Lady, it's all for your sake.

Desire has come upon me.
In all the world there isn't so clever a man,
That is able to recount all her excellence,
Her neck is whiter than the swan's,
And she is the fairest maid in town.
Such luck I have received,
I know it is sent to me from Heaven
From all other women my love is removed
And alights on Alison.
I am completely worn out from staying
awake,
Weary as water in a weir,
Lest anyone takes away from me my beloved,
For whom I have yearned for a long time.
It is better to suffer sorely for a time
Than to mourn for ever after.
Fairest under a skirt,
Listen to my song.
Such luck I have received,
I know it is sent to me from Heaven.
From all other women my love is removed,
And alights on Alison.

1208
Chapter One

"MY LORD BELVOIR, it's good to see you."

I threw my leg over my horse Fitzroy's ears and jumped down. "Matthew Steward, how are you? I hear you are a father for the first time?"

Matthew bowed low. "Aye, sir. A son. John after the king. Six months now. Congratulations to you, too, my lord, for you also have another son."

"I do, and Heavens, how the time flies."

We walked my bay stallion across the yard of the manor of Bedwyn. Hal of Potterne, my man at arms, followed me slowly with his favourite grey, Grafton, and a groom came to take them both from us.

Looking up at the sky, I said, "Another fine day, Matt."

"Yes, my lord. My wife tells me it's set fair for the whole month of September."

"Is it now? She knows these things, does she?" I said with a smile.

"She's very good at weather, sir. Her own bones tell her, she says," he chuckled.

I laughed out loud. “So how is Bedwyn faring, Matt? It must miss its old master and mistress terribly?”

“Aye, sir, so it does. God keep them in his bosom.” Matt crossed himself. “He was a fine man, and she was a wonderful lady.”

I followed suit. “Yes, they were.”

We were speaking about my father-in-law, Toruld Congyre, the father of my first wife, Cecily, who had been murdered in 1200. He had owned Bedwyn until his death last year from a prolonged disease. My mother-in-law had died of lung congestion shortly after.

I had inherited the village and demesne and Matthew Steward had run it with the help of the manor’s able staff for quite a time. I was well pleased with how he managed it. Bedwyn village had always had an independent status in the forest of Savernake and it was still so.

“I’ve come to look at the birds, Matt? Shall we go round?”

We took the path around the great barn and made for a smaller building tacked onto the end.

Here were the mews for my father-in-law’s prized falcons.

I had no birds at Durley, which was just three miles to the southwest and was the village where I lived. For many years, if I had wanted to hunt with birds, I had come here to my father-in-law’s home and hunted with him and his hawks. It was his passion, and he had the money to devote to it, for it was an expensive pastime.

Now they were mine, and I was determined I would visit them more often.

This, however, was only my fifth visit since he’d died. My work had kept me from the pleasure and I’d not been to the mews for a while.

“Where’s Roger, Matt? He’s usually here to meet us.”

“Oh, he’ll be somewhere about the village, my lord. He never leaves the birds for long.”

Matt opened the door of the mews.

There was a fluttering of wings as the birds, standing on their perches, anticipated company. I saw one bird was hooded.

We peered into the gloom of the building. Small windows high up in the wooden wall threw a beam of sunlight down to the floor and dust motes danced in the disturbed air.

The smell from the birds also escaped the door; not a too unpleasant smell, I thought, though there was an added tang I couldn't immediately identify.

I made for the corner where the falcon I favoured most was sitting hooded with her head cocked.

"Ah, my proud Gilda," I said. "How are we today?"

I took a glove from a peg and slipped my hand into it. As I did so, my eye caught a dark patch of something on the floor in the corner.

I ducked under the bird slowly so as not to startle her and eased myself around her bow perch.

"Matthew!"

"Aye, sir?"

Matt came scuttling into the building and screwed up his eyes in the gloom.

"Come here for a moment."

He, too, ducked under the perch.

"What's this?"

Matthew bent and put out his hand to the sand scattered on the floor.

"Blood, sir."

"Not from the birds' food?"

"I can't say, sir."

We returned to the light from the door.

"Find Roger, will you," I said, „He should know...."

As I spoke, I turned to the space behind the open door

where various items for the birds were stored and hung on pegs: the jesses, braces and cadges.

A humped figure lay against the base of the wall.

I threw off the glove. Matt caught it and his eye travelled swiftly to where I'd looked.

"Jesus, it's Roger," he said.

I was now on my knees in the sand before the sprawled man. He was slumped against the end wall of the building, his head on his chest.

I lifted the slight body to the light.

It was Roger Hawkes.

Blood coated his bald head, face, neck and upper body. He wore a thin shirt, braies and hose and his shirt had been torn to shreds. Blood had soaked into it.

"Is he alive, sir?" asked Matt breathlessly.

I sat back on my haunches.

"No, Matt. I'm afraid he's dead."

There we are, Paul, my scribe. We begin another tale. A tale which I shall relate to you, and you shall write down for me, for I can no longer write with my ancient and misshapen fingers.

Yes, you are right. It does seem odd. But as you may imagine and will have learned from all those stories you transcribed for me before, this scene was not as it first seemed.

Do you know, the details of that picture are scratched into my brain as cleanly as a stylus scratches into a waxed tablet? The morning sunlight, the smell of the mews, the shadows, all as clear as crystal to me, even forty years later. Yes, you're right, boy, I do have a good memory, particularly for a man of seventy-three.

That might be one of the reasons why King John required me to look into the crimes in my area; the felonies in the Forest of Savernake and elsewhere in north Wiltshire, in the lands of which I was lord, still am lord, though I allow my sons to run the whole thing now.

I had an inquiring mind and a good memory then and I can recall the details of each mystery I solved.

Let's carry on writing, shall we, until the light fades?

Hal, my man-at-arms, came into the shed quickly and bent over my shoulder.

"Looks like 'is birds 'ave 'ad 'im!" he said.

"That is indeed what it looks like, but..." I caught my lip with my teeth and looked around.

"They are all as placid as the perches on which they sit and aren't flying free, angry or upset."

"Would a bird do that, sir...I mean...go for a man they know well and attack 'im, to kill 'im?"

"If the birds had young and were protecting them, they might. However, we have no such thing here, Hal," I answered. "These aren't wild birds. These are birds used to people. And kill him? I really doubt it."

I looked over at the four perches where the falcons and hawks sat; my favourite Gilda, a saker and the only one hooded; Parsifal, a sparrowhawk; a lanner, whose name was Flitch; and a female goshawk known simply as Brownun. There was a strict hierarchy of which bird might be flown by whom. A knight might own and fly a saker or a lanner; a lesser man, a goshawk. There were no birds for the higher order of noblemen in my father-in-law's mews.

I scoured the ground under the perches. There were the

usual droppings and a few feathers, nothing unusual.

I picked up the falconer's hand.

"See here, Hal, if Roger had tried to defend himself against the birds, he would have been scored about the arm and hand."

"'E isn't."

"No."

"Just the 'ead and chest."

"When you are taking wild birds from the nest, Hal, to rear for yourself, the parents dive at you and attack you about the head. They don't, as a rule, score you on the front of your chest. If you have any sense, you turn your back or defend yourself with, let's say, a buckler held above you."

"Or if you've even more sense, you go when the parents are out."

"Just so."

"You mean, my lord, that someone wants us to blame the birds for Roger's death?" asked Matt with a face as grey as putty.

"I think that's what we are being led to believe, Matt," I said.

I stood up. "Master Steward, can you send someone for the coroner? Hal, might you go back to Durley and fetch Johannes from his room? He needs to see this."

Johannes was the doctor of Marlborough, the largest town in the area. He had been staying with us for a few days, for he was uncle to my second wife and godfather to my three children. He, Hal and I had had much experience looking at corpses.

Hal straightened up and stroked the twin peaks of his long grey beard, worn long in imitation of his Viking ancestors.

"Why would anyone want to kill ol' Roger? He was as quiet as a settin' 'en."

I shook my head. "I don't know, Hal, but I don't think it was the birds."

Matt screwed up his face. "Are you quite sure, sir, about that? I mean, really sure? The scratches and gouges—they look like the birds' talons."

"No, I'm not completely sure, but my thumbs are pricking and when my thumbs prick..."

"Ah," said Hal. "Take it from me, when 'is thumbs prick, then you jolly well know that it's goin'ta be a murder, Matt. No doubt about it."

"What do you think, Johannes?" I asked a while later when the doctor had bent over the body. There was more light in the little shed now, for we had opened wide all the windows—mere wooden flaps over openings in the walls—and the sun had crept around the right side of the building.

Johannes clicked his tongue. "I know nothing about birds, Aumary, but I can tell a knife wound when I see one."

"Where? Show me?"

"Here, in the neck. It was meant to be covered by the scratches but failed to be hidden well enough to fool me."

I leant over the body of Roger Hawkes.

"Yes, there...I see it. Where the neck meets the shoulder."

"A major bloodline runs up there."

"So he bled to death?"

"Until I get him somewhere where I can really examine him, well, I can't say exactly, but yes, I think so."

"When the coroner comes, we shall take him into the large barn and put him on a trestle."

"Aye, a good idea."

"I have looked around the bird shed. There's nothing. No knife." I looked around again.

"We'll need someone to look to the birds. I must go and ask Ralph."

Luckily, Roger's son Ralph was all prepared to step into his father's boots. This was often the case, for the position of falconer was handed down from father to son.

The young man ran his sleeve over his eyes and nose and stood as I entered his house.

He knew that his father was dead. It was all over the village, but I told him more of the unfortunate circumstances surrounding his father's death since it was I who had found him.

"I am so sorry, Ralph. I will do my best to investigate and bring the perpetrator to justice."

"Aye, sir. I know you will."

"Meanwhile, do you think you might carry on looking after the birds?"

"Aye, sir. It's what I've been trained for."

"Good man."

"Do you want to take one of them out today, m'lord?"

"No...er, no...not today, Ralph. Not after what's happened."

He nodded and looked away, tears in his eyes. "Who would want to kill my ol' da in such a way, sir?"

"Did your father argue with anyone, Ralph? Is there anyone you think might have had something against him?"

He closed his eyes. "No, sir. No one."

I looked around the cottage. "Your mother died last year, didn't she, Ralph, and your sister is married and living away? It's just you and your father?"

"Aye, sir," he sobbed. "And now...it's just me."

I left him to his grief.

Johannes had told me that it was likely that the man

had been dead for two or more hours when we'd found him, for he was not yet stiffening, not even in the jaw, which is the first place which shows the rigour. I needed to find out if anyone had seen Roger that morning.

One thing puzzled me...nay, two.

Why was Roger partially clothed?

And why was just one of the birds hooded—the bird called Gilda, with which I liked to hunt?

I walked about the small village for the rest of the day, talking to the villagers. Did any of them have an idea why Roger might have been attacked? None did. No one had seen the man that morning.

The reeve, Henry du May, a man in his forties with a bright red beard which covered his throat, shook his head.

"He was a very quiet man, m'lord. Most of these falconers are. Calm, quiet and keeps themselves to their work."

"Friends or enemies?"

"Oh no, sir. He didn't have any special friends. In boyhood, yes, Yves of Harbook. Boyhood friends they were, coming from the same place, but he certainly didn't have any enemies."

"He always seemed to me a man wedded to his birds, Henry. Especially when his wife..."

"Lison, sir."

"That was her name, wasn't it? When... Lison died."

"His is a sad story. Five sons. All but the youngest, dead."

I crossed myself. "Sad indeed, Henry."

Henry du May recounted for me the deaths of Roger's sons. One drowned accidentally at the age of six; one died in his twenties of a cut which went bad; one taken off by some kind of fit aged fifteen; and the fourth an infant death. Ralph was the only survivor.

"There is the one daughter..."

"Ah yes, Richildis. I remember."

"Yes, sir. She went off to be married. Lives in Ramsbury town."

"She's the wife of a merchant, isn't she? I don't know much about it."

"Yessir. They have a fine house on the High Street near the church...a new one. Not been married all that long."

"Hmm. You know of no quarrel that Master Hawkes may have had with anyone?"

The reeve pursed his lips. "No, sir. Nothing."

I turned to leave.

"Except...well...well, it was hardly a quarrel."

"Ah, yes?"

"It was over that marriage, m'lord."

"Who did Richildis marry, du May?"

"Master Mansur Grover. You know that he is a wealthy man, sir."

"I'm told that he owns a large iron forge in Ramsbury. I have never met him."

"Aye, sir. Iron smelting. Much money in that, I'm told."

"And he argued with Roger?"

"His daughter, sir, ran away with the man."

"I remember she was quite a good-looking girl, Henry."

"Oh, ah,... sir. She could have had her pick. She picked ol' man Grover."

"And her father was not happy?"

"Wasn't much he could do about it, m'lord."

"Oh?"

"Well, it went like this, see..."

"I remember," said Hal suddenly. "The girl disappeared one night, didn't she?"

"Yes, and her father, Roger, pursued them to the town. He'd no idea this amour had been going on. His friend told him where they were, I believe. They thought it was going to be a rape marriage."

"But it wasn't?"

"Oh no, sir. Ol' Roger eventually caught up with them."

"But they were already married, weren't they?" said Hal.

"They were, and by then, the man Grover had had the girl's maidenhead," said the reeve.

"Too late to do anything about it then," said Hal with finality.

"And so this man Grover was not popular with our dead falconer, du May?"

The man shook his head. "But the girl seemed happy enough, and Roger had to accept it. So, like I say, it wasn't really a quarrel."

"Hmm. Seems like a good reason to hate a man, all the same."

"But if that's so, sir," said Hal, "why is it that it's the falconer who's dead? Surely ol' Hawkes would want to widow his daughter, not the other way round."

"Perhaps they fought and this was the result?"

Johannes shook his head. "I don't see any evidence of a fight...certainly not in here, and this, I think, is where he bled to death." He pointed to the bloodstain.

"So if this is where he fell, why is he lying against the wall?"

"Crawled there, I s'pose?" said Hal, sadly.

"Hmm. And what we want to know is why did Hawkes dislike this fellow so much in the first place? Now, in that answer, we might find some bones, ol' Hal."

"Bones, m'lord? Meat and gravy, sir, meat and gravy!"

I needed to find and inquire of the other people involved in this tale. Before the coroner had come and gone and his jury of twelve men over fourteen had pronounced it murder, I sent a runner back to Durley to tell my wife Lydia that I would be staying at Bedwyn that night.

Off I went to Ramsbury with Hal in tow early the next day. My first call was to the forges worked by this wealthy man, Grover.

These were special forges in which the pulverised rocks holding the iron ore, brought from Seend, near Devizes, were heated to allow the metal to be released and melted.

Hal and I clopped down the main street, which ran parallel to the River Kennet. About two-thirds of the way down the long main street and not far from the church, we heard the sound of the workings and passed into a stockaded yard, about which many men bustled.

A man came to take our horses and gestured to a long, low building at the edge of the workings.

We scratched on the door and called out.

"Enter."

A young man with sparse brown hair and a small beard of the same colour rose from behind a table. He wore a brown capuchon hood and a short brown tunic and sported a tanned face. It seemed he was all brown. His face was smiling and showed a jolly disposition.

"Good day to you. Might I be speaking to Master Grover?"

The man chuckled under his breath.

"Ah, no, sir." He scratched his forehead with a rather dirty finger. "The master isn't here yet."

"I am Sir Aumary Belvoir, warden of the Forest of Savernake. I am also the constable of the county, and I am come about the death of my falconer, Roger Hawkes."

The man bowed low. "Ah, yessir. We heard that he'd...died."

"How did you hear? It's scarce a moment since the coroner made his pronouncement."

"Someone from Bedwyn came, sir, and spoke to Mistress Grover last evening about her father's death. It's hard to keep that sort of news silent after that."

"You are?"

"John of Burridge, sir." He bowed again. "I am the overseer of the men here."

"Well, John, is the mistress at home?"

"She is, sir. The house is the first by the church - you will not miss it, it's..."

"Tell me, John of Burridge, did you ever see my man Roger Hawkes here at the workings?"

"No, sir. Never."

"You know him then, how he seems?"

"Aye, my lord. You know how it is round here. Everyone is related to everyone else. I knew Roger. He's…he was...my sister's husband's uncle."

I turned that relationship around in my head.

I heard Hal chuckle softly in his beard behind me.

"The man was stabbed in the throat."

"Oh!" John of Burridge blinked a few times. "We heard that his birds killed him."

"Then whoever came from Bedwyn to tell you that he was dead told you awry, for it's murder."

The man swallowed.

"And I am investigating, as is my task as constable of this county."

The man fiddled with his fingers, nervously massaging his thumbs.

"I can't tell you anything about it, sir."

"Where do the men who work for you live, Master Burridge?"

"Most of them are Ramsbury men, m'lord."

"The rest?"

"Here and there around about."

"Any from Bedwyn? Free men?" I asked.

"A couple, sir."

"Then I'd like to speak to them. Now, please."

Burridge scurried around the end of the table. "I'll see if I can find them, sir."

The man left us, wiping his brow with the back of his hand.

Hal and I looked at each other.

"Jittery sod, i'n't he?" said Hal.

"Ah, well. Murder makes some folk nervous, Hal."

"S'pose it does. Whereas you and me, we'm used to it," he said philosophically.

I chuckled at him. "Sadly."

I looked down at the table. There was a pair of pincers lying on the surface. I picked them up.

"Expect to find that sorta thing, wouldn't you?" said Hal. I nodded as I replaced them.

I looked over the tabletop again and noted, amongst other things, a long sample of iron shaped like a spearhead. Then, I picked up a dried piece of what looked like turf. I turned it over in my hand.

"What's this...? Ah, yes, see how the iron ore glistens. It's trapped in the moss-rich, red soil of some areas."

Hal looked over my shoulder. "Is that the stuff they make this iron from then?"

"I heard that sometimes it can be found in abundance in bogs, Hal. If I'm not much mistaken, this stuff is known as bog iron."

"Iron found in bogs? Nah, go on, you're 'avin me on, sir."

"No, Hal. In some places, that is where it's found. In bogs."

"You are quite right, sir," said a deep and resonant voice from the doorway.

I put down the peaty sample and brushed my hands together. We both turned as one, and Hal took in a quick breath. The man came into the building, out of the sunlight, ducking his head as he moved under the lintel.

"Sir Aumary Belvoir, isn't it? Warden of the forest."

I nodded. "And constable of the county."

Hal had his mouth open and was staring.

I smiled.

"Master Grover?"

"I am Mansur Grover, sir," he bowed, "Ironmaster."

I took a deep breath.

"I am pleased to meet you, sir."

The man before me was black of skin. Not tanned with wind and weather as some of the forest folk were, but dark, as if he had been painted with a black dye.

Hal cleared his throat. He whispered,

"Devils and demons."

Grover chuckled.

"Yes, my good man," he said smiling, "And the black goes all the way through." And he waved his hand down his body.

Chapter Two

WE SAT DOWN companionably in his office and he told me about himself in his luscious, deep, dark voice.

I was not as surprised as Hal, for though I had not seen a black man before in the flesh, I knew that they existed. Had not my grandfather described the Saracen to me when I was a boy? His father had seen such men in the Holy Lands while on crusade.

The man was about thirty-five, big-boned and tall with handsome features and a nobly chiselled nose. His lips were full and purple pink; his forehead well formed, his hair curly like my own hair, though cropped very short, his dark brows profuse but well shaped, and he wore a small dark beard.

He had, he said, come from North Africa as a child, when his father had returned from the crusade. His mother was an African, and his father was a man of our area.

My memory was now teased, for I recalled a story that went about the forest when I was young, about a man who had returned from the wars in the Holy lands, a man who had taken a black wife. I had not heard what had happened to their child.

"Before his enlistment in the crusading army of King Richard," said Mansur, "my father was a smelter. It was natural that I should carry on his trade after he died."

"There is always a need for steel, Grover," I said, smiling.

"You know, of course, that there has been smelting in Ramsbury since the days of the Saxons, my lord?"

"I did know that, yes."

He nodded and sipped his ale.

"Then you know a deal more than many who have lived in this town all their lives, sir."

I smiled. "I know that Ramsbury was an important place once. More important than it is now. I know that it has its own bishop, and that the church was very important and old; indeed, it had a bishopric. I know, of course, that the bishop had a palace here."

"Then you do know our little town, sir," said Mansur Grover, smiling, his perfect white teeth shining in the darkness of the shed.

His smile disappeared. "But you have not come here for me to lecture you on the importance of Ramsbury. This will be about the death of my father-in-law, Roger."

"You have heard that he has been murdered?"

The man's body stiffened. "No, sir. We had heard that he had had an accident."

"Then I must disabuse you, sir, for the man was stabbed where the upper chest meets the neck, and he bled to death."

Mansur whispered, "Murder?"

"We heard that you and Roger were not exactly friendly?"

"I married his daughter without his consent, yes. He did not approve of our marriage."

"I bet 'e didn't," said Hal quietly.

Mansur Grover sighed. "Whatever is said about our marriage, my lord, Richildis and I, it is a love match. She is happy with me, and I am happy with her. I married her with her full consent."

"But not that of her father? There was bound to be bad blood," I said.

"Does that make me his murderer?"

"Not necessarily."

"Why should I kill him?"

"I don't recall intimating that you did, Grover."

The man looked down at his folded hands.

"I had no enmity for him, my lord. He was a good man. He just didn't want a black man for a son-in-law."

"Aye, he was a good man," I said quickly. "I knew him for many years but he was a quiet and introspective man; it was hard to get to know him well."

"As folk will tell you, he kept to himself."

"He worked latterly for my father-in-law, Toruld Congyre. When Congyre passed to his eternal rest, I took on the manor of Bedwyn."

Mansur nodded. "This I knew, sir, and, of course, I know of your role as the Warden of Savernake, but so far, our paths have not crossed."

I shrugged, "The forest is a huge place, Mansur. I rarely come to Ramsbury."

"It lies just outside your area as warden, does it not, my lord?"

"It does, and as you know, it was once the property of the bishop, but the manor is held by the Lord Roger of Durnford now."

"You know him?"

"I do."

Mansur Grover put down his cup.

"Not only am I the Lord of Durley and the warden of the forest, Grover, the king has appointed me constable of this part of the county. It is my job to inquire into murders committed on my ground."

His eyes narrowed. "And so because this is murder, you come to me to ask…?"

"Where were you before dawn yesterday morning?"

"I did not go to Bedwyn and kill my father-in-law."

"It was not a quarrel which escalated, and you perhaps…"

"NO!"

"You are a big man, and Roger was small."

"I did not kill him."

"Then where were you?"

"At home."

"You have people who will say that is so?"

His nostrils flared, "I do."

There was a flurry of sound outside the door.

"Come in, Burridge…don't loiter there," said Grover.

The door was pushed open.

"Sir, the Lord Belvoir asked me to find the men from Bedwyn."

"Send them in."

We questioned these men, but they could tell us absolutely nothing about the death of Roger Hawkes.

At last, we stood outside in the open for a moment before taking our leave.

Hal scrutinised the man in the brightness of the sunlight.

"Well, here's a man burnt by 'is own profession," he said from the corner of his mouth and quietly in my ear.

I smiled at his observation.

Grover had heard him and chuckled loudly into the air.

"Rather burnt by the fierce African sun, master. I must say summer here is fine when it deigns to give us summer, but sometimes my bones yearn for the heat of my native lands. I do so hate the winter with its howling wind."

"Hal and I have never experienced the heat of the desert, Master Grover, though we have friends who have.

We Englishmen, too, hate the winter. I think you can tell how heartily we hate it for the number of songs we sing praising summer and how many songs heap scorn on the cold weather."

We all chuckled.

"Might I go up to the house and speak with Mistress Grover? Do you think she has sufficiently recovered from the shock of being told about her father's death?" I added.

"She will be pleased to receive you, though, of course, she does not know that her father was murdered. I would ask you to keep that from her. She would..."

"Ah, no. I am sorry, Master Grover, that I cannot do. There are questions I must ask which will depend upon her knowing the truth."

The man sighed, a deep, heartfelt and sincere expression.

"Yes. I suppose it cannot be helped, and she will hear it soon enough from the gossip of the town."

"When I am gone, find me some people who will swear that you were at home when Hawkes met his death. Send me word at Bedwyn or Durley."

"I will, sir."

He strode to the gate. "Perhaps I should come home with you."

"Ah no, Grover...you stay here. I would prefer to see the lady alone."

Richildis Grover lifted her pretty face to mine.

"Murdered, sir?"

"I am so sorry to be the bearer of this awful news, madam."

She sat down on a bench and stared at her hands. "I was told..."

"No, madam, what you were told was not the truth. It was made to look as if your father had been clawed to death by his own birds, but he was stabbed in the neck by a man whose talon was a sharp-bladed knife."

The woman's maid, an older lady in her forties, came and laid a hand on her shoulder.

"Why would anyone want to do that?" asked Richildis Grover.

"Madam, your marriage to Master Grover was not popular with your father…?"

The maidservant scoffed and looked away.

"It's all right, Margaret, you can go," said her mistress with tears in her eyes.

The older woman shuffled her feet, "But…madam…"

"No, I will be alright. The constable is an honourable man."

The door clicked shut behind us.

Mistress Grover smoothed down the skirts of her cherry red gown. "She is very protective of me, but she is one for gossiping."

"She has been with you since you were a child, I suppose."

She nodded, and the bright white, almost transparent linen of her head cloth fluttered with the action. The perfect oval face was framed by the full wimple which she wore with grace and elegance. It was held in place by a band of woollen ribbon, woven wool in yellow and white of a geometric pattern. Her skin was perfect and flawless, her brows arched above limpid brown eyes. I judged her to be not a day over sixteen.

I saw a band loom in the corner attached to a house post and suspected that this woman was one who kept her fingers busy. The loom was loaded with cherry red yarn and with black threads. Her own work or perhaps that of her servant.

"Tell me all, spare me nothing, my lord," she said.

I recounted how I had found her father's body. She gasped when she heard how he had been killed.

"Do you have any idea why a humble falconer should meet such an end, madam?"

"No, none," she answered with an absent expression. "It is a complete mystery to me."

"Your brother, too, is at a loss."

"Oh, poor Ralph. He will feel the loss much more keenly than I, for they worked together. I have Mansur to console me."

"We have met him, Mistress Grover. Your husband."

"Then you will know why my father did not approve of me marrying him, why we had to do so in secret."

"He was not trying to annul your marriage then? He wasn't going to the king perhaps to seek redress for the wrong done to him, as he saw it?"

"He did not say so."

"What did he say?"

She lifted her head to look me squarely in the eye. "He wanted me to marry his friend. But my heart was already captured, sir. Please do sit down...how rude of me not to offer you..."

"No, not at all. We prefer to stand. Tell me, he knew absolutely nothing about your...affection for the ironmaster, madam, before the night of your marriage?"

"We managed to keep it a secret. My maid Margaret knew. Mansur's friend and right-hand man, Master Burridge, knew, sir. No one else."

"I wouldn't be too sure about that," piped up Hal behind me.

Richildis tilted her head to look around my arm.

"Well..." Hal scratched his nose. "Someone told yer father you were missin'. "

She did not answer at first.

"My father called Mansur a thief."

"A thief…the thief of his daughter?"

"He told him he had bewitched me with foul potions and spells and that if I were in my right mind, I would not go off with…off with…such as he."

"It did not come to blows?"

"No, sir. My father visited the house just after we were married, but there was no violence."

"So he went away…content…or…?"

"No, sir. Not content, but he realised that I had made my own choice and that, quite contrary to his concerns, I was not afraid of this black man. I told him so. I told him that although he'd given me life and cared for me these many years, I now had another master and that I loved him and would stay with him until the sum of my days. In the end, he was forced to give us his blessing."

"And that was it?"

"It was, my lord."

"This man whom your father wished you to marry? Who is he?"

"A man called Jocelyn Pinter, sir. Of Marlborough."

"Ah…I know him, he is the man responsible for the regulation of weights and measures in the town. Reputedly a good man and of a good family."

She looked down. "I…I did…not like him, sir."

"Hmmm."

She stood up and lifted her chin. "It is done now and cannot be undone."

"Neither can your father be brought back from the dead, madam," I said.

"No…no, he cannot. But you, sir, I know, will do your utmost to find the person responsible."

I nodded my head. "I was fond of your father, Richildis.

He was a good servant and a fine falconer. I'll not see him unavenged."

"Then begin with this Jocelyn Pinter, sir. I..." the woman stopped and seemed unsure. "I think he has been so in love with me that he would allow the devil to take possession of him, and I cannot say what he might do if..."

"You think that the fact your father promised you to him and failed to deliver you, that he would be so incensed as to exact such a revenge?"

Richildis Grover took her lip in her teeth. "That is my fear, sir."

"Surely his wrath would be for the man who stole you from him?"

"If he can injure my father for failure, sir, then can he also not make an attempt on the life of my husband? I am afraid for Mansur."

I looked at her intently, and her pretty face blushed.

"Have you heard Jocelyn Pinter threaten anything, madam?"

She looked down at the floor. "No, sir. I have not. Not yet."

Outside the house, Hal shook his head and shoved his thumbs into his belt.

"I've never heard such sower," he said.

"Rubbish, Hal?"

"Aye...Pinter kill Roger? It's rot."

"Not the man we know of, Hal."

"No...But then...'ow well do we really know Jocelyn Pinter?"

"We'll need to have a word or two with him."

We made for Bedwyn in the heat of the midday, keeping to the cooler paths under the trees.

"I am a little concerned, Hal," I said," we need to talk to Father Godfrey about burying poor old Roger and with the interdict in place, he can't be laid in the churchyard at Bedwyn."

In his quarrel with our monarch, John, the pope had laid the whole country under an interdict in March of that year, 1208. No man could be buried in consecrated ground, nor could any word be said over him to help him to Heaven. The churches were locked and no baptisms, marriages, or confessions could be performed there or anywhere.

"I did 'ear Father Godfrey saying that he would open up a bit o' ground by the back of the manor, but..." Hal shrugged, "It won't be 'oly will it?"

"No."

"The longer this goes on, the more folk the sextons'll 'ave to dig up come the liftin' of the interdict and bury in the right place."

"Or make the places they are buried consecrated ground after all. Doesn't bear thinking about, Hal."

"I'll try not to die till the pope comes to 'is senses then, eh?"

I chuckled at his dark humour.

We rode slowly under the trees surrounding the path to the manor.

I happened to glance at the churchyard to my left as I rode through the gate.

"What the...?"

I jumped down and ran up the path, closely followed by Hal. We slid to a halt beside the largest tree in the graveyard, scattering the little pebbles of the path and peered upwards into the branches.

Hal crossed himself.

The slight breeze stirred the leaves of the old ash; the grasses underneath rippled. The sun dappled the plants around the bole of the tree, a tree which held an unusual and macabre fruit.

> *Yes, Paul, you are quite correct, this happened in a few places over England in the years of the Interdict, I'm told.*

There, hanging by ropes, was a coffin. It swayed gently in the breeze, tilting from side to side. It had never been in the ground, for it was splinter-new and clean. The rope had been wrapped around a large projecting branch and it was secured with several knots.

However, beside it, hanging upright, there were two other bodies without coffins which had, there was no doubt, been dug up, even if they'd only been in the ground a short while. Their bindings were stained with earth and covered with soil and oozing putrefaction. Flies buzzed about them in droves.

I looked around the graveyard and towards the church.

There was no one about. No one was obviously watching us.

"This a protest, sir?"

"Aye…I think it might be, Hal."

"Well, you can't blame 'em now, can you?"

I walked backwards, looking to see if there was anyone trying to observe us at the rear of the tree. There was no one about.

The two of us turned and walked into the house by the church.

Father Godfrey was on his knees feeding a kitten.

"I'm sorry to disturb your good works, Father, but might you come out into the graveyard with us?"

The man struggled to his knees and, with a perplexed

expression, accompanied us outside.

"Oh my! Becket's sainted...soul."

"This, I believe, is the coffin of Roger Hawkes...?"

Father Godfrey nodded.

"These two are...? I asked.

Father Godfrey crossed himself and shook with anger. He took one involuntary step back.

"Old Mother Parfitt and Elias of Shawgrove. They died this summer, about three weeks ago. I think, yes. I think it's them."

I rubbed my forehead where a headache was beginning. This happened to me at times of stress and had done so for the past few years after I had been hit on the head by a mad woman wielding a log.

"We need to get them back in the ground, father," I said, "or they will become a problem."

"Aye," said Father Godfrey distractedly. "I'll get...the grave...I'll get them put back where I had them. Of course, Roger has not yet been buried, but we shall do it quickly."

"I do not want to know who has committed this...act," I chose my words carefully, "but I do not want a repeat of it."

"Aye, m'lord. I will make that known around the village."

"Hal tells me you have made a small area available to the villagers for the burying of its dead."

"Aye, I have, but people just don't want their loved ones to go into unhallowed ground, sir, with nothing said over them."

I perched my backside on the flint wall of the churchyard. "Father, I beg you, can you not see your way to speaking some simple words over your piece of ground? Your flock will not know what you say...it does not have to be the word of God...though he will understand, I'm sure, what you are trying to do."

"God hears all, my Lord Belvoir."

"I'm sure he does. But your people will not understand the Latin. For them, it will be enough to keep the souls of their loved ones from the clutches of the devil. Please, I fear we will have a repeat of this if we cannot give them some crumb of consolation. They so want their people to lie in hallowed ground."

The old man's face crumpled as if he would cry, and he said, "God forgive me..."

"Please."

"The pope has..."

"I know what the pope has decreed. He doesn't have to live with the despair of the people who have lost loved ones. It's bad enough losing them—Heavens, I, of all people, know that..."

"Aye, m'lord, you would know."

My first wife and eldest son had been murdered within a few months of each other, and I knew what it was to mourn.

"But not to have them lie in consecrated ground, prey to everything a simple village man most fears. It's a double blow."

Father Godfrey looked up at me and threw his hands to his face, "Oh, God forgive me...I will do it."

"We cannot have a repeat of this, Father, we cannot."

"No...no, we mustn't."

He suddenly drew himself up and straightened his spine. "I'll find someone to put them away where they belong and I will, as much as I am able, speak over some ground...I will," and he wobbled off towards the village street.

Hal and I led our horses into the yard of Bedwyn manor.

"Matthew, where does Yves of Harbrook live? Is he a Bedwyn man?"

"Aye, he has a house on Church Street, m'lord. He rents it out now. He has another in Ramsbury, I believe. You'll find him there mostly, for he is bailiff to the Lord Durnford.

Yves was born on the farm at Harbrook and took his name from there, but he's a Bedwyn man, really. Until he went to the town, that is, and became the bailiff."

"Then it's a trip back to Ramsbury tomorrow, Hal."

"What about this fella Jocelyn Pinter?"

"We shall make a journey to Marlborough to speak to him and we shall set out from home…which is where we shall make for now."

We were back in Durley by late afternoon. The golden glow of the sun on the walls of the manor pulled at my heartstrings as we clopped slowly down the road to the gate.

I fell tiredly from my beautiful bay stallion Fitzroy's back and gave him into Cedric Groomsman's hands.

"Sir…?"

"Yes, Cedric?"

"Might I have a word?"

"Certainly you can. Can it do here, or must you come up to the hall?"

"The hall, sir…it's an important thing I have to ask and so…"

"I will wait for you there, Cedric."

Hal, a look of puzzlement on his face, screwed up his eyebrows and released them again in a comical gesture of questioning.

I shrugged and we climbed the manor steps.

I had just reached the screens passage when my nine-year-old daughter, Hawise, came running down the hall and skidded to a halt by the doorway.

"Oh, Dada, I thought that it was you."

"Ho, ho…I am Dada again, am I?" My daughter was growing up fast and had lately begun to call me 'Father'. Today, she had slid back to her old favourite.

"What do you want, that your ol' father must be called Dada again?"

"Please, Dada, don't joke."

"What is it, sweetling?"

"It's Holdfast...I think...she is very ill...Plum is with her now in the stable..." Plum was my houndsman, and he looked to the care, health and breeding of all my dogs.

"Ill?"

"I think she is going to die," she blubbered.

I walked into the hall. Three men were sitting there and they all rose as I entered, as was right and proper.

John Brenthall was my chief wood warden, responsible for the working folk of the forest and all the forestry that went on in it. His son, sixteen-year-old Peter, his apprentice, sat by him with his hound Maxime.

My priest of Durley was the third man: Crispin Darrell of Chilton. He would have been a good person to speak to about the murder of the falconer, but he had been away a long while in Salisbury and had spent years as an aide to the bishop. He had returned to us four years ago.

I backed Hawise onto a bench. "Tell me what has happened."

"She would not eat yesterday, and then she kept drinking and drinking, and she will not rise. She just lies in the stable, panting, and Plum thinks...that she has something wrong with her insides and she will die."

"I will come...where is your mother?"

"In the stable with Holdfast and Plum."

"Then go to them." Out of the corner of my eye, I saw Cedric bowl in behind me and stop to take in the sombre mood.

"I will be there in a moment."

She nodded and ran shaky fingers over her eyes.

"I can't see her being so ill, Father; she is usually so happy."

"Aye, she is."

Holdfast was my little white gazehound dog and she was the same age as Hawise.

I pushed my daughter gently towards the doorway to the screens passage.

Hal took her arm and accompanied her to the outer door.

I turned to Cedric.

"Yes, Cedric, what can I do for you?"

The ginger-haired young man scuffed his feet on the flagstones.

"Come on, man...you were all for spitting it out a moment before..."

"I want to get married, sir."

I blinked.

"I mean, I'd like to get married, sir," he said, grinning.

I took his shoulder and moved him away from the other men, though I was sure they'd all heard what he had said.

"And I have come to ask your permission...if that is all right."

"It is all right, Cedric. Yes, indeed. Who is the fortunate girl?"

Again, he looked at his feet.

"Alysoun...Alysoun Backs of Marlborough...she who works for the town reeve Nicholas Barbflet, sir."

I remembered the girl. Indeed, she worked for the Barbflet family on Crook's Lane. I also remembered that a few years ago, she'd had a beau who had died in a dust blast at the town corn mill. He'd been a miller at the building owned by my good friend Nick.

"You have asked the girl?"

"No, sir...not formally. I have said that I will ask you first."

"You must ask her master too, Cedric."

"Aye, sir, I know."

Cedric was a freeman and did not need to ask my permission to marry, but I could see why he was doing so. The girl, who was also free, would come to live in Durley, and they must have a house.

"Then ask Master Barbflet—it's a courtesy—and then your girl, for I give you permission to bring her here to Durley," I burbled on "Do you want to be married here or in Marlborough? You will have to ask Father Torold if you wish to do it in the town...oh, no...it cannot be, can it? No formal marriages whilst this interdict has us in its grip."

"We don't mind, sir. We can do a handfasting with witnesses."

"We can do that here if your girl is willing. She lives at the western end of town, does she not?"

"Yessir. She lives with her grannie on Back Lane when she's not at the Barbflet house."

"Will her grannie let her go to you, Cedric?"

"Aye, sir, she will."

"Well, then. We'll see what we can do, young man."

The young man's freckled face lit up. "Thank you, sir. Thank you." He backed out, repeating his thanks and bowing his head.

Oh, I said to myself, that it was always so easy to make people happy.

I stood for a moment looking at the door through which he'd disappeared. Into my mind's eye came Cedric as a lad of twelve, haring up the stairs screaming at the limit of his lungs, for Cedric had been the person to see the block of stone fall on my poor five-year-old son and kill him.

I could never forget that moment.

Lydia, my wife, had had Holdfast moved up to the solar. I stood and watched as my little white gazehound lay before the cold fire, her favourite place, and panted furiously.

"What is it, Plum?" I asked.

"I think, m'lord, it's the insides…you know she has never had pups."

"Aye, I know it. She would never allow a dog near. It wasn't for the want of trying to mate her."

Plum, my houndsman, smiled, the red birthmark for which he was named creasing on his cheek.

"She is a one, sir! She'd have bitten the tarriwags off…"

"Yes, Plum…I understand," I nodded to my daughter, who was on her knees, cradling the dog's head.

"Ahem," said Plum, looking abashed. "She wasn't fer havin' it, sir."

"And so because she has had no offspring, there is something wrong with her insides?"

"It happens, m'lord, to bitches. They go bad inside, for the Good Lord means them to have children, and if they refuse, the womb shrivels and dies, and the dog…"

Hawise turned a tear-stained face to Plum."

"She will die, won't she?"

"Aye, sweetling, I think she will," I said.

"Uncle Johannes could save her. I know he could."

My daughter did not really bother with my bigger dogs on the estate, the alaunts, lymers and wolfhounds, though she was kind to them, but this little dog she had known all her life, and she was very fond of her. Hawise played with the puppies, but as they aged and grew tall, her interest in them waned.

She stroked the dog's muzzle. "Now, now, Holdfast. I will ask Uncle Johannes to…" she said.

"Hawise, Johannes knows about people. He doesn't know about dogs," said my wife, Lydia in a very sad voice. "He will not be able to help her."

"We could ask him…we could…couldn't we, Dada?"

Hal was standing in the solar doorway. He would come no further unless asked.

"Do you want me to go for him, sir? Bring him back. See if there's anything he can do?"

Hawise leapt up, "Oh, Hal, would you do that? Would you? Tell him that Holdfast…"

"Wait…wait…" I put up my hands. "Uncle Johannes has many draws on his time, Hawise. He cannot just drop everything and come to Durley for a dog."

"But she's my dog…"

"Oh…I thought she was my dog?" I said under my breath.

"Please, Hal…as quickly as you can," moaned my daughter.

Hal looked at me under his grey brows.

"Oh, go on then…but only if he feels he…"

"Thank you, Dada," said Hawise, tripping up to me and embracing me around the middle. "She must get better, she must."

"Your Uncle Johannes cannot work miracles, Hawise," said Lydia softly.

"No, I know. I know he can't. I must go to the chapel to pray…God can work miracles. And we have the relic of St Margaret in the chapel." This was a family possession brought back from the Holy Land by my great-grandfather.

"The chapel is locked, Hawise."

"Oh nooo!" She burst into tears. "Then I must go and pray by the door of the chapel. God will hear me if I shout loud enough."

And she was off in a flash of red skirts.

Johannes came in at suppertime.

He strode up to the solar.

"I'm sorry. I had to do it. Hawise is in such a taking over her."

"I know how much she loves her," he said smiling.

"You know that I would not call you for a dog no matter what, Johannes."

He smiled indulgently at me. "Holdfast is part of the family; let us see what we might do."

I left him to his ministrations and went down to the office to scribble down everything I'd learned about the murder of Roger Hawkes that day.

A little while later, Johannes scratched on the door.

"Plum is correct; her womb is gone bad."

"Then she will die?"

"She will die if I do not do something about it."

I must have looked completely bemused because Johannes chuckled and sat on the stool in front of my table.

"She has but one chance."

"That is?"

"I remove the womb."

"Oh, come on, Johannes...that will kill her anyway. In the most horrible way."

"You don't trust me?"

"Of course I trust you," I said, "but Holdfast is but a dog...she..."

"They are the same as us inside, Aumary. Well, the same as women."

"They are?"

"They are...I must not tarry if I am to save her."

"What will you do?"

"Can you move her to a trestle in the stables and find me someone to help?"

"I'm sure Plum will help. He knows all there is to know about dogs. And Tostig is a good man in a crisis."

He stood and made for the door…"She will not feel it, I promise."

"It is not to me you need to make that promise, Johannes, but to Hawise."

I will not go into the detail of that amazing evening.

No, Paul, I will not…

I have told you before that Johannes of Salerno was the most astounding doctor I ever met. He lost fewer patients than any man in his profession. He used his skills for any man, woman or child, and because he was a wealthy man, he rarely charged for his services, only billing those whom he knew could pay.

That evening, he carefully removed the diseased womb of a dog. He told me later that he had done it before in Salerno, Italy, where he had learned his doctoring. In this country of ours, it is not permitted to cut up the body of human beings to see the workings under the skin, but in Salerno, in his youth, they had no such bans. They had also looked at the inner complexities of animals and learned much from it.

Yes, he had done it before and so he knew what lay inside our little Holdfast.

We sat in the solar, Lydia, Hawise and I, and chewed our fingers for a few hours. Our brave Holdfast lived up to her name that day, for she remained with us another six years and was as sprightly as she had ever been after a time of quiet and rest to recover.

No, Paul, I do not know what Johannes did; I do not want to know. I am glad he did it, for, you will learn in another tale, this is not the only time he had to do this and the next time he did it, I was greatly pleased that he had practised on Holdfast.

I promised Hawise another puppy, a small dog, to be a companion for Holdfast or a replacement should she not survive. And the acquisition of him led to me discovering something interesting about the death of my falconer, Roger.

Hawise began to smile again.

Chapter Three

THAT EVENING, the rain came down in a steady drizzle, and folk went to their beds early. The nights had begun to draw in, and tasks were not so easy to accomplish in the twilight. If there were labours to be achieved, they were those managed inside the home.

I sat up talking to Johannes in my office about the murder of the falconer whilst we listened to the drip of the rain from the roof.

"His life was simple, Johannes."

"Nothing for which anyone might kill him?"

"Not revenge. Well, I think not. People say not. Not money, nor property at stake. He did not seem at odds with anyone."

"Not even this new son-in-law, you say?"

I shrugged. "There was nothing he could do about it."

"I noticed that he was out in just his braies, his hose and shirt?"

"That struck me as odd, I must say, for he would have dressed fully before going to his work with his birds."

"And he had hooded just the one bird and they do this to... what?"

"Keep the bird calm when she is taken out. Their sight is far better than ours, Johannes, and when they are out on the glove, they will be distracted by many things."

"Did Roger know you were going to see him that day to fly the birds?"

"No."

"So why had he hooded the one bird you almost always chose?"

"That is a mystery."

"This daughter of his tells you she thinks it's the town pinter?"

"I think she is speaking out of some kind of dislike of the man, though I can't think why. She can hardly have known him living in Bedwyn as she did."

Johannes leant forward, put his elbows on his knees and rolled his wine cup between his palms. "Women can be strange, Aumary." He shook his head.

"You are beginning to sound like Hal!" I chuckled.

Johannes' face creased into a grin. I noticed there were more lines around his eyes than previously.

"She tells you that her father wanted her to marry him, and yet you only have her word for it as yet. What if it was the other way round and Pinter would not marry her?"

"You mean that she married the Moor because she was spurned and ran off to spite both Pinter and her father?"

"Stranger things have happened with women, Aumary."

"Hmmm. I shall discuss this with Pinter tomorrow.

"And the other person involved?"

"A man called Yves of Harbrook. He was a boyhood friend to our falconer. The man who knew...however he did have that knowledge... that Richildis was away from home that night, the night she disappeared."

"Then you must find out how he knew."

"She has a gossiping servant by her own account, Johannes."

"It might be that."

He stretched. "I will think about what I found with the falconer's body and get back to you, but now, I'm for my bed. I will be back in town early tomorrow."

"Ah yes…it's market day."

Johannes of Salerno was always busy on market days.

"Thank you for your help with Holdfast," I said simply. "Let me pay you."

He tutted and shook his head.

"Dogs are tough creatures, Aumary. Holdfast should be fine if she doesn't take a wound fever, and I am doing my best to make sure that doesn't happen."

"You treated her as if she was one of our children."

He smiled. "Is she not?"

The town pinter was a serious and exact man in his late twenties who lived in a house on the town green. It was his job to make sure that all measures sold by the suppliers of food stuffs in the town were in line with those rules laid down by the town council and stipulated by the government of our noble King John.

I approached his hall the next morning and heard his voice in earnest conversation with another man.

"A pint is a pint, Master Green and should be sold as such."

"Aye, but…"

"You say your ale is thick and that they bring you odd-sized vessels. Pah! Then you measure it as I have said…"

I poked my head round the door.

"Master Pinter, have you time to speak to me?"

Both men turned and bowed. Master Green, who ran

the only alehouse in town, looked relieved.

"A warning, master, a warning. Next time, it will be a fine."

The keeper of the Green Man passed me in the doorway, nodding a bow.

"Morning, my Lord Belvoir." His eyes rose to Heaven.

"Morning, Green."

Jocelyn Pinter shook his head in resignation, then smiled broadly at me. "What might I do for you, sir?"

"I have come to know about the death of my falconer, Roger Hawkes, Master Pinter."

"Ah...yes... I heard. It's very sad. Killed by his own birds, we hear."

"What makes you say that?"

Master Pinter's eyes grew round. "Is it not true, sir? I did think it was strange, I must say."

"Tell me what you know."

Pinter's eyes roved over my pale blue cotte, took in my sword and knife and settled on my face once more.

"Please take a seat, sir, and I will try to help, for you look as if you have come to ask for help."

"I do?"

Pinter threw out a hand to a chair sitting by the window and took up a small stool for himself. He parted his cotte, shoved the stool between his knees and lowered his backside onto it. He tossed back his long, thinning brown hair.

"My Lord Belvoir, it's part of my job to know when a man is lying. It's part of my job to see what's on a man's face. Now Green..."

"The alehouse master?"

"Aye, Green, he is a devious sod, sir; one look at him, and I know what he is trying to do. I know if he's lying or covering up...I know when he's wrong."

"You're trying to tell me, Pinter, that you are a good

judge of men and have guessed that I have come to speak to you about the falconer's death because...?"

"There is something sinister about it. I know your role, sir. I know you would not be asking questions if it were a simple matter of the man being mauled by his own birds."

I smiled. "You're quite right, Pinter. He was murdered."

The man reeled back on his seat. "Murdered! Oh, God's blood, that's awful!" He crossed himself.

"It was made to look as if the birds got him, but there was no way this could ever be the truth. Whoever killed him knew little about falcons or about how they will behave, it seems."

"How, may I ask, did he die then?"

"He was killed by a knife blow to the neck, which severed the blood line here," I pointed to my own throat, "and he bled to death."

"God take him to his bosom." He crossed himself again.

"The damage to his head, which was made to look like talons ripping into him, was done when he was unconscious or dying to try to disguise the manner of death. Did you know him well?"

"No...not well. I am, as you will no doubt know, a Bedwyn man, and I am a little behind him in age. I knew him better in our youth, better than I know him nowadays."

"I hear that he'd promised his daughter to you."

The man's brow furrowed. "I had mentioned to him that I was looking for a wife. I am well established here in the town now, m'lord, and am of an age to marry and settle to providing myself with heirs, but it was not something we had seriously discussed."

"I have heard differently."

"From whom?"

"Never mind."

"He was looking for a good match for his daughter Richildis, and he did say that if she'd have me, I might be that man, but no more than that."

"You have met the girl?"

"A few times."

Jocelyn Pinter languidly put one knee over another. "She's a pretty piece. Young. By all accounts, a good housekeeper. Capable, kind. Her father was concerned to find her a decent man."

"There was no hurry to this? He didn't scout around. He could no doubt have had quite a few suitors for her hand in marriage here in the town, could he not? Or Bedwyn, or even in Ramsbury?"

"I was in no hurry, though. Roger did seem to want to do the deed fairly quickly."

"Why was this, do you know?"

"It was just a feeling I got, m'lord," said Pinter.

"There was no..." I loaded my words carefully and heavily, "pressing need for the girl to be married?"

Jocelyn Pinter smiled, "I do not think that she is with child, sir. No. Not that."

I smiled. "It wouldn't be the first time a father has foisted a pregnant woman onto an unsuspecting bridegroom, Pinter."

"I am not that man, sir. It would be hard to fool me."

Somehow, I almost believed him.

"Well, you know that she married secretly, the Moor who owns the smelting works at Ramsbury."

"It's gossip about the town, my lord, but unless I hear it from a reputable source, I shall not repeat it."

"I am your reputable source then, Pinter."

"Ah."

"You're not surprised?"

He shrugged. "The one thing I didn't say about

her, sir, was that I got the impression she was a little, erm…wayward."

"Ah. And still, you think that there is no possibility of a child even though she is as you describe…wayward?"

The pinter laughed. "No, sir. I have a feeling she has been rather spoiled by an indulgent father and mother. She will have her own way. If that means marriage to a man who is, for want of a better word, my lord, on the edge of our society here in Wiltshire, then…she will marry."

"You think she did it for…what - notoriety? They both tell me it's a love match."

Pinter shrugged again. "Perhaps it is. Let me say, though, I am glad I didn't pursue it with Hawkes. Like I say, I had a bad feeling about it all, sir."

"You now have another girl in mind, Master Pinter?"

"You are perceptive, sir." He nodded his head.

"So, who do you court now?"

Pinter laughed. "I have my sights set on the eldest daughter of Master Fletschier, sir."

"Ah…yes. Her name is…er…"

"Henriette, my lord."

"Yes, that's right, Henriette. I wish you well with it," I said, thinking to myself, 'that he'd wasted no time there.

"Now, she is a girl who has been brought up well, sir. Quiet, but who can speak with grace when she needs to. A girl with restraint and a good demeanour. The right kind of wife for the town pinter, my Lord Belvoir."

He sat back and looked pleased with himself.

"Going back to our murdered falconer…you have no idea why he might have been killed? There was nothing in his life you can see which might have led him to such an end?"

Pinter pursed his lips. "No, sir. If I think about John, I cannot find anything in his life which would make someone wish to kill him.

"This Moor, Mansur Grover, have you met him?"

"No, sir, never."

"Might he have some quarrel with my falconer, Pinter? Over and above the enmity over a stolen daughter?

"If he did, sir, then I know nothing of it."

"It was very sudden, this wooing and marriage of the iron master and Richildis Hawkes, I think."

Pinter shrugged again and made a moue. "I think she will tire of him, sir, soon enough."

"Richildis of her husband?"

"Yes, my lord. She will, I am sure, be looking for someone younger and more handsome soon. Mark my words

"Why do you say this?"

"They will age, but she'll never catch him up. She is but sixteen years of age, and he is well on his way to forty. I suspect many find him not the most handsome of men. I'm sure there are plenty of other men such young girls would be interested in. I don't think she will stay faithful somehow."

"You don't think she's a girl with particularly high morals then?"

"Would she have married such a man in such a way if she were, my lord?"

I looked him over. He was quite sincere in his words.

"I'm told she is very much in love with the man, and he with her, Pinter."

"Perhaps they are, sir. Now. But I doubt it will last. Summer is short, my lord, and they will enjoy it while it's here, but winter comes soon enough. Then let's see how happy they are. As I say, he is forty. He's nearly in old age. Food isn't plentiful in the winter...if you catch my drift, sir. "

I cleared my throat. 'Hang on, Pinter, I am thirty four,' I said to myself, 'and I am nowhere near an old man.'

"You visit many folk, Pinter, here in the town and round about. Keep your ear to the ground. I want to know if you hear anything about this matter."

"Aye, sir. I can keep my eyes open."

And now to talk to Master Yves of Harbrook.I found him by chance in the buttery at Bedwyn Manor, speaking to Matthew Steward. They both bowed as I entered.

"Good day to you, Matt. All goes well with you?"

"Aye, sir. Thank you," he answered. "Master Harbrook, you may not know, this is Sir Aumary Belvoir, Warden of Savernake, son-in-law to Master Congyre and now lord of this place."

The man bowed low, and a lock of auburn hair flicked over his forehead. He tossed it back as he rose.

"Your Lordship."

"I'm glad I found you, Harbrook. Might we have a word? I am looking into the murder of my falconer, Hawkes. I suspect you probably know that."

"Yes, my lord. Matt here has told me. I am devastated at the news. Please ask me anything. I will do my best to help you catch the black devil that killed him."

"Might we sit in the hall and talk?"

I led the way. Harbrook threw a comment over his shoulder.

"I'll be back, Matt. Then we'll organise for you to come up and choose which dog you'd like."

"Right!" said Matthew Steward.

I sat myself on a chair and gestured for the other man to sit on a bench. I watched him carefully as he took off his cloak, folded and wrapped it up methodically, wiped the seat with his hand and sat on the folded cloak.

He was of average height and build, with a profuseness of dark auburn hair worn long and swept back from his face. That visage was narrow and his cheekbones stood out sharply from a shaven face. Thoughtful, light brown hazel eyes gazed out from deep-set sockets.

"You know then that Roger was murdered, Master Harbrook, a knife to the neck here." I showed him where the knife wound had lain on his friend.

He winced.

"And the slashes he received afterwards were made by the murderer to confuse us, to make us think that the birds were the culprits."

"They would never harm him, sir. Never. When Matt told me, I knew it could not be so."

"You knew the man well?"

"In our youth, sir, we were the best of friends. I went to work for the bishop at Ramsbury and rose to bailiff. I didn't see him as often as I might have liked, but we shared an ale jug now and again."

"You know the family, I hear. The daughter."

Harbrook wriggled in his seat. "Aye, I knew them all. Know them."

"And what do you think of her?"

"Think, sir?"

"You know that she has married…"

"Yessir…I know that. It broke her father's heart."

"I hear that you were the one to tell him of the girl's flight to Ramsbury. Mind telling me how it was that you knew when Hawkes himself had no idea what was going on?"

"Oh, I knew what was going on," said Harbrook with an edge to his voice. "The little hussy throwing herself at the Moor. Simpering over his tales of far-off lands, whispering in corners and touching…and…"

"You were witness to this?"

"My sister was, sir."

"Your sister?"

I pictured the earlier scene at the new house in Ramsbury, with the older woman in company with the girl Richildis.

"Ah...I see...she is the companion and maid to Mistress Grover?"

"Yes, sir. She told me. And I told her father."

"How was it they contrived to meet and carry on this courtship, then? It cannot have been easy. A young girl protected and chaperoned..."

"You think so, m'lord?" He shook his auburn locks. "I warned Roger. I told him he had given her too much freedom," said Harbrook. "When her mother died, it was easy for Richildis to slip away."

"And with that freedom, she managed to meet and engage with the iron master?"

"She did, sir. Were he a truly honourable man, my lord, he would have gently rebuffed her. Sent her back to her father."

"Did Grover ever appeal to her father? Did he ask for her hand in marriage in the usual way?"

"No, as far as I'm aware, he never did. It was all so underhand. That's why, when I found out, I had to tell Roger what was going on. That's the pity of it."

"Your sister told you that Mistress Hawkes had gone to the black man that evening? The evening she disappeared?" I asked.

"She told me that she thought it was about to happen, and she had become worried. I merely told Roger, but we were too late to stop the marriage because Roger wouldn't believe me, sir. He argued that his daughter wouldn't do such a thing. He wouldn't believe me."

"Hard to believe ill of a beloved daughter?"

He nodded sadly; the auburn forelock dipped once more over his eyes, and he brushed it back again.

"How did that evening go? Tell me."

"I thought I had seen Richildis leaving Bedwyn on foot, sir, with a few things tied in a bundle. I asked my sister where she was going and found that she was leaving home and that Margaret was sworn not to speak out and say anything. I asked Roger to go home and ensure that Richildis was there."

"She walked the five miles?" I asked, disbelief tinging my voice.

"I have no doubt there was someone to meet her, sir, somewhere in the forest, with a horse. It was well planned. She will not have had to walk far."

"And the vows...?"

"It was all arranged beforehand. The man has money. He bought witnesses to their pledging. You know, sir, that the churches are closed to marriages, but you also know that if two people pledge themselves before witnesses without a priest, then that marriage is as valid as that conducted with great pomp and ceremony at the church door. If only Roger had listened to me. Then, at last, he went home and found her gone. Stunned, he straight away took a horse to Ramsbury, but he didn't know where they were. They were not yet at the house by the church where they now live."

"You did not follow? Go with him?"

"Oh yes, I went with him to be a witness. But as I say, we had to search all over the town for them. By the time we found them, it was all over. They were man and wife, and the marriage had been consummated. It was early morning." The man's voice trembled. "The deed was done by then. My sister was called to join her a while later, for Margaret thought that if she could go to Richildis and be with her, perhaps things wouldn't be so bad. Richildis is but sixteen years of age, sir. She needs another woman around her and Mansur's home and workplace are very masculine."

"Your sister has, I was told, been with Richildis since she was a child," I said.

"My sister is unmarried, sir, and has devoted her life to the girl. She would not leave her."

"The position of falconer is a worthy one, Harbrook. Here, as on many estates, they are valued members of the household and are well paid. They can employ servants of their own. It was the case here. Margaret was Roger's servant?"

Harbrook clasped his knees and nodded. "My wife also tried to talk to Richildis but to no avail. She was besotted, bewitched."

"You are married then, Master Harbrook?" I had wondered if the man had had designs on the young girl himself.

"Yes, sir, I am married. I have been married for four years."

"Do you know of any other reason why Master Hawkes should be killed?"

"No other reason, no. I will say this, though: the black man has a temper, my lord. I was told of it that night. It would not surprise me to find that he had killed poor Roger in a fit of temper over Richildis."

"Why, when the whole episode was over, and Roger was a beaten man? Grover had his way."

"I grant you all this was some time ago, over a month since, but the resentment festered, and Roger could not let it go."

"I heard that Roger accepted the situation and tried to make the best of it, that it had not come to a quarrel."

Harbrook shook his head again. "Oh no. It was not so. Roger felt betrayed. He faced him more than once on the Moor's own ground, but each time, Richildis managed to intervene and calm the waters, I'm told. She would not return home with her father. I think Grover can be a dangerous man, sir."

"How so?"

Yves of Harbrook leaned forward and lowered his voice. "I am not the only one to have seen his temper, his fits of jealousy. He is a proud and angry man. You do not need to search far for the murderer of Roger Hawkes, sir."

I now had two conflicting reports. First, that Roger had accepted the situation and was beaten, and the second, that he was far from beaten and was actively engaged in trying to wrest his daughter from the clutches of her new husband.

One strand remained taut in all this tangle. Two men had told me that Richildis Grover was determined to be married to the Moor at all costs. It was certainly not an abduction.

"Who told you, my lord, that Roger didn't care about the fate of his daughter?" asked Harbrook.

"My reeve here at Bedwyn who knew him well. I have also spoken to Master Pinter in Marlborough town. He cannot see why the quarrel should carry on once the deed was done, either, Harbrook."

"Perhaps neither of them knew Roger as I did, sir."

"Hmm." I stood. "Well, thank you for your information, Harbrook. I may speak to you again."

The man retrieved his cloak and shook it out, smoothing the creases and carefully laid it over the crook of his elbow.

"Aw!!"

"What's the matter?"

"Oh, that's one of the problems..."

"Problems with...?"

"Hair, my lord. I keep dogs, you see. The Durnfords' dogs. Well, not me personally, but I have an interest as bailiff. I breed them, white dogs, oh and the hair...oh the hair gets everywhere." The man was beating down his dark brown cloak with the flat of his hand.

"You are too fastidious, Harbrook. A little hair never hurt anyone," I chuckled.

We walked out to the sunlight of the screens passage.

"Ah, m'lord," said Matthew Steward, coming out of the pantry. "Will you be requiring supper, or are you going back to Durley?"

"To Durley, Matt."

"If you are finished with me, my Lord Belvoir, Matt and I have a little business to conduct," said Harbrook.

"Ah…are you buying a dog, Matt?"

"Yes, m'lord. For myself." His eyes rose to Heaven. "Or rather for the wife."

"Not content with a baby then…she must have a dog?"

"Our old dog died in March, sir, and she will have another puppy to replace her. Do not fear it will be a smallish one and will be declawed."

Forest law dictated that all dogs loose in Savernake, indeed, in any of the king's forests, must have their two front claws removed so that they could not hunt the deer. Failure to comply with this rule of law meant a severe fine and the death or displacement of the dog. I sometimes had to hear cases in my manorial court and hand out the fines for infringements myself.

"Never fear, Matt," said Harbrook, "all will be done before it ever gets to you."

"Master Harbrook…what do you breed, lymers… Alaunts?"

"I have lymers, yes and alaunts too, though it's the gazehound bitch who has just given birth. Five puppies. Three dogs and two bitches."

"I promised my daughter a dog, Harbrook. Perhaps I'll send my houndsman over to Ramsbury to look at your puppies. We may be able to do business."

Harbrook grinned. "I would be most gratified if you were to take one, sir. For the warden of the forest to have one of our dogs would indeed be an honour."

"Declawed, sir?" asked Matt with a smile.

"Declawed, Matt," I answered.

I ambled home to Durley by back ways, thinking all the time on what people had said.

My roan gelding Bayard clopped gently through the forest; it was a good job he knew his way home. It was the middle of September. The forest was still green, but the tops of the trees and some of the smaller saplings were turning a little. Small gold and rust butterflies were feeding on the fermenting fruit of the wayside blackberry. The hedges were full of the red berries of the haw and the rose hips; the elderberries were bowing the stems of the elders with their profusion of black clusters. The sloe crop of the blackthorn was abundant this year.

I slid tiredly from Bayard's back and gave him into Cedric's hand.

He grinned at me.

"I've done it, sir. I've asked her, and she has accepted me. It's all arranged." He positively shone.

"And at the same time, Master Hartshorn, Rob and Mistress Giffard are going to get married, so it will be a double celebration, sir."

"Congratulations, Cedric."

I remembered that one of my foresters and the widow who brewed ale in the village, who were neighbours, had been courting for a while, since his house burned down in a raid we'd had on the village the year before. Rob had come to me just last week to tell me they were planning to marry. Not that he'd needed to. They were both free.

Mistress Giffard could marry whom she wished as a widow.

"I am very pleased for you all."

I hauled my body up the stairs and shouted back. "We need to get building you a house, Cedric."

Henry Steward met me at the top with a beaker of ale.

Hal was lounging on a bench behind him. He looked up from his whittling as I entered.

"Oh dear. You look like you've just bought a sword to find it's got no edge."

I laughed out loud. "It's only that I have just got a surfeit of information going round in my brain, Hal, and I need to write it all down to make sense of it. It's a bit of a jumble."

"Aye, jumbles are tirin'."

"How is Holdfast?"

"True to 'er name, holdin' 'er own. She's eaten some pobbies, I'm told, and is doin' well."

"I'm glad to hear it."

"The wound is clean…"

"It will be if Johannes has anything to do with it."

"An' she's no fever."

"No trouble here, Hal?"

"No, nothin' like what we 'ad at Bedwyn. No dug-up corpuses."

"I am very pleased to hear it. I'm off to my office to write everything down. Any messages?"

"Agnes says what she wishes to ask will keep till tomorrow and Johnathan Reeve has one or two queries, but again nothin' that won't keep. E's gone 'ome."

"Good."

"Oh, and there's this."

He stretched over the table and fetched up a piece of parchment.

"It was brought in by a lad from the ironworks."

I scanned it. "It's a list of folk who saw Mansur Grover

with his wife at home the morning that Roger Hawkes was killed, Hal. All have signed it with their mark." I threw it down. "One less suspect then."

"You never really thought it was 'im now, did you?"

I shook my head. "He has, as far as I can see, no motive."

"He gains nothin', does 'e? No coooee bonies."

I chuckled. A scholar I had known when I was young had told me about a lawyer of the Latin age called Cicero, who had come up with the phrase 'cui bono' - who benefits. It was something I had thought about in each of the crimes I had investigated from the early years.

"He has what he wanted, Hal."

"The girl?"

"Hmm."

I turned to go to my office and fiddled for the key, which I kept on a chain around my neck.

"Johannes was here for a little while. He was passin' through goin' to someone out at Ladywell."

"Oh?"

"'E looked in quickly on 'Oldfast and left this 'ere for you."

It was a sealed letter. Johannes rarely sent me sealed letters.

My brow must have furrowed because Hal added. "'E told me 'e didn't want to put it on parchment, but ..."

"Ah."

Hal stood in the doorway of my office as I broke the wax seal and read:

'The excellent Constable Aumary Belvoir, greetings and the bond of friendship.'

That was rather formal for Johannes.

'I thought that you should know, Aumary, what I found when I had a chance to examine the body of Roger Hawkes properly yesterday.'

Ah, yes. After the coroner had been, I left Johannes in

the barn at Bedwyn bent over the cadaver, and I had gone with Hal to Ramsbury.

'The man died, as I said, very early in the morning of the day you found him, of a wound to the neck. He did indeed bleed to death. The other wounds were inflicted as he lay dying, as I explained to you. They were caused by a knife; the shirt was torn to shreds and the skin scored about the breast, neck, face and scalp. None of these wounds were deep. If he were dead quickly, he could not have bled so profusely from these wounds and so it is my guess he was unconscious for a while. However, I found no contusion on his head where he had been struck insensible. This puzzles me, I must say. For if he were struck in the neck, he would have staggered, perhaps crawled outside and called for help. His attacker must have prevented him.

There is one other thing which you must know.

Upon examining the whole body of the man, I found that he had a large aggressive lump, which us doctors call a tumour, which was evident in the lower stomach region. It was well advanced and would have killed him in a short while, maybe a very few weeks.

Roger Hawkes was a dying man, Aumary.

Yours in love and deep admiration.

Johannes.'

I threw down the letter and pinched the bridge of my nose. This was not the news I wanted to hear. I had liked and admired the man Roger Hawkes.

My falconer had somehow managed to conceal this affliction. A capacious shirt, covering the swelling, was the garment in which he had been found and the one which a knife had shredded.

I had not seen him for some months. Had this affliction been plaguing him quietly for some while? No one had told me that the man was ill. Did he keep it from his friend

Harbrook, from his son, and his daughter? From everyone? Was this why he seemed so keen to have his girl married off? He knew he was not going to be around to care for her. Was he trying to get his affairs in order?

Master Grover. He had been suffering for some while with an incurable illness. It would have killed him in a very short while. I am merely trying to find out if anyone knew this."

Mansur Grover took this news quite calmly.

He enveloped his wife in his huge arm, sat her back on the bench and towered over her.

"An illness? We did not know this. No, we did not know."

"He would, my friend the doctor tells me, be dead inside a couple of months at the very most."

"I repeat, we did not know this. Had we known, we might have behaved...differently."

I nodded. "I can think of no reason why my falconer should have been struck down, Grover. If it was known he was dying, then if someone had wanted him out of the way..."

"It was not us, I assure you."

"Out of the way for some reason, then they need only wait six weeks or so."

The Moor's gaze hardened. "Had we known, we would have waited to marry. To save him grief."

I walked around the back of the party.

"Thank you for the letter telling us where you were the morning Roger died, Grover."

Mansur looked over his shoulder at me. "I said that I would provide us with an alibi. I do as I say, my lord. I am a man of my word."

Suddenly, there was a grumbling sound and a frenzied and violent shouting in the yard as several men rushed up to the house door.

The servant came running into the hall. "Sir, I am sorry...there is fighting at the works. They ask you to come back and deal with it."

"Fighting...whatever for?"

"It's the Durnford bailiff and your man, sir. They are

shouting at each other, and some of the men have drawn knives to protect themselves."

"What for, for Heaven's sake?"

The man shook his head. "Please, sir… they asked for you."

We exited the hall, ran down the short lane and crossed the road into the nearby ironworks compound.

Several men were ranged around the edges. In the centre, there was a crowd and much shoving and pushing.

"What goes on here?" shouted Grover.

I followed that with, "Stop, in the name of the constable!"

The shouting grew louder, but the people engaged in the fracas drew off. Hal moved towards the men and glared.

I strode into the middle of the two groups, my hand on the pommel of my sword.

"By the power invested in me by our sovereign Lord John, I command you to desist."

"Burridge, what is going on here?" shouted Grover again, coming to stand beside me.

Mansur Grover's overseer was red in the face. He pushed his way to the front of the crowd, though he had been at the forefront of the pushing and shoving when we'd entered the yard and had, we'd noticed, instantly retreated as we entered the compound.

"The man Harbrook… he came here looking for you. He pushed his way into the office. I told him you were not here. He wouldn't take no for an answer and he became abusive."

I looked around for Harbrook.

There he was, nursing a bloodied wrist. One of the men he'd brought with him was tearing up what looked like the hem of a shirt in order to bind his wound.

"And what does the bailiff want with me besides to buy

iron at a price he doesn't want to pay?" said Grover, turning a hard eye on Harbrook.

"I merely want to know where you were when my good friend Roger was being stabbed to death."

"The constable here has my answer to that and he is satisfied. Why should I answer especially to you?"

"You are a devil, Grover. First, you bewitch the innocent Richildis, then you murder her father..."

Mansur Grover's laugh rang around the compound. "You are drunk, Harbrook...go home and sleep it off."

"You will all disperse to your work here and in other parts of the town. All of you!" I cried at the top of my voice. "Or I will have you all confined!" I had to be very sure of myself, for I had little power here. This was not the forest, nor was it Marlborough town. Luckily, this was still Wiltshire, and my constable's writ was good here.

The men shuffled into groups. Some left by the main gate. Others went back to their work in the compound.

I approached Harbrook. "Who struck you, Harbrook?"

The man looked up, and his face took on a rather embarrassed hue.

"'Twas in the melee, I don't know. We were trading insults. It's nothing."

"So, Richildis is an innocent now, is she? Yesterday, you sang a different tune."

"She was, as I told you, bewitched, my lord. How could such a creature as Richildis want to marry that foul abomination." He jutted his chin at Mansur Grover, now helping to right some of their equipment turned over in the fighting.

"It is her choice and her choice alone, Harbrook, and nothing to do with you."

I took him by the sleeve and moved him to the side of the shed.

"Tell me, you were, by your own admission, friends with Hawkes for many years. Did you know he had been ill… very ill?"

"Ill, my lord? I don't think Roger had a day's illness in his life!"

"He had a large lump in his belly, Harbrook, one which would have killed him in a few weeks."

Harbrook, distracted, let go of the rag he was holding to his injured wrist. His face dropped, his mouth opened, but no sound issued from it.

"Whoever killed him did not know they had no need to, for he would have been dead inside a month or so."

"God in his Heaven," he crossed himself.

He stooped to pick up the rag, tutted, and shook it, for it was now covered in earth and gravel.

He turned down his sleeve for the wound to his arm had stopped bleeding and was no more than a scratch.

"No, to answer your question, my Lord Belvoir, I did not know."

"What do you have against the Moor that you march in here with your men and pick a fight."

Harbrook planted his feet. "We picked no fight. I am often to be found here. We buy iron for our own working. I came to negotiate. The man Mansur was not here as promised. I spoke to his man, who was obstructive and foul-mouthed. I took exception."

"And you traded insults, no doubt. You seemed insulting enough to the iron master. I heard you with my own ears."

Harbrook shook his shoulders. I deemed it something he did when he was slightly put out.

"Aye, well. My blood was up. I did want to know where he was when Roger met his end."

"I have an answer to that, Harbrook, and I am satisfied, as the iron master says. Your fears are ungrounded."

He looked at me with narrowed eyes, and I saw the change in them. He sighed and looked towards the forge master's right-hand man, the man who had argued with him, John Burridge, who was at that moment in earnest talk with Grover.

He bowed. "Then I apologise for my behaviour. It is unlike me to become…inflamed. I am most usually in control of my tempers."

"We shall forget this episode then. You are the only one hurt. Let that be your lesson. Best to stay away from Master Burridge in future." I slapped him on the back. "I will send my houndsman to you later today and he can pick out a puppy from your brood. When do you say they can leave their dam, Harbrook?"

"Another seven days, sir, and it can be yours."

"Good."

I turned away. Hal came jogging up and nodded at me. I followed his eyes.

There, on the fringe of the compound entrance, stood Mistress Grover, her eyes seeking out the tall figure of her husband.

Harbrook passed her in the gate with a bow and a few words. She quickly drew away from him and marched off to her husband.

"No love lost there then, it seems?" said Hal, grinning.

"Hmmm. Maybe."

I ambled over to the party in the middle of the working area.

"Burridge, a word."

"My lord," the man bowed.

"What was all that about? Let's hear your side of the story." I moved him to the edge of the compound out of earshot of the assembled men. Hal followed and leaned on the fence.

The man wiped his face with a rag."That man is an insufferable pecker, my lord... always finding fault with this or that. Pleasing him in this business is a hard job. He marched in here, calling for my master, uninvited..."

"The man said he had an appointment..."

"That was a lie. He had no such appointment with Master Grover. I would know this, for I'd be the one to make that appointment." His nostrils flared. "You see how he lies, and then he begins to pick a quarrel over the last consignment we sent to the Durnford estate. Once he'd exhausted that, he began to speak ill of my master. That I will not have, sir, oh no!"

"What is the source of their quarrel, do you know?"

Burridge's pinched face took on a secretive look. He leaned forward. "I think there's a deal of jealousy, sir."

"Over the woman, Richildis?" asked Hal.

Burridge nodded. "I am sure that he wanted her for himself and was baulked at the last minute."

"The man is married, Burridge."

"When has that ever stopped a man, m'lord?"

I folded my arms and stared at him. "You are saying that Harbrook had designs on his friend's daughter and that because Master Mansur stole her away, he is angry?"

"I don't think she's the only one. It's well known he's got a bit of a roving eye."

"Mistress Grover 'as no eye but for 'er 'usband," said Hal, watching the two of them across the yard.

Grover took his wife into the forge office, and the door closed behind them.

"I must go back to my work, my lord."

"Go then and stay away from Master Harbrook."

"I hope you told him to stay away from me, sir."

I watched him go.

"One of them is lying, m'lord," said Hal, smoothing

down his long grey beard and fingering the two separate points. "Or both of 'em. I can't see what's goin' on."

"I don't think these are the only liars either, Hal."

I put my arm over his shoulder. "Come! Back to Bedwyn."

"Ralph, sit down, please," I said as we entered the house of the falconer in the middle of Bedwyn village.

"I have some news for you."

The young man's earnest face turned up to mine as he slowly sat on a bench. "You have found the man who…?

"No. Sadly…we haven't, but…we must ask you…did you know that your father was deathly ill?"

His brow furrowed. "I knew that he was not well…but ill unto death? No."

I sat down before him. "The doctor tells me, Ralph, that he had a huge growth here, which in a very short while would have killed him." I pointed to my own belly.

"He was tender, it's true. He said he couldn't eat like he did when he was younger, but I never thought…I thought it was just his age. I did know he had trouble passing water…"

I stood and looked down at him. "Doctor Johannes put his remaining life span at a couple of months at the most. Did anyone else know of his affliction, do you think? Your sister was unaware, it seems."

"Tildy didn't know?"

I shook my head. "She was as shocked as you are. Your father must have managed to keep it a secret from everyone."

"It would be like him. He was, as you know, sir, a very quiet and self-contained man."

I ruffled my curly black hair as I walked about the room. "I just cannot see why anyone would wish to murder him."

"No, sir. I too …am…at a loss…"

"You saw him that morning? The morning he died?"

"No, sir…he was out before me."

"Was that unusual?"

"Well, we mostly took our morning ale together, but that morning…he'd gone."

"Nothing seemed different about the night before, Ralph?"

The young man pulled his mouth into a wide grimace. "Well… I did hear him walking about the floor the night before. I don't know why. It woke me. I don't know what time of night it was. I can usually tell because of the bells in the church. Father Godwin tolls them for the offices, but… with the prohibition…"

"Did he go out then, do you think? When he rose?"

"I don't know, I can't tell you. I went back to sleep." His voice quavered.

I laid my hand on his shoulder. "Well, he's at peace now."

"Except he cannot lie in hallowed ground, can he?" he spat.

"Ralph…God knows where he is…he was a good man, there doesn't…"

"If God were the merciful God we are led to believe, my father would not have died…not have suffered…he would still be here with us…"

"My Lord Belvoir!"

A voice broke into our conversation from outside.

"My lord, are you there?"

Hal pushed off from his leaning position by the door. "That's Tostig!"

He pulled open the door just as the figure of the steward Matthew reached for it. He fell into Hal and righted himself, pulling down his tunic.

"Sir… one of your men from Durley…"

Tostig pushed past him. "My Lord Belvoir…sir."

Tostig was one of my senior grooms.

"Yes, Tostig. I am here."

"A request from Lady Belvoir to return to Durley, sir."

"Back to Durley?"

"There's been a murder, m'lord."

We clattered under the gatehouse at Durley a short while after having ridden pell-mell through the forest. Luckily, Bedwyn was but three miles from Durley, and the road was straight and, at this season, good under our horses' hooves.

Lydia was waiting for me at the top of the manor stairs.

I took them two at a time.

There were tears in her eyes.

"What's happened?"

She nodded down into the stable where, through the open door, I could see Cedric sitting on a stool, my chief groom, Richard Marshall, standing over him. Cedric had his head in his hands and he was unashamedly sobbing.

Richard looked up and I saw him nod to Bill, who came and put his hand on Cedric's shoulder.

Tostig led out Fitzroy and Fenrir, giving Bayard and Grafton, the horses we had taken to Ramsbury, to Aelfnod, our youngest groom.

Richard came up the stairs and nodded to me. Hal followed him up.

"Sir…Cedric has just come back from Marlborough. It seems that…" He swallowed and looked back down to the open stable door. "It seems that the young lady who he was…who he wanted to marry, my lord…is dead."

"Dead? Alysoun dead? But…"

"She has been murdered, Aumary," said my wife.

Chapter Five

"MURDERED? No! Alysoun? What? Why?"

"Cedric went to meet her, sir. They met usually at her grannie's house, but according to Cedric, she wasn't there."

Tostig was standing at the bottom of the steps. He shaded his brow with his hand against the sun.

"Sir...I went into town with Cedric. We had some errands to run. The town reeve found me on the High Street and asked me to come and fetch you. I brought Cedric back with me. There was nothing he could do. I thought it best that he didn't stay but came home."

"Well done, Tostig."

"By then, poor Cedric had found his girl in the barn at the back of Nick's house," said Rich.

"The big one by the mill where the grain is stored?"

"Yessir."

"The girl is still there, guarded by Nick's men, sir. He asked for you to go straightways to the town."

"Aye...I'll go. I'll go now. Hal, Tostig - are you up to..."

"Yes sir, anything," said Tostig.

"Saddle yourself a horse."

Lydia ran into the hall and returned with two cups of ale for Hal and me.

I threw mine down my neck and wiped my mouth with the back of my hand. I had been wearing my gambeson as I did when out in the forest every day, but now I realised how warm it was.

Then the thought came into my head that I was angry... and that had made me even warmer.

I jumped down the hall steps and made for the stable.

"Cedric..." I said gently. The lad lifted his head to me and made to rise, but I pushed him down with the flat of my hand.

"No. Stay." I simply did not know what to say to him.

"Look after him, Rich," I said. "I am going into town quickly, Cedric. I will find out who has done this."

"Yessir," he hiccoughed, though I doubt he truly understood me.

"Tostig, do you know all?...Can you tell me what I need to know as we ride?"

"Yessir. I was there when Cedric...I went to the barn and ran up the lane."

I took his arm, and we walked out of the stable.

"I do not want to bother him with the details yet. I know what it's like...when..."

"Yessir."

"Then let's ride and ride quickly."

Nicholas Barbflet, the town reeve, met us at the top of Crook's Lane, where he had his house.

His face was pinched and white, showing he was still shocked even a length of time after the finding of Alysoun's body.

I threw down Fitzroy's reins and made for the town

reeve, who drew me into the kitchen door at the back of his house.

"Thank God," he said. "I have left everything for you to…see." He crossed himself. "It's such a shock, Aumary. On my own ground…the poor girl. Have we a madman in the place?"

I shook my head. "I don't know. Lead me to her, Nick."

We walked down towards the water mill. Hal and Tostig followed.

"Tostig says that Cedric couldn't find Alysoun at her grannie's, where they had agreed to meet. He says he was told that she had come to your house where she works, but when he couldn't find her there, one of your kitchen maids said that she had gone down to the barn."

Nick looked up, his face lined in puzzlement. "Why would she go there? At this season, the barn is full of grain ready to be milled. Why should she be wanting to go there?"

I shrugged.

"Cedric thought she had gone to find you with a message perhaps. That's what he told Tostig shortly after he…found her."

I scratched my chin. "There was no one in the barn?"

"No, not as far as I can ascertain. They would all be busy in the mill. The main door is locked usually. There is normally a lot of folk to-ing and fro-ing, but today it was open for a while."

"No one saw her enter the barn?" I asked.

"I have made inquiries. No, no one."

Nick nodded to the two men standing by the closed barn door. I recognised them. Both were his men from the mill.

"Grist, Waterman."

"Milord Belvoir," they nodded, looking grim.

Nick gestured for them to stand aside and move off. They turned as one and walked back to the mill, sombrely watching their own feet plod in unison and without a backward glance.

"Johannes is about town, and when he has finished, he'll come here…" said Nick.

"Meanwhile…" He pulled the handle of the large right-hand door of the great barn. It was an old door, but not a very ancient one and so it was not as hardened, perhaps, as some of the older oaken doors one finds. Being a barn, it was not studded with metal.

"Wait!" I peered at the outside. Through the wood, I'd noticed a small spike of metal just poking out from the planks.

"You will see why in a moment, Aumary," said Nick.

I touched the spike. It was very sharp at the tip. Nick swung the door.

As he swung it, Tostig came forward and put out his hand. I puzzled at this action and was about to ask him to move, but as the door opened further, I could see why he had acted so.

He steadied the body of poor Alysoun Backs.

She hung on the door, spitted through like a hog. Her chin hung on her chest, and her arms lay loose at her side. Her brown hair hung like a curtain to her breast.

Tostig let go, and she drooped a little further but did not swing as she might have done if he had not held her.

"God's teeth!" said Hal, "And poor Cedric found her… like this?"

Tostig nodded. "I was at the coopers up the lane. I was collecting a basin my wife had ordered and heard Cedric yell."

"You came down and found them?" I asked.

"I did. Ced was on his knees just here. He'd opened the door and…she'd just swung out at him."

Hal crossed himself. "Poor lad." He took a shuddering breath, "It was a good shot."

"Aye, Master Hal. Someone who knows how to throw a spear," said Tostig.

"She must have just come in the door…turned to pull it shut…turned again and wallop!" said Hal.

"She staggered back with the weight of the spear and it pinned her to the door," I added. "Slightly lifting her from her feet." I bent my knees to look.

"But what's a spear like this doing in here?"

I looked around. This was a grain store, not a weapons store.

There was only one entry. This one with two doors.

There was nothing strange about the place at all. And such a spear was not common in the vicinity.

"Who has been here today?" I asked.

"Grist and the young man who helps fill the sacks."

"Milward?"

"The younger brother of the wheelwright's apprentice. Earlier today, just before noon. There was no one here then."

"When did Cedric find her?"

"Just on nones…or it would be if the church were ringing bells."

"Aye, it's awkward without them."

"So she was killed between midday and the ninth hour of the day?"

"Looks like it," I said.

"But what was she doing here…and why kill a little house maid?" Nick shook his head. "Felicity is distraught, I can tell you."

Felicity was his wife and she treated all her staff like family.

I suddenly looked up."Has her grannie…?"

"Aye…she knows…"

I shook my head. "Terrible…just terrible."

Tostig looked out of the barn door. "Here's the doctor now, sir."

Johannes came running, but he slowed as he approached the barn.

"What have we?"

"There is no hurry, Johannes," I shouted up to him. "The girl is dead." As I said this, I felt a frisson roll along the whole lane as folk who lived and worked here heard me. I immediately regretted my words.

Johannes came up and peered around the door. He crossed himself. "God! Poor girl."

"Are you happy for us to take her down, or shall you examine her here?"

"We have informed the coroner, but he won't be here for a while, Sir Aumary," said Nick.

I nodded. "On my authority, take her down."

Hal and Tostig moved to prise the girl from the door and to extract the spear.

I went out into the lane.

People were moving about their business, but it was quiet, a Tuesday, not a market day, thankfully, and late in the afternoon. Folk were not busy about the streets.

I looked up and down the lane. Towards the corn mill, which lay right by the River Kennet, there was a row of weavers' houses with their weaving sheds in the roof. Then, the fenced-in yards of the coopers and wheelwrights were situated a short way back. Some houses faced the lane further up, and then the house of the town reeve lay at the top with a couple of small bothies leaning up against the wall. Some more houses on that side marched down in a row towards the barn by which we stood. It almost bordered the mill pool. Then, my eye found the mill again.

The back of the houses on the High Street faced this lane, but their higher windows were small, and the spaces in the attics were mostly for storage or for sleeping in. It would be unlikely for anyone to have been staring out and notice who went into the barn.

Johannes came out, wiping his hand on a small piece of cloth. "As Hal has told me…a clever blow, straight to the part of the ribs where lies the heart. She hardly knew what had hit her."

"Small mercies," I said.

"When, Johannes? Can you tell?"

"Very difficult. Tostig tells me they found her on nones."

"Yes. About nones."

"Then I would say that it happened only a very short time before. She has been dead about three or four hours."

I looked up at the sky. The heavens were a screen of haze, and the sun was not visible, though it was warm and sticky.

"It is now about the twelfth hour… or just past," said the doctor.

I took my teeth in my lips. "Why?"

"Was she coming here to meet someone?" asked Johannes.

"If it was so, then she must have thought Cedric was here, for it was he she was supposed to meet."

"God that he should find her so."

"This will not be good…you realise…?" said Johannes.

"Aye, I know. He saw my son Geoffrey die, too. Poor boy. Why is it some folk have all the misfortune and others just sail through life, Johannes?" I asked gloomily.

The doctor smiled a rueful smile.

"If I knew that, my Lord Belvoir…I would be God."

Tostig came out of the building with a frown on his face and with the spear in his hand.

"It's a boar spear, sir…why would anyone in the town…?"

"It might come from the castle, Tostig."

"Ah, yes."

"Anyone from there might have taken it. Or perhaps the armourer in town has one missing from his workshop."

"Not many hunt boar, sir. It's not a common weapon. And you'd get some strange looks carrying one down the High Street."

"We have some at Durley, Tostig, and there are also some at Bedwyn. But no, they're not common."

"Possibly more of them about than you might imagine, eh?" said Johannes as he took it from Tostig. "But not in the town.

"Why these lugs on each side, Sir Aumary?"

"Boar 'ave the 'abit of pushin' to get their tusks in you, you see," answered Hal quickly. "These 'ere are to stop the creature gettin' at you once you've stuck 'im. They'll ride down the shaft at yer, fierce little buggers, even though that means them getting well and truly spitted."

Johannes grimaced. "But it's long enough to pin a slight housemaid to a door."

We all stood there in silence for a moment. Nick Barbflet, shaking his head, left, turning for the top of the lane with a wave of his hand.

"Leave the spear, Johannes, for the coroner. Let us go and speak to Felicity Barbflet, the girl's mistress. Perhaps she can shine some light on this terrible thing."

"No, my lord. I cannot tell you anything," said Felicity, sniffing into a square of rough linen. "It's all so baffling."

"It was her day off, you say."

"She comes in every day but Sunday, and she has a day off every so often, like everyone else. You know that she lives up on the Backs with her old grandmother."

This was the small lane which ran at the back and parallel with the High Street, up the hill.

"Yes, I do know that."

"Her parents died in the dock fever outbreak, and there was just Alysoun and her old grandma left. Her siblings died then, too."

Many folk had had family die in that terrible outbreak of fever a few years ago. We had not escaped it at Durley.

"Who knew that it was her day off, and who knew she was meeting Cedric, Fliss?"

"Everyone in this house. I can't think anyone, particularly outside, would know their plans beforehand. Cedric and Alysoun would meet at her grannie's and then walk about town or go down to the river to sit…or…" She dropped her chin and snivelled into the linen screwed up in her fist. "It's all too awful."

"There was no real pattern to it, Sir Aumary," said Nick, patting his wife on the shoulder. "They just arranged it when they could. If Cedric came into town on an errand, as he did today, then they'd meet for a short while."

"Aye 'e told me a while ago that they shared a pie an' a flagon of ale by the river sometimes," said Hal sorrowfully.

"Has she been seen in anyone's company lately? Anyone that was new to her, perhaps?"

Everyone present shook their heads.

I took a deep breath and let it out again in a gesture of bafflement.

"Did she seem her usual self today, Fliss? Was there anything bothering her, do you think?"

"Bothering her…well…no…not as far as I know, sir."

"She was her usual self this morning?"

"Yes…just pleased to be seeing Cedric. I saw her in the hall before she left."

"If it was her day off, why was she in your kitchen?"

"She came to fetch a flask of ale," said Nicholas Barbflet.

"So where is it?"

"I…Fliss, do you know where it might be?" asked Nick, a look of bewilderment on his face.

"I wasn't here in the kitchen just then, but Aelfwine was," said Felicity Barbflet.

The girl Aelfwine, who was tearfully standing in the kitchen doorway, came forward and squared her shoulders.

"Yes, mistress, I saw her."

"Aelfwine, can you tell me how she seemed? Did she seem to you happy and content or…" I asked.

"She was smiley, but…"

"But?"

"Well, she said that she was happy to be seeing Cedric, m'lord, but that he wouldn't like what she had to tell 'im, sir."

I stood up straighter. "She was about to tell Cedric something?"

"She said it was important and that…"

"Yes?"

"And that he had to tell you, m'lord."

Nick, Johannes, Hal and I all looked at each other and blinked.

"Have I got it right, girl? Alysoun was going to tell Cedric something he wouldn't like, and Cedric was to tell me."

"And you wouldn't like it either, sir," said Aelfwine. "But apart from that, she was as happy as a lark." Then tears began to course down her cheeks silently.

I cleared my throat. "Did she have a flask of ale, Aelfwine?"

"Yessir." She wiped her eyes with a shaky hand. "It was one of our black leather ones. She took it with her."

"Then where is it?"

We went back to the grain barn. The flask was nowhere to be seen.

All the way back to Durley, I listened to the chatter of Tostig and Hal, but I heard not one word they said. Round and round in my head went the statement of the little maid Aelfwine. Alysoun had had no chance to tell Cedric her news. She had been killed before she could impart it to him. Or he to me. In a way, I was grateful for that, for if Cedric had known, he too might be dead.

What was this news? What had little Alysoun heard or seen which had got her spitted like a boar on that barn door? Was this anything to do with the death of my falconer?

Once more, but this time, as the sun was setting over the forest, we clattered under the stones of the Durley gateway. Two grooms, Richard and Bill, came out to take our horses. I could see Cedric furiously raking the muck from an empty stall.

"What is he doing, Rich…? He should…"

"I can't get him to stop. He keeps busy. The whole afternoon, he's been busy. He won't rest or stop to eat or drink," whispered Richard.

"I nodded. "Yes, it dulls the pain a little. It doesn't make it go away, and when you are forced to stop, it comes back, but for a while, it is lessened."

Richard Marshall nodded.

"I'll speak to him, Rich."

I put Fitzroy's reins into his hands and went into the gloom of the middle stable.

"Cedric."

I saw his back stiffen. "Yessir?"

"Come here for a moment and speak to me. Sit on this stool."

Cedric turned to me; his face was pink with exertion, his brow was sweaty, his eyes were red with crying, and his nose was snotty.

"I am not fit company, my lord."

"Put down the rake and sit."

"I cannot answer your questions, m'lord, without..."

"Cedric, you and I have been through a great deal together over the years." I saw his brow lift.

"If we cannot speak to each other about our sorrows and through our grief after all this time then it's a poor friendship. Sit."

He wiped a hand across his nose, put down his rake and sat.

I saw him shuddering to breathe steadily.

I threw myself down onto a pile of new straw. I felt it best to be matter-of-fact and straight. Both of us would be lost else.

"This afternoon, I found out that Alysoun knew something that she was bursting to tell you. This thing was so important, Ced, that she needed to tell you so that you could tell me. Do you have any idea what that might be about?"

Cedric sniffed. "Something to tell me that you needed to know, sir?" His face was blank.

"She may have lost her life over it, Ced? Any idea what?"

Cedric stared into the space just outside the stable door. My other stable lads had taken the horses in by other doors to give us peace. We heard them quietly working in the next part of the building.

"What might Aly know, sir? She worked for the town reeve; she lived at the top o' town. Her friends were those at the reeve's house. She went to church at St Mary's. She was a quiet girl with no enemies. I ask you...what might she know?" His face had now paled.

"Does she know anyone in Bedwyn, Ced?"

"No, sir. I don't think so. She was a town girl."

"So you don't think she knew the falconer, Roger."

"Him that was murdered, m'lord?"

"Yes."

"No, sir."

Cedric's freckled face and ginger hair were caught by the westering sun, dipping over the wall of the manor.

"I don't know why she was killed and in such a brutal way, Ced, but I am trying to place her in the same set of circumstances as my falconer. Two murders in four days, I cannot think they aren't connected."

Cedric looked down at his feet. "Aye, sir. I see what you mean. Alysoun didn't know him, no."

"Why did you go down to the barn?"

"Because, sir, Aelfwine told me that she had seen her going that way."

"But why did you go in?"

Cedric looked away, and his pale face reddened in the cheek. "We sometimes went there. If it wasn't being used. It was a quiet place to…to…"

"I see. So you thought she might be waiting for you there?"

"Yessir. We'd been there before. It's just a matter of picking your time. We never stayed long. Just for…you know…a kiss and a cuddle, nothing else. She was a good girl, sir."

I smiled and rubbed my hands through my curly black hair.

"If you think of anything…anything, Ced…"

"Yessir."

"It's almost supper time. Finish now, and then go to the hall for a bite to eat."

"No, sir…I'm not hungry."

"Go anyway. You need to be in company."

Cedric stood up. "I'd rather be alone."

"Aye, I know you would. But it's best we aren't. Your

friends need to see you, Ced. You need them."

He shuffled his feet and scuffed up the straw. "My lord?"

"Yes, Cedric?"

"Is that what you did?"

"Did?"

"When the little lord Geoffrey was murdered and Mistress Cecily died? Did you keep in company?"

"Aye, I did."

Cedric brushed his hands of straw and muck. "Then...I shall go up to the hall."

"Good man."

He walked past me with his head held high.

"And Ced...?"

He stopped but did not turn.

"I have investigated many crimes, as you know."

"Yessir, I know."

"And in every one, I have brought the culprit to a justice of some kind."

Cedric Groomsman stared out at the golden glow of the courtyard.

"I will find them, Ced. I will. And you will see them punished. This, I promise."

Chapter Six

PLUM HOUNDSMAN came back the following morning from his trip to Ramsbury.

He had reserved a gazehound dog for us, and he would fetch it in a week's time. I pictured Hawise's happy face and that of my elder son, the almost three-year-old Simon, who loved to rough and tumble with the dogs. They would be elated when they saw their gift.

We were down at the open-fronted shed where Plum kept my dogs when they were not free about the manor and gazed upon them sleeping in the sunshine. Mildred, one of my wolfhound bitches came to me immediately and nuzzled my hand, for she knew that I would have a piece of dried liver in my purse for her.

"Ah, m'lord," said Plum, laughing. "You spoil these creatures, you do."

"And yet, Plum, they are not spoiled. They are well-mannered, biddable, happy dogs, and even left to their own devices, they are no trouble about the manor."

"No, none at all. I see to that, m'lord."

"I take no credit for it, Plum. You are a veritable wizard

when it comes to training dogs. How did you find Master Harbrook's kennels?"

"Fair enough, my lord. Though we should not be so harsh with our dogs."

"Harsh?"

"Very little kindness or comfort there, sir, but it will not matter. Our dog will be away before he can experience too much of their unkindness, and we shall be able to undo any harm that may have been done."

"Oh dear...were we right to have one of their dogs, Plum?"

He smiled indulgently at me. "The kennel master drinks, sir, and is not the kind of man I would have in charge, but... our little lad will be fine. I have never found hardness the best way with animals. You get more out of them if you are kind."

"A fair word, Plum. We need a name for him, don't we?"

"Perhaps the little Lady Hawise should choose, sir?"

"Aye, I'll put it to her. Did you get to see much of the place, Plum...about the manor of the Lord Roger of Durnford?"

Plum took off his coif and scratched his almost bald head. "I saw the mews; I saw the stables; the dogs were close by. There was another man there looking at the dogs. I talked to him a little. He came from the town, he said. We both remarked on the tidy state of the place...not everyone is as fussy as us when it comes to our whelping, now are they? But this place is run as tight as a tick."

"You saw both dam and sire?"

"Aye, this man and I, we saw the parents. Good creatures both, and the bitch is a good mother."

"Did you know this other man? Did he seem as good a judge of hounds as you?"

"No, sir. He said his name was erm..." He scratched his

pate again, "Pinter, that was it...lived in Marlborough, and this was the first dog he had in adulthood. That's why we struck up together, sir. He wasn't a good judge, but I helped him out a bit."

"Ah yes...I know the man. That was kind of you to give him the benefit of your experience."

"Well, can't have him paying too much for a little squirt, sir."

"No, indeed."

"He did seem to know the bailiff well, though. They talked about that black man..."

"The iron master?"

"Aye. Master Hal told me about him."

"What was said...did you hear?"

"It seems neither of them likes him very much."

"The town pinter told me that he didn't know the Moor."

"Oh no, sir...that can't be right. Maybe you misheard."

"I specifically asked him if he knew him and he said he'd never met him."

"Well, that i'n't right because they both of them were calling him from hill to vale. They definitely agreed on the words they'd use to describe him, sir," said Plum, winking at me in a rather suggestive way.

"Well, well. Choice words, eh?"

"Choice and fruity, sir..." Plum chuckled at his own words. "I don't think there's a sin he 'aint tried..." He snorted down his nose. "According to them."

I smiled. "The man seems perfectly ordinary to me, Plum, but...perhaps they know him better. Well, we look forward to seeing our new addition, whatever the Lady Hawise comes up with, for his name."

I walked back up to my office with a puzzled expression on my face. I needed to write down everything that everyone involved in these deaths had said, or I would forget. Doing that sort of thing enabled me to look for flaws in their stories, for inconsistencies.

I was scribbling at my desk when I heard a hard-pressed horse ride in through the gateway. It skidded to a halt, and I heard footsteps slapping rapidly on the flagstones of the yard and up the stairs.

I looked up and through my open door. Into view came a panting Nicholas Barbflet. I jumped up.

"Nick...what's amiss? Something's wrong?"

Nicholas, the town reeve, rarely came into the forest. He was a town man, and although he could ride, obviously, he rode abroad infrequently.

"Aye...there is."

I reached over and poured him a beaker of ale.

"Tell me...drink."

I pushed the ale towards him.

He sat down sloppily on the stool in front of my table, his limbs loose and tired. His face was set in a grimace. I wasn't sure if this was because he was unused to riding or if the news he was about to impart angered him. Gradually, his breathing steadied.

He swilled the ale around a dry mouth.

"Not content with taking our little housemaid from us, Aumary...the man has Alysoun's grannie now."

"How do you know that?"

"She hasn't been seen since Alysoun's death was reported to her..." He swigged again.

"Ah, but wait! Has she not just gone off somewhere? Her granddaughter has been foully slain. She..."

"No, Aumary, the woman was seen after Grist, Fliss and I went to see her to tell her. Then suddenly she disappeared. The house door was left open, her drop spindle is still lying on the table...food on a platter on the table untouched..."

"Her mind has turned, perhaps, and she is walking

about in a daze? That is sometimes how it happens."

"No one has seen her, and we have all been looking out for her this past day or so. Her neighbours are worried." He shook his head. "I have a feeling in the pit of my stomach..."

"Have you searched the house? The town."

He nodded into his ale.

"Not a peep or a flicker of her. But..."

"But what?"

He leaned sideways and fiddled in his purse. "This..."

It was a small scrap of material, a heavier gauge linen.

"A head cloth?"

"Aye, we think so...and..." He took it back again and searched the piece, folded it over.

"Here. Found stuck into a splintered internal door frame."

I saw what he'd shown me and pursed my lips in thought.

Walking round my table, I took his shoulder in my hand. "What can I do?"

"Come and look, my friend. You may find something we have missed. You are used to looking. We aren't."

I nodded.

I yelled for Hal as I stuffed the small bloodstained piece of material into my own purse.

"And she hasn't been seen since yesterday evening?"

I raked my practised eye over the cottage's largest room. It was a building of three rooms. A place to make food to the back, a hall and sleeping room in the middle, and to the front, a room where weaving and spinning could be done. This cottage was one-storeyed, and the window to the front room was large to aid in the major industry plied here. Cloth making.

"Gudrun also comes to us to help Fliss in the house,

cleaning mostly, two mornings a week, and I know she works for Master Pinter some of the time," said Nicholas Barbflet. "That's how we know she is definitely missing. She didn't arrive this morning. Even after we had told her that she must come and be welcome, no need to do any work…just come and be with us. Eat with all the staff in the kitchen."

All was as Nick had said. It was as if the woman had simply stood up from the table and walked out. There was a blanket which served as a cloak behind the door and outdoor pattens by the hearth. However, this weather, they would not be needed.

Hal opened another shutter.

"She worked for Master Pinter, you say?"

"Yes, and us. The rest of the time, she was a weaver for Master Chapman."

"The door was open?" asked Hal.

"Yes. And the shutters …three in all, one closed. I opened one…you have just opened the other."

I hunkered down by the fire. The ashes were cold. No food lay in the pot. The pottage the old woman had been about to eat was on a trencher on the table. Cold. The bread on the plate was hard. There was water in the jug. The cups were clean. The whole place had a cared-for and house-proud look about it.

Her distaff lay on the other end of the plain trestle. In the front room, was a large upright loom set with blue wool, beautifully fine and expertly woven. It was two-thirds finished.

A small barrel of wool to be carded lay on the floor. The carding tools lay close by a stool to the side of them. On a small chest by the door were some smaller samples of woven wool.

I picked up some household equipment, fingered it and

put it back onto the wooden shelf fixed to the daub wall: a nice yellow glazed jug; a wooden platter with a wavy pattern incised around the edge; a small wooden press for cheese-making; and a pottery salt box.

It was all very tidy. This house was owned by a woman who liked order, someone who placed things squarely and exactly. The distances between the items were pleasing to the eye. Everything was placed as if to satisfy the most exacting person.

"A good housewife and very tidy. To the point of utter exactness. Nothing out of place. Too tidy. It's almost as if it's not lived in."

Nick's eyes roved over the place. "She made a good housemaid. Makes."

"I can see that she would."

I walked into the middle room. My eye came to rest on a large chest of oak, which lay on the wall by the inner door to what passed for a kitchen. I stared at it.

Once more, my eyes ranged over the room. "Perfect... not a piece out of place. One could almost measure the distance of each thing from another, and it would be found to be exact."

It made me think of the little starlings on the manor house roof and how they would all gather there of a morning and evening, thirty or forty of them all along the ridge. They would shuffle up; another one would join them; they'd shuffle some more until every bird was accommodated, every bird the exact same distance from its neighbour.

The chest annoyed me. In a perfect room, with perfect things, this chest, with its large hasp of blackened iron and its bands of metal reinforcement, stood out as odd.

I gestured to the chest. By my reckoning, it was at least two centuries old.

"That's a strange thing for a cottager such as Gudrun to own."

"Not so strange if you know the history of the family, Aumary. Gudrun comes from a family of old Anglo-Norse stock. Her family was wealthy once. Under the Confessor, I believe."

"And this is a relic of that day?" I said, standing over the large chest and staring down. Small decorations that looked like little people carved in simple lines marched over the lid.

I frowned. "In a room of perfection, this is strangely out of place."

"I don't know..."

"No, I mean that it isn't straight. It's shifted from its usual place. See the gap at the back where the right-hand side does not meet the wall. Two inches, at least. I think she would not be a woman who would stand that for very long. And there is a fringe of floor dust where it's been moved."

I took the lid of the chest and pulled. It was heavy. There was a hang lock in the metal hasp, and I realised that it wasn't fixed shut but simply laid there to secure the two parts. However, the lid would not budge with it in place, and I fiddled it out.

The hasp on the lock caught, and I had to prise it up stiffly.

I inched the lid up until it was resting against the perfectly whitewashed daub wall, and looked down.

Gudrun's pale and unfocussed eyes stared at me. Her mouth was drawn back in a grimace. Her finger ends were clawed, and her nails bloodied where she had tried to lift the lid and had scratched at the wood in an effort to part it from the body of the chest. There were scratches on the wood and her knees were raised, her torn and bloodied head cloth awry.

I crossed myself and stepped back. Hal dipped his head to look in.

"God's ditties!"

"Christ's bones!" said Nick as he peered into the pit of the chest. "Has she suffocated to death?"

"Aye, hit on the head, stunned, woozy and then bundled in here and left to asphyxiate."

Nick sat heavily on the bench by the table.

"Fetch Johannes, Hal, will you? We shall need him."

"A horrible and slow way to go. Panic sets in. You breathe even harder, taking in what remaining air you can ..."

"Can we lift her out, Johannes?"

We put our hands to her shoulders and legs, her head flopped back and Nick Barbflet held it gently as we laid her on the floor.

Johannes carefully looked her over.

"A blow to the side of her head incapacitated her but didn't kill her. She would have been unstable and dizzy. Her murderer lifted her and jammed her into the chest. I take it she fell over there, where the piece of her head cloth was found?"

"Would she cry out?"

"Oh, no doubt after a short while, when she regained her wits."

"Then none heard her, Nick?"

"No one has reported it, no."

"Ask around again. See if anyone's memory can be jogged." Nick nodded.

"Mind you, this house is isolated from its neighbours. They might not have heard the cries of a weak woman, prisoned in a heavy wooden chest, yelling for help."

I walked out into the sunshine of the day and looked up the hill.

"Nothing but sheep up there and crops over there.The noise and bustle of the street that way. The neighbour to the left…who is it, Nick, do you know?"

Of course he knew.

"Master wheelwright's man, Jerome."

"Out at his work early till late."

"And to the right, over there, the cutler Master Lorimer's assistant."

"Also out. Are there wives?"

"Not the cutler but the wheelwright Jerome, his wife works for the Caspars. She's a carder."

"Ah, so also out at work," I said, scrubbing my beard.

"Johannes, when did she die?"

He came to stand in the doorway.

"Well, from the lividity and the rigour, I'd say late Tuesday afternoon or early in the evening, maybe later. Not long after her granddaughter and after Nick came to tell her the sad news."

"So folk would be coming back from their work, perhaps?"

I looked back into the house as Nick Barbflet found the cloak behind the door and covered the woman's remains.

I stood there for a while.

"Right then. Can we secure the door, and when the coroner comes, can you unlock it for him? I must go and speak to a few people. Will you be the first finder, Nick?"

Nick took in a breath to speak. I thought he was going to refuse, and then, "Yes…I can do that," he said. "Of course I can."

Pinter laid down his pen very slowly and deliberately.

"She's dead, you say?"

"Yes, Master Pinter."

"I heard, of course, that there was a search for the poor woman, sir. She didn't come to her work here this afternoon, and naturally, I thought that…that she…"

"Was too distraught over the death of her granddaughter…"

He steepled his hands before his face. "To stir outside her house, yes? I have told you, sir, that I do not listen to gossip, and although there was talk about the town about poor Alysoun being found, I listened, I'm afraid, with half an ear. "

"When did you know that the rumour about her granddaughter's death was true?"

"When I visited the Fletschier house, sir, earlier today. Master Fletschier confirmed it was so."

I walked around the man's table and looked out of the window at the Green.

"And yet you do not listen to gossip, Master Pinter?" I turned back.

His face creased into a supercilious smile, "That is so, m'lord."

"But you are quite capable of indulging in gossip yourself, it seems."

Pinter looked affronted.

I looked out across the Green again. Clouds were massing over Granham Hill. Two women were nattering under the trees to the edge of the road.

"Oh, no, sir…you'd never catch me indulging…in."

"When will you take possession of one of Master Harbrook's dogs, Master Pinter?" I turned to face him.

"Dogs, m'lord?"

"I have it on reliable authority that you are to have one of the pups from the Durnford's estate at Ramsbury, Pinter."

His eyebrows flew up into this thinning hair. "I am, sir…? How did you…Ah…" He looked a little embarrassed at last.

"My houndsman tells me he gave you some help to choose the dog, Pinter."

Pinter had recovered. "Ah, that was your man. Yes, indeed he did." He laughed self-deprecatingly. "I have no idea about dogs, you see."

"Then why do you want one?"

"It is for my intended, sir. A gazehound. A gift for the fair Henriette. A lady's dog, don't you agree?"

"No …" I rubbed the side of my nose. "Not exclusively."

He looked away rather bemused, trying to give himself time to think.

"You spoke with Master Harbrook about the iron master, Grover."

"We did? Ah yes, perhaps we did."

"It seems you are not, as you assured me, a stranger to the man."

"Ah no…not entirely, sir."

He rose and made for a table at the back of the hall. He lifted a jug towards me,

"Ale, my lord?"

"No, thank you. Why did you lie?"

He came back to the main table, lifted the cup to his lips and spoke,

"I did not wish it to be known that I had been… erm…elbowed out of the way by…one such as he, m'lord." He drank.

"So you did indeed talk to my falconer seriously about wedding his daughter, Richildis."

"I did, sir, though I changed my mind fairly quickly, as I said."

"Hmmm. Where were you last night, Pinter? Where were you, in fact, between the later hours of the afternoon and the early evening? At home, I hope?"

I spent the later hours of the evening in the Fletschier household, at supper and returned here just past the fourth hour of night. I am not accustomed to being out too late," he said.

"Can anyone corroborate your story?"

"I did see Master Cowper, sir...wending his way from the Green Man, but that is all. We waved at each other."

"It's on the way to your house from the Fletschiers', isn't it...Back Lane...the old woman's house?"

"Yes, sir, but I didn't go the Back Lane way. Master Cowper will tell you that, sir."

"Pinter, did you know that Roger Hawkes was a dying man?"

"Dying m'lord...n...n...no...I..."

"A stomach malady for which there was no cure, alas. Dr Johannes confirms it. It might provide us with a reason why Roger was so keen to have his daughter married quickly."

"No...I knew nothing of this."

"No one did, it seems."

"So, to be married before he died...?"

"But she took matters into her own hands." I watched him for a while. He was far away in his own thoughts.

"Master Pinter, do you have any idea what it was that Alysoun Backs or her grandmother knew? It was information so dangerous that they would both lose their lives over it."

His eyes rose to mine.

"Why ask me, my lord? I scarcely knew them."

"Like you scarcely knew the iron master, and yet I find you knew him enough to dislike him and speak ill of him?"

The man's gaze wavered but he did not answer my question, "Surely, m'lord, you cannot think that I would murder an old woman and a young girl?"

"At present, I do not know what to think, Pinter."

"Why, sir? What possible reason might I have?"

I shrugged. "At the moment, I know not why anyone should want to kill them." I marched to the door and took it in my hand. "Or kill my falconer."

I passed out onto the Green. "But rest assured, I shall find out." And I closed the door quietly.

I wandered back to Johannes' house, where I had left Hal and my horse.

We had dinner together, and we discussed, as was customary, all aspects of the deaths in the town and my manor of Bedwyn.

"If we could find out where that boar spear came from, sir…might we know who the devil is?" said Hal.

I looked towards it, propped up in the corner of the kitchen by the door.

"It really should go to the coroner as deodand."

"Ah."

"It has no particular distinguishing marks. Might have been made anywhere."

"Right you are, sir."

He looked carefully at it, "But it's quite a distinctive shape, in't ,it with its narrow and triangular lugs?"

"We know who hunts boar hereabouts? Who has permission…?"

"Who pays the king a fee, that is?" said Hal.

"Well, we ought to know, Hal, for it's our job to issue the warrant which says they have permission. Or rather, it's John Brenthall's job. Is there anyone…ah no…"

Hal shook his head "No…not quite the season yet, is it?"

"No, not quite."

"I suppose anyone might have had a spear like it?" asked

Johannes. "Not just a man who hunts boar."

I shrugged, "As we said before, you might get a few strange looks wandering around the town with a boar spear, and it's not that easy to disguise."

"Why would you choose it specially to kill the poor girl? Why not a sword, a knife, strangle 'er...why throw a spear?" said Hal.

"Perhaps to keep your distance?" I offered. "You don't have to get close to your victim."

"To implicate someone else, perhaps?" said Johannes astutely.

Hal and I blinked at him.

"But who?" we both said together.

"Ah well", Johannes stretched out his long legs, "Find the man who hunts boar with such a spear and you will know who our murderer is trying to implicate."

We stared at him open mouthed.

"Any more ale in that jug, Aumary?" he asked.

Before we made our journey home to Durley, I stopped at the barn on Crook's Lane and wandered up and down.

Nick, with his arm around the shoulder of Algar, one of the young lads who ran errands up and down town for the master miller, came up the lane from the mill.

"Ah, Nick...tell me...carts? Have there been any carts up and down here, to the barn recently, let's say, in the past week?"

Algar laughed behind his hand and then flushed red up to the roots of his hair.

"M'lord, do you know what it is you ask?" said Nicholas Barbflet, putting his hands on his hips.

"Carts...passing by?"

"Dozens, Sir Aumary. To the mill, to the barn, to the

wheelwrights and the cooper, the weavers...it would be better to ask when there hasn't been a cart passing down the lane."

I rubbed my forehead..."Ah yes...I see."

"Why do you ask m'lord?" asked Algar.

"I had a thought that someone might have concealed the boar spear which killed Alysoun on a cart and then hidden it in the barn for later use."

The two millers looked at each other.

"Would it not have been easier to just...?"

"Yes...a knife, a sword...? I have been through all that, and there is a reason I think it is a possibility."

Algar screwed up his forehead.

"We have weekly carts from several places. The wheelwrights get them all the time, and the coopers now and again. Both bringing wood. But of course, none of those come down the lane this far to the barn except the grain carts."

"Would you recognise all these carts and their drivers?"

"Mostly yes."

"If they come to the barn or the mill, Algar will be here to open doors, help unload, that sort of thing," said Nick.

"Did you see anything unusual, lad?' asked Hal.

"Unusual, Master Hal...like what, when?"

"Well, perhaps a cart which you didn't recognise?" I added. "Any that shouldn't be here?"

Algar twisted his face into what he obviously considered a thoughtful expression.

"Ah, well...none what I don't know. Old Master Hoggs' handcart was here, I saw that... But that's one I do know. But it was a bit unusual. He normally comes midweek."

"Hogg?"

Hal and I looked at each other. "Hogg as in pig, Algar?"

"Aye, him."

"What was he doing here, Algar?" asked Nick with a frown.

"He came to see Old Mother Webber about her eggs," he tossed a hand behind him to indicate where the woman's house lay.

We looked bemused.

"She keeps chickens," said Algar. " Lots of 'em. Good layers."

"Why would he bring his cart? Has he a particular reason to bring it down the lane?"

"Well, see, he comes and brings her feed for her hens and she gives him eggs. They bin doing it for years."

"Ah."

Algar looked shiftily over his shoulder. "Mind you, that i'n't the only thing Old Hogg's been gettin', if you see what I mean, m'lord."

Hal smirked. "They have an… arrangement, do they?"

"Well, he comes nearly every week…and he doesn't always have eggs…" Algar tailed off and looked sheepish. He glanced at his master. "He comes on a Wednesday - market day - but this week, it was a different day.

"You've been watching then, Algar?" said Nick, folding his arms.

The lad flushed to the roots of his hair again. "Well… yes…I suppose I have. I thought it was odd."

"Why?" I asked.

Algar squirmed a little, "That's the day Old Master Webber goes to market."

"There's a Master Webber, is there?" asked Hal.

"Oh yes."

"The woman isn't a widow. That much I know." This was Nick with a smile on his face.

"So the man came down the lane with his hand cart and stopped…where?"

"Ah, now that I didn't see, sir," said Algar confidently.

"Where can we find this Master Hogg?"

"Bottom end of the Marsh, m'lord. By the ropers."

On our way home to Durley, we passed by the Marsh. Hogg lived in a tiny cottage squashed between a turner's house and a dyer's workshop.

The pigs rootled around at the back of the property in a long yard. We heard them snorting and scuffling around.

The man shook like an aspen leaf and seemed not to hear well, for we had to repeat ourselves, but eventually, we got it from him. One wondered what on earth Old Mother Webber could possibly see in this specimen of manhood.

He had been approached by a man. When he went to town, could he take this boar spear in his cart to the barn and hide it? It would be picked up later. He would receive a whole penny for his effort. A boar spear in a hog cart. Oh, the irony of it.

"Well, you would, wouldn't you, m'lord. An' I was goin' there anyway. I told 'im."

"This man…describe him to me."

"Describe him, well I'm not sure I can…"

"Tall, fat, bald, what?" shouted Hal. "Aw, c'mon, man!"

The man's face took on an angry hue, "Bit like you… ugly!" he shouted back.

I took a penny from my purse.

"Old, young…dark, blond…?"

I waved the silver penny in front of his face.

"Ah well… if I can remember right…" The man sucked his grubby thumb nail.

"'E were quite well dressed, though he weren't a nob…"

"No?" I smiled.

"Erm…'E were bearded…no 'e weren't, 'e were clean-shaven…an 'e kept callin' me, 'my friend'."

"Did 'e indeed?" said Hal.

"I weren't no friend of 'is."

"Anything else? Do you know where he comes from?"

"Well, when I goes out to the forest to take me beasts…"

"Pannage?"

"Aye. I have the right up on Forest Hill. I sees him sometimes. I never usually speaks to 'im. Good day, and that… But that day…"

"Where? Where do you see him?"

"'E comes down into town on a fine 'orse."

"From?"

"Bedwyn, m'lord," said Hogg. "I think…or was it Ramsbury? Or it might be 'Ungerford. I did 'ear 'im say it once."

"It would help if you could describe him further."

"Oh my…well, you see, me memory only goes so far for a penny…it gets stuck…I'm old, see, and me memory…"

"I took out a halfpenny and held it before his eyes."

"Long hair. Fancy like. Rides like he doesn't like his backside coming in contact with the saddle. Holds the reins like they'd give him the plague," he chunnered.

Hal grinned at him "'Arbrook?"

"Oh, I don't know the name."

"Was he alone or in company?" I asked.

"Ah well, you see my head don't quite go to that…cos…"

"Your old and yer memory doesn't run to it," said Hal sarcastically.

"This is your last penny," I said… "Tell me, or they will both go back into my purse."

The man grinned up at me, showing his few black teeth.

"Company. Iron men."

Chapter Seven

"WELL, that dun't make any sense at all," said Hal as we rode home.

"That Master Harbrook is the man who planted the spear or that he was seen in company with the master of the iron forges and his people, Hal?"

"They quarrelled. We saw 'em. There i'n't any love lost between the Durnfords' man and the Moor."

"Ah, no, Hal. What we saw was something quite different. What we saw was a quarrel between the iron master's foreman and Harbrook."

"But 'e insulted him."

"Like I do when I call you old Hal or when Tostig tells you your beard has shrunk in the rain, you ol' devil… No."

"You mean it was all a joke? Nah!" he said, shaking his head, "'e called him a foul abomination, sir."

"They did not come to blows, Hal. The iron master laughed it off. There was no real animosity in any of it. It was with the man Burridge that Harbrook had the quarrel. The rest was a tussle between the Durnfords' men and the forge men. I have a feeling it doesn't take much for any of them to argue. There's many a man who speaks sweetly to the face and sourly behind one's back."

"So, you think that it is likely that the Moor's folk or even the man 'imself kept company with Harbrook down to the town?"

"Until I have it proved otherwise, Hal, it's a possibility."

"Well then, answer me this…why is Harbrook hiding boar spears in the grain barn?"

"We don't really know it was him."

"That man said the fella doesn't like his arse to touch a saddle. That Harbrook is a fussy devil. Just like him…"

"Are there no other men that ride as if they preferred the horse were made of wood, Hal?"

"Hmph."

"Of course, the other thing to think about is this…"

"M'lord?"

"Was it Alysoun who was the intended recipient of the boar spear, or did someone throw it, not realising it was she who had come through the door?"

Hal looked at me with his mouth open, laughing. I dug my heels into Fitz and cantered off.

"You mean someone else was supposed to come through that door, and the killer just let fly? Nah. You have to see who it is you're throwing it at," he said, catching up with me a moment later.

"The door was in darkness, Hal. It faces east. The sun was over the forest to the south-west at that time of day. If you'd arranged for someone to come and meet you, you would expect them, and not a girl keeping a tryst with her lover. You would see the dark shape and let fly."

"It makes more sense than Alysoun being the intended victim. Yes, it does."

"Of course, I could be completely wrong," I said.

We arrived home to find that we had guests.

Hal and I looked at each other in surprise as we dismounted and left our mounts to the grooms.

Two horses were being walked around the courtyard by a pair of young men who were obviously brothers, the likeness was so acute.

"Who's this then?" asked Hal from the corner of his mouth.

"I recognise them, Hal, for they were in the yard of the iron forges when we had the altercation there."

"Ah. Good lookin' pair, in't they?"

They were indeed good-looking, with long, straw-blond, wavy hair, regular features, muscled arms and perfectly proportioned bodies. Not a pair you would easily forget.

They bowed their heads as I passed and made my way up the steps to the hall.

"Sir Aumary, my lord," My wife Lydia came hurrying up the hall to meet me.

"Here is Mistress Richildis Grover come to visit. She wishes to speak to you, and I asked her to wait, knowing that you would return home soon."

"I hope you have not been waiting long, mistress?"

"No, m'lord, your wife very kindly entertained us. She is such excellent company."

"Well, that's good." I smiled at Lydia.

"Here is Mistress Harbrook also, Rousalie, the bailiff's wife. She insisted on coming along today. She is Mistress Grover's friend."

"Ah...I see." I nodded to her. "What can we do for you, mistress, that you must travel specially to us here at Durley? Please sit once more."

"I have heard that..." Richildis swallowed, "that there

have been some murders in the town, sir."

Hal, who had followed me into the hall, turned in the action of pouring ale.

"Well, that news was quick across the ground!"

"The nature of gossip, Hal. Yes, madam, it's true. I am trying to link these deaths to that of your father, but as yet, I cannot do so. Have you have any information which might help me?"

"Oh, no, no. We have no news of that sort. It's just that. I am so very concerned, so worried. I thought if we could come to talk to you here, you might be able..."

"Richildis is very concerned for the safety of her husband, my lord," said the older woman.

She was a dark-haired beauty of about twenty-four with fluttering eyelashes and deep, mysterious eyes. She wore a green bliaut with small white embroidered flowers decorating a band at the neck. Her hair was covered with a white veil held in place by a white band, and her hair was caught into a net of the same colour at her nape, visible as she moved. Her voice was low and musical.

"Why, madam, should you be so worried about murders in the town?"

Richildis wriggled in her seat uncomfortably. "I hear that the woman who lost her life lately was that old woman who worked for Master Pinter, m'lord. I remember telling you that I did think that Master Pinter was... if not completely guilty of my father's death, then implicated in it. The woman worked for him..."

"At the moment, madam, as I say, I cannot connect either Master Pinter to the deaths in the town, nor to that of your father. He has an alibi for each time the murders were committed."

"Then he lies, sir."

I looked stiffly at her, frowning. "Why do you dislike

the man so?"

She fiddled with the stuff of her dark green gown. "I do not...dislike him...I merely..."

"Seems like it to us," said Hal, "Like you say, this isn't the first time you've tried to get 'im into trouble." He threw himself down onto the other end of the bench where Mistress Grover was sitting. She moved away and glared at him, squashing herself in the corner.

"Mistress Grover is concerned about Mansur, m'lord. He has not been himself these past few days," said Mistress Harbrook, taking over the conversation.

"In what way?" I took a sip of my ale.

From the corner of my eye, I saw Lydia move closer to my chair.

"He's quiet and lacking his usual humour, sir. He doesn't speak to me, and his temper flares at the slightest thing. This is most unlike him," said Richildis.

"He is lately evil-tempered with his men, my Lord Belvoir," said Mistress Harbrook, "and that is most unusual. He never shouts at them, but today..."

"He threatened to put Master Burridge from his works, sir," said Rousalie. "That would never do, for Master Burridge has been at the works, boy and man, since Mansur's father's day."

"He would truly be lost without him, and the man is Mansur's good friend and chief worker," added Richildis.

"You can account for nothing which has brought about this change in him?"

"Perhaps he is worried about some aspect of business," said Lydia quietly. "I know that the Lord Belvoir can be introspective when there is something which bothers him..." She looked at me and smiled sweetly. "Whether it be in his role as constable or a problem with his forest."

I looked over my shoulder at her.

"My lady wife is correct. Many things make a man quiet or uneven of temper."

"Sir...I have been married but four weeks. My husband has been nothing but sweetness and has been so loving towards me in those four weeks. It is such a shock, for suddenly, this week, he is cold and ...harsh..."

"I heard it, m'lord," said Rousalie. "It was...uncalled for. Richildis had done nothing to warrant the tongue-lashing she received today, sir." Rousalie set her lips in a hard line.

"You are sure there is nothing you can have done which might make him angry with you?"

"No, nothing. And then why should he be angry with his men?"

"What did he say to you?"

"I cannot repeat the words, sir. I cannot." Richildis Grover put her head into her hands. "I fear that he is afraid for his life, and so...must be harsh and unkind to everyone. Including me."

"Do you know if Mansur has seen Master Pinter lately?"

"Perhaps he has."

"How do they know each other?"

"It is not a long nor a deep acquaintance, sir. It is through the Lord Durnford and his men, I believe."

"What is the pinter of the town to do with the Lord Durnford?"

"Pinter grew up at Bedwyn, m'lord. He knows the folk there," said Mistress Harbrook. "And he knows some folk in Ramsbury."

"Master Pinter tells me that he knows Mansur but a little."

"But that is not entirely the truth, for they do hunt together, sir. Along with my husband, who is the bailiff to the Lord Durnford."

"Tell me, madam, do they hunt boar?"

"Why, yes, they do. They are going to hunt the lord's land soon, I believe. Hunt in the Lord Durnford's woods as soon as the season begins," said Richildis.

"And that is soon, I think," added Rousalie.

"I cannot imagine why, madam, but I thought that your husband was not in good favour with your own man." I nodded to Rousalie.

"They do business together and are not too often in each other's company, but there is no outright hostility. Or at least..."

"Yes?"

"There was not. Until my father was killed."

"Yes, Master Harbrook did seem to wonder if Master Grover had something to do with that," I said.

"As you saw, sir, the other day, Rousalie's husband, who was a very good friend of my father, was concerned that Mansur had perhaps..."

"He seemed to want to accuse him of murder, madam, but had not the words or proof."

"We were there, remember," piped up Hal.

"Oh no, sir. He merely asked him where he was at the time." Richildis Grover fiddled with the gloves tightly clasped in her hands. "He did not mean to accuse him, I'm sure. Mansur had nothing to do with it. But Pinter...he is a man of a different mould."

I sighed. "What am I to do about it?"

"Arrest the man Pinter..."

"I have no evidence upon which I may hold him, madam."

"Must you have evidence?"

"I am afraid I must."

Richildis Glover stood up, and two bright spots appeared on her cheeks.

"I have no wish to be widowed, my lord. If I must keep a wary eye on my husband, then I shall. I tell you that his life is endangered, and I know who the foul fiend is who wishes to remove him from my life so that he can have me as he wishes…as he wished before Mansur came into my life."

"That would be against the law, madam. A widow cannot be forced to marry anyone she does not wish to marry."

Richildis pouted.

Mistress Harbrook put her hand on the girl's arm. "Hush, Richildis. The Lord Belvoir knows how you feel. I am sure that he will give the matter some thought and…"

"What is there to think about, madam?" I stood up and looked down on them both. That is easy for me to do, for I am a full six feet in height.

"I have no doubt that Grover has much on his mind. Keep a polite distance from him for a while, and I am sure he will come back to you the same man he was before."

"This may go on such a time, my lord, that my husband will forget the love and respect I have for him and perhaps forget me altogether."

"That will not happen, Richildis," said my wife. "You will again be his darling, I am sure of it."

"I will do what I can to bring you into his mind, Richildis, whenever I can," said Mistress Harbrook. "I will ask my husband to do so too…when they are at the hunting, perhaps."

Richildis turned up her pretty nose.

"There is something going on. I know there is. I am just warning you, my lord."

I sighed. "There really is nothing I can do except carry on looking into the death of your father and these unfortunate two women of the town."

"I wish you well, my lord." Richildis Grover bowed her head and rushed from the room.

The other woman stood and smoothed down her gown.

"I am so sorry, sir. One must remember, she is but sixteen and prey to all manner of fears and hurts," said Rousalie Harbrook. "Many of them are flights of fancy, I'm sure, but this..."

I smiled at her. "I am sure it's something time will mend, madam."

She curtsied nicely and then turned and left with a "God keep you, m'lord, m'lady."

Hal sniggered into his cup. "We've become marriage menders now, have we?"

I shook my head. "It's in their heads, I'm sure, Hal."

"Well, I don't think it is," said Lydia archly. "Like she says, there is something going on...I feel it bubbling under the surface. Something sinister."

Hal and I laughed at her.

But she was right.

To and fro to town I went for almost a whole week inquiring and searching, and I came up with nothing.

No one had seen or heard anything. Everyone had an alibi for the time that Alysoun was killed and that her grandmother was murdered. No one who could be guilty was in Bedwyn when my falconer died.

I was almost about to give up and tell Cedric I knew nothing and could not keep my promise when an incident with Harbrook, the dog breeder, set me off on another track.

My promised hound had arrived from the Durnford kennels. Hawise had given him a name. For the first few days, the little beast would not leave Hawise's heels. As she moved about the stable, where he was confined for part of the day, or the hall where she took him sometimes, he was to be found nipping at her heels, pawing at her, stuck to her like a cleaver…that little plant of the forest which produces prolific and clinging tendrils and little round sticky seeds. And so he became Cleaver.

Hawise and I were standing in the end stable one afternoon, watching Plum put the dog through his paces.

He was a handsome dog, completely white but for a black patch on the nose and one black foot. He watched Plum carefully as the dried liver was fetched from the pack and waved over his head with the instruction, 'sit'. Cleaver watched the piece go out of sight over his ears and sat back to keep it in view. Nine times out of ten, he would overbalance and end up wriggling on his back, and Hawise and I would giggle.

A shout from outside the gate made me look round.

"My Lord Belvoir!"

I walked out into the warmth of a sunny mid-September afternoon.

It was the reeve of Bedwyn, Henry du May.

"My Lord! My Lord!"

"Henry, whatever is the matter?"

"There has been a terrible accident in the forest." He came round the corner, breathing hard.

"Accident, Henry? Where? Who is hurt."

"We have him here, sir. We came to Durley because it was the nearest place."

"Bring him in, Henry."

I turned to my Durley steward, another Henry.

"Find Hal, Henry. Also, see if you can locate Mistress Janet…she should be somewhere about the village, probably at home this time of day." Janet Peddler was the woman we trusted to see to injuries about the place when doctor Johannes was not in the village."

I looked around the courtyard. "Tostig…open up the end room!" I gestured to the little room, the end of a row which I'd had built as lean-tos onto the wall of the manor some years ago. "We shall take him in there."

Six men came in with a man strung on a cloak carried at four corners. The two middle men, the two brothers I had met recently with Mistress Grover, cradled the injured man's body in the centre.

"Merciful God!" I said to myself out loud. "Mansur Grover!"

In truth, I could not see the body on the cloak, for the six men obscured him, and there were many further men milling about the courtyard.

Tostig ran to open the door, and they carefully squeezed themselves inside.

"Du May, what happened?"

"A boar, m'lord. I am told they had her at bay, and she broke away. The dogs did not hold her."

"The mastiffs let it go?"

"We had mastiffs, yes...they were not bold enough to hold the beast at the ear. It was a large creature, sir."

"So what happened?"

"Two were tossed aside, and one gored. The boar raced up and struck."

"You did not manage to get a spear into it? Not one of you?"

"Master Mansur managed it, sir...but..."

I heard another scream come from the room, and we all shivered at the severity of it.

At that moment, Janet came in at the gate. She stopped to listen, then ran on.

"Janet 'tis a goring by a boar...there may be nothing we can do." She nodded and moved on.

"You have come from where?"

"Toteham, m'lord, close by Toteham."

"Wait!" I clutched at his sleeve. "You are telling me that

they were hunting in Savernake?"

Du May squirmed. "They were, yes, sir. I..."

"Du May, you know that is forbidden."

Henry hung his head, "Yessir, I know."

I looked at him sidelong. "Were you with them, Henry?"

"Just to..." His utterance was cut off by another terrible scream.

"Thank goodness you were not further away."

"No, sir. We took the decision to come here."

Another man touched his forelock, "A few of us had followed them, m'lord, but before we could do anything, the boar had struck."

"Where are the rest of your hunters?"

"Some fled. Some are still outside, and some have returned to Ramsbury and Bedwyn, m'lord," said the man named Ash.

"I heard you were hunting on Lord Durnford's land. Had you always planned to hunt in Savernake?"

"No, sir, but we...we..."

"You realise you'll pay dearly for this du May?"

The man hung his head.

"We strayed following the boar...until we were in Savernake and off the Ramsbury estate land."

"Foolish man. Right, fetch the rest in." I called to Henry, "Ale for the party, Henry, in the hall."

"Aye, sir."

Another terrible scream rent the air. We all held our breath as it bubbled away.

"It is forbidden to hunt Savernake without permission and I have not given permission. You know that, and you are a Savernake man."

"Yes, sir." Du May shuffled his feet in embarrassment. Then he added, "We could not extract the spear head, sir, so we broke it off as short as we'd dared."

I nodded. “This was not well done, du May. Go and get some ale.”

I made my way to the small room on the south wall.

Hal was standing there in the doorway, grimacing.

“Wait…!” I turned in puzzlement to question du May, but he was disappearing into the screens passage.

“He said ‘boar spear’. The wound was made by a spear?”

“Aye, I saw it stickin’ up,” said Hal, his face creasing into a frown.

“But he also said that the boar gored the man.”

“Oh…”

“So which is it?”

I pushed my way into the room. It was a wonder the man had survived the breaking of the ash pole to which the spear head had been fixed. Ash was a hard and difficult wood to break. I thought then that the man was not likely to survive. It was amazing he had lasted this long - a journey through the forest and the movement of the spear - the man was very tough, I thought.

The injured party was writhing about on the bed. Janet was trying to still him.

She turned to me, and our eyes met. Her look said that there was no chance that the man would live.

There was a bubbling cough and another scream, this time much reduced in volume and the man lying on his back on the bed straightened.

Suddenly, he stretched his legs out stiffly to the full limit, the breath bubbled in the back of his throat, his body softened and he lay still. Janet got up and moved away, her hands covered in blood.

“I’m sorry, m’lord.”

“Thank you, Janet, you did all you could do.”

I looked down at the dead man now lying in stillness on the bloodied blanket of the small bed; his head turned to one side.

It was Yves of Harbrook.

I felt a presence behind me and looked round. Mansur Grover entered the small room, dipping his head under the lintel.

He crossed himself.

“Too late?” he asked.

“Too late,” I answered.

Chapter Eight

"SO LET ME get this right..." I said. "You decided to hunt in Savernake despite this being against the law? You began in Ramsbury on the Durnford estate but strayed into Savernake?"

The men looked at each other, some shamefacedly, others rather defiant.

"You will be fined heavily for this, you know it."

"Yessir, we know it," said Mansur Grover

I passed my hand over my forehead. "So tell me again what happened."

"We..." Grover fell silent, and no one else spoke.

"You, Grover, were waiting in the brush to throw your weapon at the boar?"

"It escaped the dogs, m'lord and came on without check."

"So you threw your spear. So did you, Master Burridge."

"And so did I," said another man of the Lord Durnford's retinue.

"My spear missed...I must say, I am not a good shot, sir," said Burridge, rather embarrassed.

"Mine hit the mark and wounded the boar," said Mansur.

"I was there merely as a guide, m'lord," said du May. "I

had no weapon and stayed back."

"Mine…My spear, I know not what happened to it. The boar turned at the last minute and made for Harbrook," said the other man.

"I had another spear and waited for her to come up, planted it ready to take her body, but the beast keeled over within a few yards, and I did not make contact," added Grover.

"By then, the pig has stuck poor Master Harbrook," said Burridge.

"As I saw it, Yves was gored, and then this spear came out of nowhere," said Mansur.

"No, no, no, sir," said the Lord Durnford's man named Master Abbeye. "The spear took him first, then the boar."

"No, I saw it, Thomas, you are wrong. The boar was first, then someone threw the spear, and it hit Yves."

"How many of you loosed weapons?"

They looked around the party, "Five, I think," said Burridge.

"Then where are the five spears?"

"That's what I was about to say," said Abbeye, "We recovered two from the undergrowth, one from the boar, and one is in Master…" he tailed off, looking down at his shoes.

"No, there was no spear in the boar, though it lay dead."

"There are two unaccounted for."

"Who was closest to the boar when Master Harbrook was gored?"

"I was, sir," said Mansur Grover. "I was a little to his right and behind him."

"What did you see? I want a detailed account, Grover," I said.

Grover ran a hand over his sweating brow. "I yelled that the dogs had let go of the pig. I threw a spear and hit it.

Here." He touched his right shoulder.

"That didn't stop the beast?"

"No, sir, it came on."

"Then?"

"It hit Master Harbrook, Yves, and threw him backwards onto a tree trunk."

"No, no. It was the spear which threw him backwards onto the tree trunk," said Abbeye.

I turned to face him. "And where were you?"

"To the right side of the boar, so I had a good look at her putting her tusks to Master Harbrook's lower belly and then trying to toss him. He did not fly, for he had already staggered back with the spear wound and was pinned to the tree. The boar went in under it."

"And it was then you threw your spear."

"I had already thrown my spear and sadly missed. I had another in reserve, though I have to say, I would not have had time to prepare myself for a charge if the boar had turned my way."

"None of you were mounted?"

"We had been, sir," said Mansur. "Harbrook had already given the beast a poke with his own spear from horseback, and the boar charged off. We followed on foot, thinking that it was wounded and would be held by the dogs. And there is great honour in following the boar on foot, my lord, as you know."

"Never underestimate the tenacity of these beasts, Grover. They are the most fearsome creatures of the forest. Especially in the breeding season. First-time mothers give birth at this time of year, and if a sow thinks you threaten her piglets, you are unlikely to get away with a simple warning."

He looked away.

"You think, Master Abbeye, that the spear hit Master Harbrook first?"

"From where I stood, it looked like it. He was thrown backwards to the tree, and then the boar came on and gored him."

"What did you see, Master Burridge."

"Oh…me…? Well. I think I saw the boar, but I'm not sure about the spear. There were so many of us, you see, all ready to loose. I was more concerned about not hitting anyone. I had already missed with my first spear."

"Hmmm. Well, someone hit him."

"Yes…I see that."

I turned to Janet, who hovered in the hall doorway.

"Janet, in your opinion. The spear wound…was that the fatal wound?"

"They both would have been fatal eventually, sir," she said. "Though I'm sure that Dr Johannes can tell you more than I can."

I smiled at her. She returned me a shy smile and looked at the six or so men crowded up by the dais.

"I will set my foresters to hunt for the missing spear, and we shall recover the one which is in the body of Yves of Harbrook."

I walked out from the middle of the men and looked back at them all ranged before me, ale cups in hand.

"The coroner will wish to speak to you all.'

"But, sir, surely that doesn't need to happen. Master Harbrook was killed by accident," said Abbeye.

"The rule is any unexpected death, Abbeye," I said. "Regardless. His jury will decide if it was an accident. Being the Lord Durnford's man, I should have thought you'd know that."

"Accident…or what, sir?" asked Mansur Grover, his cup to his lip.

"Or a deliberate act."

The men shuffled their feet and growled amongst

themselves.

"Sir. A deliberate act...How could that be?" asked Burridge.

I swivelled and took Mansur's eyes in my direct gaze.

"Grover...you were closest to Master Harbrook. Might that spear have been designed for you?"

There was uproar as the six men shouted denials.

"Your wife was here yesterday, and she was concerned that you might think your life was in danger."

Mansur Grover blinked several times and screwed up his nose. "My life...why would she think that?"

"She feels that you have been under some strain lately. She can think of no other reason but that you are afraid for your life."

Master Burridge elbowed his way to the front of the men. "Master Mansur is afraid of no man, sir."

"Burridge is correct...I have no fears. This is a mere womanly silliness, my Lord Belvoir."

I shrugged. "Nevertheless, she came all the way from Ramsbury with Mistress Harbrook to tell me of her anxieties."

Grover tossed back his ale.

"This is foolish talk, sir. You must remember my wife is a spoiled girl of sixteen. She is vulnerable to all manner of fancies."

I looked carefully at each man. "The coroner will speak to you all. I, too, will come when we have distanced ourselves a little from this event and speak to you, one by one, and I will be lodging a report with the justices in eyre. You WILL all be tried for this breech."

They all looked uncomfortable.

"The justices, sir...? Surely you can hear this in your own court?" asked Abbeye.

"A man has died, Abbeye." He looked down shamefacedly

at his feet. "Meanwhile, I ask you to leave all spears here with me, every one which any of you carried today."

"Why, m'lord?" asked Burridge.

"Because I ask it, Burridge, and because I want to look at them all."

He swallowed and gestured to the back of the hall. The lesser men who had collected there came up and, under Hal's direction, placed all the spears that had been out in the forest that day along the boards of the dais. Some dashed down to the horses where there were others stored.

"One or two have gone back to Ramsbury, and no doubt Bedwyn, with the men we sent home, m'lord. Those, however, were not taken out or used."

I nodded. "I am content. Master Abbeye, please convey our condolences to Mistress Harbrook on the untimely death of her husband. We shall send his body to Ramsbury as soon as we are able."

The man bowed. "Thank you, my lord." He backed out of the room and disappeared, followed by some of the servants.

"I think it would be best if you all rode home now. Do not say anything about this event. It will be huge news soon enough. I will speak to you tomorrow."

They all bowed as a body and then, one by one, made for the hall steps.

Mansur Grover watched them go and did not stir.

"There is something more you wish to say, sir?" I asked.

The man rapped his cup down on the table. "No, My Lord Belvoir, nothing at all." Folding his cloak around him, he left.

Hal let out a stertorous breath. "Well! Here's a bloomin' bundle o' breedbate!"

I chuckled at him. "What is that supposed to mean, ol' Hal?"

"Oh, that's Wiltshire speak for something which causes strife amongst folk."

"Then breedbate it is."

"What do you think 'appened."

I sat down and stared at the pile of spears.

"Poaching is an offence under the law, Hal, be it deer or boar."

"Aye, I know that, 'course I do."

"Grover is certainly unsettled, though somehow, if he were worried for his life, I doubt he would go off into the forest where someone could easily pick him off."

"D'you think someone 'as tried it? You did ask if you wondered if the spear was intended for 'im."

"Or, for some reason, Hal, Grover wanted to get rid of the Lord Durnford's man."

"I s'pose there is that too."

Hal filled his ale cup. "But why? Why would 'e?"

"I don't know yet, Hal."

Hal put down his cup and picked up a spear. "What are we looking for?"

"Are these any of the same type of spear that we had stuck through poor Alysoun, Hal?"

"I have it in the undercroft…wait I'll get it."

I sat on my chair, turning these latest problems around in my head. The door above me opened, and Lydia's head poked out of the gap.

"Aumary…what's going on? I heard some men in the courtyard. I didn't want to disturb you when you were talking, but…"

"It's all right, my love. We have a dead man delivered to us from the forest, but when Johannes has seen him, then the body will go back to Ramsbury."

She came out of the door, pulled it to, and stood on the little landing of the first step.

"No. Not Master Grover?"

"No, not him. Master Harbrook. He that bred little Cleaver and works for the Lord Roger."

"Oh no…poor man. Did I hear someone say it was a boar?"

"A boar or a spear, the result is the same. The man is dead."

"Oh, poor Mistress Harbrook." Lydia crossed herself. "Whyever men do such dangerous things for sport and fun, I do not know."

I chuckled into my ale cup. "Sport with a boar is, they tell me, the absolute test of a real man."

"Then thank all the saints that you are not a real man, Aumary Belvoir," she chuckled.

I snuffled into my ale. "I have done my fair share of pig-sticking, Lydia. When I was younger but …not now, I have dependents and a manor to run and frankly, I value my life!" I chuckled.

Hal returned with the spear we had taken from the grain barn in Marlborough.

He began to search through the spears left by the hunting men. "What are you doing, Hal?" asked Lydia.

"Looking for a similar spear to this one, m'lady," he said. "One like that which killed poor Alysoun."

"Oh, how terrible," said Lydia.

Our younger son Phillip, at that moment, screamed as if he were being stuck like a pig, and Lydia grimaced. "I must away to feed Phillip." She turned. "I hope you find the answer."

"Ah…" said Hal as I heard the upper door click.

"There is one?" I said, sitting up from a lounging position on my chair.

"Aye, there is…there's two."

"Do we know who laid them down there?"

"I was watching carefully. I made 'em all lay 'em down in separate piles."

"And these belonged to?"

Hal looked up. "Mansur Grover's party."

I looked up at the rafters. "Shall we send for Johannes, Hal?"

On the morrow, the weather turned, and we woke to a slight mizzle. The forest was dull and dripped with silver droplets. Autumn had fully arrived.

I stood on the top step of the manor, waiting for my horse to be saddled and gazed up at the grey heavens. A lazy winged heron flew across, making for the Oakhill pool, I supposed, which lay a little way to the north west of the manor.

First, we would visit Bedwyn and speak to the men there.

Some men had gone as beaters and taken their leashed dogs out, but none could tell me very much for they were not close enough to the action.

Master du May, too, had been hanging back. He admitted to me that he did not like boar hunting. It was, in the main, a sport of nobles and rich men, and my reeve was neither. He was simply there to guide folk around the area, he said, as they were not all familiar with the terrain.

"But Harbrook was a Bedwyn man. He would know where he was. Why stray into Savernake from Durnford land?"

"I think the men knew it was Savernake. They just didn't think anyone would find out."

"Why you, du May?"

"I was asked to come to Ramsbury."

"By whom?"

"By Master Harbrook, sir."

"Even though you know it is illegal, Henry? Why didn't you tell them that they were no longer on their own land?"

Du May dropped his chin to his chest in embarrassment. "I was carried away by the...excitement of the chase, I suppose. And I wasn't hunting, sir. But I did say. I did tell them."

"Not forcefully enough, du May!"

"I was merely helping..."

"Pah...just helping!" I frowned at him.

"But I would not have been able to reason with them, sir, anyway. They were determined to follow the pig into Savernake." Henry's lip quivered. "Master Burridge was very...persuasive, sir."

"I see that Ralph Hawkes was also with you. He kept to the shadows, did he not?"

"Yes, sir. He came with me. He, too, knows his way around the forest."

"He must do, he is my falconer," I snapped.

"He insisted he come, sir."

"Hmm. Do you know why?"

"He..." du May looked away, "He told me he wanted to take a look at those men who were connected with his sister's marriage and his father's death, sir."

"His sister's husband, Grover, and Master Harbrook, Roger Hawkes' friend."

"Those men in particular, sir, yes. If you want to know why, you must ask him yourself, for I do not know," said Henry du May with a remorseful smile. "But he, too, knew that it was forbidden to hunt the boar in Savernake, m'lord."

I nodded. "I will ask him. But not today." I had other things to do today.

"Henry...Since you have been so foolish, let's see if you can redeem yourself. I'd like you to help me..." and I took him by the shoulder and turned to walk him to the stables, "If you will."

Hal and I, with a few of my forest men, were at Toteham, an area of terraced common with birch trees scattered thickly over the ground. One or two old oaks punctuated the serried rows of silver trunks.

We were looking for the missing spear, which Master Burridge said he had tossed into the confusion of boar, bodies and beaters.

I also wanted to see for myself where the accident happened and, as was my usual habit, picture the scene and how it may have come about.

With us, we had Henry du May, who had been at the place when the boar had attacked.

"So, where exactly were you?"

"I was over there, m'lord, with the horses. With Ralph and the grooms. I could see up to here but not beyond at first because of the dense undergrowth."

"What did you hear?"

Du May pursed his lips. "A grunting and squealing—that would be the injured boar, sir—the men shouting, Master Harbrook yelling..."

"What was he yelling? Could you hear?"

"Something like, 'Grover, get her or stick her', or something like that, sir."

"It was an instruction to throw his spear?"

"The boar was within sight and was ranging round the men circling it, I thought. There was stiff competition to stick her, sir."

"Hmm. You didn't see the throw...any of the throws or thrusts the men attempted?"

"No, sir. I came up after the boar had gored Master

Harbrook. I heard him scream and then ran up."

John, my chief wood warden and the best tracker in the forest, came up to my elbow.

"M'lord. We have found the tree where Master Harbrook was pinned."

"Good. Show me then."

We walked a few yards and stopped before an elderly birch. Its bark was scored at the level of about four feet, and there were traces of old brown blood on its light surface.

John hunkered down.

"Many feet ran to and fro in this area. There is the mark the boar left on the ground." He stood and swivelled, "There is the place where the boar died." He paced four steps, "and here Yves of Harbrook lay as they broke off the spear, I think."

"Mansur's spear caught the beast on its shoulder."

"After Harbrook 'ad stuck it on the back from 'orseback," added Hal.

"Was the spear still attached to the beast when you saw it, Henry?"

"There wasn't a spear in it, no."

"But Mansur's blow didn't kill it, for it ran on and gored Harbrook," I said, scratching the dark beard of my chin. "So whose thrust killed it?"

Henry looked at me a little bemused. "I...don't know, sir."

"My Lord Belvoir!" It was Tostig's voice.

I ran up to him. He pointed upwards. "A spear m'lord. Up there."

I followed his pointing finger.

Up in the branches of a large oak tree, the weak sun caught the metal cross point of a spear lodged in the leaves.

"Can you get it down, Tostig?"

"Aye, sir."

One of the younger foresters climbed the tree and handed the spear down to Tostig. He gave it into Hal's hand who looked at the tip.

"Blood," he said.

"I wish I knew what happened here, John," I said, looking around the glade. "Thank you for your help. You may now all go home. Be prepared to give your accounts to the coroner." I turned to leave. "Let us go to Ramsbury and see what they have to say to us."

I called to Hal, swung off, mounted my horse and rode for Ramsbury town.

We cantered down the main street and had come to within a few yards of the iron maker's yard when Mistress Grover came flying out of the gate. She saw us, her face crumpled, and she ran across the road and up to her house by the church.

Hal turned in the saddle to watch her.

"Well, what's that all about then? She were outta there like she'd seen a moonin' monk."

"Ah…here might be the answer, Hal."

Mansur Grover was standing, flexing his fists and staring out of the gateway at the receding back of his wife.

Many of his workers about their business had stopped to watch the drama unfolding in the gateway.

Grover saw us enter and dismount, turned his back, and stomped off into the office, waving his hand angrily at his workers to return to their tasks.

We followed.

"Master Grover, good day."

He bowed his head. "A good day, m'lord? I hope so. The weather, however, seems to have decided it will not be."

"We are in poor humour today, Master Grover?"

"Forgive me, my lord, I have much on my mind," he answered.

"Well, perhaps you will have yet one more thing to think about when I tell you that the spear which killed the young girl in Marlborough, Grover, came from your stock."

He looked around the office to see who was there and jutted his chin towards the door. Men went scuttling away. Master Burridge stayed.

"Out, Burridge!" yelled Grover, and the man slunk off with a scowl.

"How do you explain that, sir?"

"I cannot explain it. I did not take it to the town to kill a young girl."

"Where do you keep your weapons, sir?" asked Hal.

"In a shed at the back of my house. All locked up and safe. Myself and Burridge are the only men who have a key."

"You have not perhaps noticed a theft from there. The lock has not been forced?

"We took our spears from there yesterday when we went out to the forest, m'lord. There was no evidence of the lock being broken then."

"Who looks to your stocks?"

"I do it myself, along with Master Burridge, and I have to say he is beyond reproach."

I nodded. "You noticed no theft?"

"Nothing."

He sat down wearily behind his table and gestured for me to sit at the other side.

"Why would I wish to murder, in such a heinous way, my Lord Belvoir, a young girl I have never met?"

"You are sure you've never met?"

"Quite sure," he said with authority.

"What about her grandmother?"

"No, sir. I know very few people in the town. I try not to go to Marlborough town too often. They are not, in general, sir, tolerant of the colour of my skin, nor my power in the

Ramsbury countryside, not least my wealth."

I nodded. "Master Harbrook? How well did you know him? It seems, according to your wife, that you have not been on as good terms with him as before..."

"My wife is an ingénue, sir. What does she know of life? Of men? Of my relationship with them?" His voice was bitter.

I leaned forward. "You, sir, I think, knew this when you whisked her away from her father and married her. It was no doubt part of her charm?"

The man sighed.

"I know that you had words with Harbrook. I hear from other sources that you were recently unhappy with him."

"What can I say, sir, to convince you that I am not a murderer? That I did not know these people?"

I sat back. "What was the cause of the recent quarrel between you and Master Harbrook? I cannot believe that it is simply his suspicion that you killed his friend, your father-in-law."

"We had no quarrel, m'lord."

I watched him for a while.

"And yet the man was heard to speak ill of you."

Mansur looked up quickly. "When...? Where? With whom did he speak? Who is your informant, sir?"

"I believe it was with the Pinter in the town."

Grover scoffed. "I hardly know the man, though I do know that he had a desire to marry my Richildis and that he changed his mind."

"Do you think that your wife felt abandoned by this man? She seems to want to draw my attention to him. She seems to think that the man desires your death."

"That is nonsense, my lord. I cannot think where Richildis has obtained this notion." He shook his head, "I will speak with her later and make her see her error, sir, make her aware that she must learn to be more circumspect…in what she says."

"She is worried for you, Grover. Does that not make you…"

"And I have told you, my lord, that my wife is worrying for nothing."

The man stared at me, and the brown eyes did not blink.

Hal shifted his backside on the stool upon which he sat, and Mansur was distracted and broke his gaze.

"Mansur, who hates you enough to try to frame you for these murders?" I asked.

"Hates me?" The man laughed out loud, and his laughter went on and on, ringing in the close confines of the small wooden building.

"Why everyone in the world, sir…everyone. Or have you not noticed? My black skin conceals a devil. I am a monster, a defiler of young women, a black beast with untamed appetites and violent thoughts."

I tilted my head. "Are you?"

"I have a …reputation, sir. An undeserved reputation."

I sat back and looked at him again: his proud head, his handsome face, and his open expression.

"I suspect when the doctor digs the broken spear from the body of Yves of Harbrook, it will prove to be one of your own."

"I didn't kill him. I was, however, in close proximity to him. I thought the boar would make for me and was readying my other spear to take it. The beast reared away and then fell dead…"

"After he had gored Yves of Harbrook."

Mansur Grover closed those dark brown eyes. "Aye, after."

"You did not see who killed the beast?"

"All eyes were on the man Harbrook, my lord."

"Except those of the man who killed the boar."

I stood and slapped my riding gloves on my hand. Tell me, what happened to the boar's carcass?"

"Men took it home to Ramsbury."

I nodded. I would not be able to examine the beast's carcass, of that I was sure.

"Think on it all, please, Grover. If you can recall anything which might be relevant, let me know."

"You will not arrest me, my Lord Belvoir. For the murders?"

Hal opened the door. "The Lord Belvoir doesn't arrest people without 'e 'as good evidence, Master Grover," he said. "Just you be glad that ' es the constable and not some other less careful bugger. They'd string you up soon as look at you."

He turned in the doorway. "Mind you…if I was the constable, on the evidence of the moment, I might be inclined to be one of them buggers."

I smiled.

"No, Grover. I am not about to arrest you. Not yet. You do have a reason, I think, for desiring the death of Master Harbrook, but perhaps you aren't the only one."

He stood up and bowed his head. "Thank you, m'lord."

Mistress Grover was sitting sobbing into her hands when we made the hall of the house by the church.

The older woman, Margaret, her face bloated and red with crying, tried to block our entry, but Hal and I politely moved past her.

"Madam, we are so very sorry to hear about the death of your brother."

Margaret of Harbrook sniffed and shrugged at the same time. "It is a shock, sir. Yves was a difficult man, but he was my brother." She wiped her eyes and looked back at her mistress. "Perhaps that's why the poor girl is in such straits…Master Grover is…"

"He, too, is shocked at the death of his friend," I said quickly.

"Shocked! Well, I dare say he is, but he doesn't need to take his moods out on her, sir."

"She knew Master Harbrook from a child, I think?"

"She did, sir…" Margaret twisted her hands in front of her. "My younger brother was a special friend of her late father, and we did wonder at one time if my brother and Richildis might be married, but…"

"Ah, so there was perhaps a time when this was thought to be a possibility?" I asked.

"Many men have desired Richildis, m'lord. She is a very beautiful girl."

"Your brother, Master Pinter? Who else wanted her?"

"A few others…I don't wish to talk about it if that's alright with you…this is a house in mourning."

"I would not intrude on your grief mistress, but I must speak with your lady," I said in a tone that brooked no argument.

I looked past the bulk of her body.

"Mistress Grover, a word?"

Richildis Grover lifted her face. I saw the beginnings of a bruise forming on her cheekbone.

"Go find a cold cloth for your mistress, Margaret," I said. "Now."

Hal had already gone to look down at the girl. Margaret passed him and tutted.

"Who struck you, lass?" he asked.

Richildis lifted her chin in a poor effort at defiance. "My husband. It is his right, is it not?"

"Is 'e in the 'abit of striking women?" asked Hal, his

hand tensing on the pommel of his sword, his face grim.

"No, sir, just his wife, it seems."

"Why, Richildis?" I asked, hunkering down before her.

"It seems, sir, I am a whore, play him false with any man upon whom I set eyes and…and I have a closet full of wicked secrets. Yet, my lord, I kneel and pray like an honest woman."

"These are things he said to you?"

"And more, my lord. I begged him on my knees to explain to me why he was so furious with me and what I had done to anger him."

I looked at Hal. He raised his grey eyebrows.

"You thought that worry had turned his brain, did you not? What can have made him so hostile to you, Richildis? This must be some misunderstanding between you."

"This morning, when I heard of the death of Margaret's brother, I cried sir. Not particularly for myself but for Margaret. She is such a sweet soul and loves me dearly, and, of course, I was unhappy for her. Mansur flew at me, saying that I was enamoured of the man Harbrook and that I was crying for the loss of my lover. It was not true."

"Ah…he is jealous…"

"He has not been so before."

I stood. "Let's dry your tears and get Margaret to tend your bruises, and we'll see what we can do."

"I swear he is accusing me wrongly."

"I have no doubt of it."

I lifted her by the elbow. "Come, sit here in the light and let Margaret bathe your face."

The servant had returned with a cloth and a small basin.

"I had come to ask you about the origins of the hostility between your husband and Harbrook. You have answered me without me asking the question."

Richildis groaned as the cold water touched her face.

"There was nothing until a few days ago…I cannot see what has caused the difference in him."

"Murders about which he has been questioned. It would distemper many a man. Not least one of…his tender nature."

"Tender nature, sir?"

"You have not thought then that he feels himself out of place and alone here? "

"Out of place?" she said tremulously.

"'E's constantly on 'is guard, lass," said Hal, "always defending himself against folk who think bad of him because of the colour of his skin."

"Even those who profess to be friends are…less than complimentary out of earshot. Master Harbrook, for one. In my hearing, madam, and I have heard it from others too."

"Are you telling me that Mansur would have a man killed because he has slandered him? That he killed Yves of Harbrook because behind his back, he told tales about him?" She rose from her seat, and the water spilled onto the floor and over the woman Margaret. "That he killed him because he believed I was his lover?" She stood up tall. "That is ridiculous, my lord."

Margaret's face was white, and she got up slowly from her wet knees. "No. Mansur would not kill my brother," she said.

"No, I agree. I don't think he would, but someone might try to make it seem as if he had."

Margaret dropped the bowl, which clattered to the floor, splitting into two pieces.

Richildis, wide-eyed, stared down at it.

"Someone wants him to hang for a crime he did not commit?"

"That I believe is the nub of it, yes," I said.

Richildis Grover crossed herself. "Almighty God, aid us."

"My brother wasn't gored by a boar then, sir?" said a

tearful and shocked Margaret of Harbrook, her lined face creasing into a frown. "He was murdered. We heard the gossip but didn't dare..."

"He was killed, I think, by a boar spear, and almost simultaneously, the boar was able to gore him. He would, I think, have died of the first wound eventually. I will not be absolutely sure until the doctor has seen him and reported what he finds."

"But it could be a simple accident... someone loosed a spear, and it happened to hit your brother," said Hal.

Margaret staggered to the table and felt for the bench, sitting, her wet skirts draping her gown tightly over her large knees.

"Then who did it, my lord? Who killed him?" she whispered.

"Someone who hates Mansur Grover to the ends of his fingertips, mistress."

Chapter Nine

JOHANNES CAME IN to us at vespers, or it would have been vespers if the church bells had been ringing.

He came out of the little room on the south wall, wiping his hands on a rag and walked up the steps with us.

"I have removed the spear head as you requested, Aumary. It had lodged in the ribs and that's why it was so hard to get out."

"Did it kill him, Johannes?"

"The boar took him in the belly. The spear went in at an angle and, with all the movement, lodged in the ribs. When he thrashed about, it then pierced the heart, and this dealt his death blow, but he would have died from either wound eventually. Do you want to see it?"

"Yes!" shouted Hal from behind me coming up the hall steps.

"Hal suspects that Master Grover is guilty of the murders of his father-in-law and the man Harbrook, Johannes."

"And the two women?"

"Ah well...he argues for an accomplice to Master Grover in the town, helping out," I chuckled. "He is not enamoured of a man who strikes his young wife merely for looking at another man, or crying at his death."

"Did he?"

"It would seem so."

Hal took the spearhead from the doctor's fingers and scrutinised it with a narrowed eye and looked at me in irritation.

"Ah, there we are! Just the same. It IS Grover's."

"All that we can say, Hal, is that it came from Master Grover's stock...no more. We cannot say who threw it."

"Good enough for me. Get him in and ask a few more questions, sir." He turned his hand as if he were twisting a knife in a wound, "Screw 'im to the chair."

I sat back on my own chair and leaned comfortably with one leg over the arm.

"I think I'll let them all stew."

"'E's always doin' this," said Hal to Johannes, cocking his head in my direction. "'E talks to 'em, lets out a bit... just a bit mind...and then leaves 'em to it," he chortled. "'E calls 'em, 'is old boilin' fowl."

"All involved are under pressure, Hal. They react in different ways. As you know, doing this sometimes provokes the murderer to act again in a panicked way. Sometimes that allows us to trip them up."

Johannes rubbed the side of his nose and blew out his cheeks, "And we all know what happened last time he tried that, Hal."

Hal chuckled deep in his beard. "Aye...he nearly became the next victim."

I ignored them.

"We need to speak to Master Hawkes Junior."

"Aye, what was he doing on the hunt?" asked Hal, "It wasn't a bird hunt."

"He wasn't too fond of his father's old friend, was he?"

"Harbrook? What does he have against him?"

"I don't know. We shall go to Bedwyn, seek him out and ask him."

"And 'e's not the only one, is he?" said Hal. "I think we should go and ask a few questions in Ramsbury too."

Ramsbury was quiet as we rode down the High Street and into the iron workings the next day. Men turned to look at us with suspicion but carried on with their work. For a short time, I watched a man pulling a bellows up and down. Flames shot from the top of a cylindrical clay oven or kiln, almost singeing his beard.

Hal and I walked solemnly to the shed.

Master Grover was away at the Durnfords' manor, I was told. Since the death of the bailiff, Master Harbrook, the business had been in some disarray. Grover had gone there personally to sort out the need for iron for the lord's farrier.

"He will be back, I'm sure, my lord, about the fifth hour of the day, if you would care to wait."

"No, Burridge, we shall also be visiting Ramsbury Manor. Perhaps we shall catch him there."

"As you wish, m'lord," the man bowed and carried on with some work of his own.

"Tell me, Burridge. You did not like Master Harbrook? Why's that?"

The man looked up at me under thin brown eyebrows and wiped dirty hands across his forehead, leaving a black streak. "He was an unpleasant man."

"Explain to me your meaning of the word 'unpleasant', Burridge."

Burridge put down the tally stick he had been holding. "I think I told you, sir, that he was a man most difficult to please. He would find fault at the tiniest thing. One had to be very careful when dealing with him."

"'E was an argumentative sort, was 'e?" asked Hal.

Burridge scoffed, "Quite so, my friend. Caused trouble wherever he went."

"I always found him polite and affable, Burridge," I said.

"To you, sir, I suppose he would be, seeing you are the warden of the forest and a lord, if you don't mind me saying."

"Tell me more about him. For instance, was he... er... over fond of other mens' wives?"

Burridge opened his mouth to speak but then his eyes slid away from my face. "There is gossip, sir. There was..."

"Ho, ho, then tell me. I'm all for gossip."

Hal gave me a sidelong look, knowing this was not the truth.

"No man's wife was safe, they say."

"Ah, and who are they, Burridge?"

"I'm sure I don't know, sir. People about. Ramsbury folk."

I folded my arms across my chest. "Are you married, Burridge? Was your wife one who was not safe from Master Harbrook?"

He looked up again. "No, sir. I am not married."

"So the only reason for your dislike of the man was purely a business one?" asked Hal.

"I did not like him, no, my friend. I didn't. But that doesn't mean I would kill the man."

"Who hated him, Burridge?"

"I doubt he was very popular with the folk at Ramsbury Manor, my Lord Belvoir. He was a hard master. He had... some strange little habits...he could not stand disorder of any kind. He hated dirt," Burridge laughed. "It took him all his time to cross the threshold of the works here. As you can no doubt see, smelting is a dirty, smelly business." He held up his black smudged palms.

"So there may be someone, perhaps amongst the

servants who were at the boar hunt, who might have had a disagreement with Harbrook."

"I have no doubt, sir."

"Hmm. And anyone who was perhaps angry with him over the pursuit of their spouses?"

"I can't say, sir."

"Tell us, Burridge," said Hal. "Do you know anyone in Marlborough town?"

Burridge pursed his lips. "No, I don't believe I do... though naturally, we do business with many places around. I don't personally know anyone...no. I go there so rarely."

"However, you do know folk in Bedwyn?" I asked.

"I think I told you last time, sir. I knew your falconer. I have a nodding relationship with a few Bedwyn folk since I come from close by. I still have family there, but I rarely visit."

"You do know Master Pinter, though, Burridge?"

"Aye. I know him. I forgot, I do know him."

"But you would say you do not know him well?"

"No, sir."

"Well, perhaps we'll now go and have a word with the widow and..."

"I doubt you'll get the real truth from her, sir," said Burridge, starting from behind his trestle.

I turned back. "Oh? Why's that?"

"She was besotted with her husband, sir. She saw no harm in him at all. It seemed that she was one of those women who was truly in love with her spouse and couldn't see his little idiosyncrasies, his strangeness, his dalliances."

I smiled a somewhat disingenuous smile. "Ah... would that all wives were so loyal, eh Hal?"

Hal scoffed. "Why I 'int never been married, see."

"Someone has to think we are wonderful after all, eh?"

Burridge grinned. "Your lordship," he bowed.

Mistress Harbrook was at home supervising some servants packing belongings for a journey.

"You are leaving, Mistress Harbrook?"

Rousalie looked up sadly. "I am returning to my home in Bedwyn, my lord. It was only Yves' business that kept me here." She sniffed. "I think you know we have a house there. It is part of my dowry."

"Yes indeed. We are most sorry for the death of your husband. It must have been a great shock."

The woman's eyes filled with tears. "Yes sir. But then, no woman knows when she will be made a widow, does she? We had four happy years together. That is what counts."

Hal cleared his throat but kept his mouth closed.

"Mistress Harbrook, do you know if your husband had any enemies? If anyone was so at odds with him, they might wish to kill him. Were there any animosities within the Lord Durnford's staff here at Ramsbury?"

"Enemies, sir? No, only the usual rivalries and mislikes that any man of office may build up over years. Yves was well-liked here. He was a fair and well-organised man. No one could hold a grudge against him."

"'E had not to turn off any man for bad work or..." asked Hal

"There were times when he had to do this, yes. But kill him for it? A man must be mad to do that, sir."

"There was no man angry with him because he had made free with their spouse?"

The woman's face was suffused with blood. "Sir, begging your pardon, that is a most wicked thing to say about a man who cannot defend himself."

I shrugged. "Some rumour I have heard."

"Is it?" she answered sharply, "Well, there is no truth

in that rumour. My husband was a good man and a loyal spouse. He would never look at another woman. You have been led by the nose, sir. It is malicious gossip." She started to sniffle, and I must admit I felt rather uncomfortable.

"Please, madam. Do not worry yourself. If the gossip is untrue, I have already forgotten it." But of course, I hadn't.

"Yves and I were a love match, sir. As much as Mansur and Richildis are."

"And yet, Mansur Grover struck his wife, we hear. Unless that too is vile gossip, madam?"

Rousalie's face hardened. "I do not know what has got into the man. He is usually so careful and kind. Lately, he has been…harsh, sir. I think I told you that before. I thought at first it was the imaginings of a young girl, but no, I have heard it with my own ears."

"What did you hear?"

"He called her a harlot, my lord. Plain and simple and accused her of fraternising with the men of Ramsbury town."

"With your husband, madam?"

She looked affronted. "No, not with Yves, but with others."

"We had it from Mistress Grover that her husband accused her of having an affair with your husband, madam."

The two servants helping with the folding of clothing, stopped stock still and watched.

Rousalie Harbrook spun around. "Off both of you. There are things to do elsewhere."

The two of them fled at her sharp tone and severe look.

She turned back to me. "That too is wicked gossip, sir. Richildis has no interest in my husband and neither did he have any care for her beyond the fact that the girl was his best friend's daughter."

"He did not once wish to marry her?"

"No. Of course not. She is little more than a child. He

has seen her grow up."

"Her husband is almost thirty years her senior, madam," I said quickly.

"Yves would not wish to wed a young girl. His interests lay with more…mature women."

"Nevertheless, this is what is said, madam."

Rousalie Harbrook became suddenly angry. "Why do you persist? I tell you, Yves and I were happy, we had no need of other consolation. Neither of us was enamoured of others."

"So if this nonsense has no basis in fact. Why should Master Grover call his wife a whore?"

"I do not know, sir."

"Then perhaps we shall ask him to his face, Mistress Harbrook. I wish you well with your move back to Bedwyn."

"Thank you, my Lord Belvoir, she said frostily."

Hal and I stood on the doorstep.

"So 'oo's tellin' the truth then? Burridge, young Hawkes or Mistress Harbrook, or for that matter, the servant, Harbrook's sister?" He scratched his cheek. "I'm blowed if I know what's going on."

"That the iron master is a jealous man is beyond doubt, Hal…"

"They say, don't they, that there's no smoke without flames…?"

"They do indeed. But what we need to know is, who has been feeding the fire?"

"Uh?"

"If there's no truth in the rumours, who is behind them and why? And why is Master Grover so ready to believe that his wife of merely a few short weeks is a harlot?"

Hal moved off towards our horses, mumbling. "Is everyone lyin' then? Everyone?"

"People are telling us what they think to be true, Hal,"

I said, taking the reins from a groom. "But whilst what they think is sincere, as they see it, it may not exactly be the truth."

"Gossip, then?"

"Mere gossip and hearsay."

We walked our beasts to the centre of the collection of buildings, which comprised the Manor of the Durnford's. My friend Sir Roger was away from home, staying at one of his other manors. His bailiff was dead and there were few staff left at the house. After a short walk around, we met Mansur Grover exiting the main building in a hurry and with a stony face.

"Well met, Master Grover!" I shouted. "I had hoped to have words with you before I must return to Bedwyn."

"My Lord Belvoir, I…I am really very busy at the moment…I have no time…"

He pushed his way past me and beckoning a couple of his men to follow, he made for the gate."

"I, too, Master Grover, am a busy man." I took hold of his sleeve.

He shook me off.

"Since the death of the bailiff Harbrook, I have…" he began.

"You have what?"

He stared angrily at me but did not answer my question.

"What do you here?"

"I came to see Rousalie, to offer my condolences."

"Ah…" I took his sleeve again. "Come, let's walk a little. I have some questions to ask you."

"I have no time for walking, my lord."

I held onto his arm. "Walk you shall, and you will answer my questions. Or I can take you to the castle and ask my questions there. Why are you being so evasive? I might almost think that you had something to hide."

"I have nothing to hide. I have told you all I know about Hawkes and about Yves."

"Your tempers seem very uncontrolled at the moment. Your wife tells me..."

"Ah no, not that again, sir." He rolled his eyes. "What is between my wife and I, is a private matter. No one, not even the Constable of the county, has the right......"

"Sadly, Grover, when it involves murder, I have the right to question anyone and expect answers. Truthful answers."

A small tic began by the man's right eye and he looked away. His men milled about by the gate, watching us carefully.

"Go back to the yard," he yelled. They gave him a surly look and turned on their heels.

I walked a little ahead of him. Hal lagged behind.

"About Master Harbrook. I have heard that he has a reputation for being the sort of man who was tempted by another man's wife. Might you know anything about this?"

Mansur Grover folded his arms across his ample chest. "I have heard the rumours but have no first-hand knowledge of it."

"And yet your wife tells me that you accused her of being involved with the man. We were there shortly afterwards, you remember?"

"You gave 'er a stripe across 'er face, I think," said Hal from behind us. "Funny way to show your affection for a woman...'ittin' 'er."

"How I treat my wife is entirely up to me," said Grover through gritted teeth. "It is, as I say, private and between ourselves."

"You called her a harlot in another's hearing," I said.

"I did not. Whoever said that is a liar."

I sighed heavily through my nose. “My temper, too, can wear thin,” I said. “You are, I’m sure, not being truthful with me. Tell me, what is troubling you?”

“My petty marital problems can have no bearing upon your work, my lord. I have told you, there’s nothing troubling me. My wife is an untried girl who needs a firm hand now and again. Have you never needed to discipline your own wife, my lord?”

I laughed aloud. “Er…no, actually, never.”

“I’d like to see ’im try,” said Hal quietly through his teeth.

A horse whinnied and I was momentarily distracted by a movement at the gate. I turned to see a horse enter at a fast pace and slide to a halt.

“Tostig! What are you…?

Tostig jumped down from Fenrir’s back. He nodded his head. “M’lord.”

“What’s the matter?” My heart sank to my boots. “Please, no more ill news.” I had seen his face, and his expression was grim.

Tostig’s eyes slid to the tall, black ironmaster. “For your ears only, sir.”

“And mine I ’ope,” said Hal, rocking forward on the balls of his feet.

“Aye, and yours too, ol’ Hal…just not… anyone else’s.”

Mansur Grover took this as his moment to escape. He bowed and strode quickly out of the gate after his men.

I shouted after him, “I’ll need to speak further with you…soon!”

“You know where I’ll be, sir,” he shouted back.

I turned to Tostig.

“Sir, the town reeve’s man has been looking for you. He went first to Durley, of course, and then when it was known you were at Bedwyn, he followed there.”

“Yes?”

"Sir Andrew Merriman at the castle requests that you return to the town, sir."

"Why, Tostig?"

"He's found a body. A body in the moat, sir."

"She was weighted down with stone," said Andrew. "Large blocks from the building works just outside the western wall."

"Where?"

"West side of the moat."

"First finder?"

"Perkin Fisher, poor lad."

"Aye, she's not a pretty sight."

Our corpse was lying on a trestle in one of the small rooms at the back of the castle stables.

"Has he made a statement?"

"I got Alfred the scribe to write it down, such as it is."

Young Perkin was the lad who fished the river for our suppers on Fridays and provided the castle with some of its supplies. He was just thirteen.

"'I was fishing by the sluice gate when my net caught on something and as I pulled, up came a dead body. I rowed for the bank and came to tell the officer of the watch. I didn't recognise the girl,' is what the clerks wrote down," quoted Andrew.

"Right."

"I shall never eat fish again," Andrew said under his breath. "Looks like they've made a banquet of her."

"Aye, they would. There are some large pike in the moat."

I peered at the body on its makeshift bier; the remainder of her hair and the cloth in which she was wrapped still dripping now and again.

"Have we sent for the doctor?"

"I sent a message as soon as she was taken out, but he is obviously from town, or out and about in it."

"He will get the message soon. He returned from Bedwyn this morning - he's been with us." I scanned the small body or what was left of it.

"So what do we know?"

Andrew blew out a breath from between his lips. "Young, small, female, that's about it."

"No clothes?"

"As naked as the day Eve tempted Adam."

"Wounds?"

"Hard to say. You look at her and see if you can see what killed her. She has been in the water so long, I think, it's going to be difficult."

"Hmm."

There were no obvious wounds; her face was unrecognisable, fish and other river creatures had devoured her flesh, and the corpse was bloated.

Hal was standing at her head. "Can I just see a little bruising around the neck?" He pointed. "It looks …odd. Was she wurried, do you think?"

I moved as close as I dared, taking a deep breath against the smell and looked carefully at her throat. "Yes…perhaps. Yes, maybe she was strangled." The little bone which Johannes had told me lies in the front of the neck looked depressed.

"I have asked Nick Barbflet who has been reported missing in the town," said Andrew.

"Just one girl."

"You know?"

"Aye," I stood up and slowly raised my eyes to his, "a friend of our murdered maid, Alysoun."

Andrew made a moue, "Ah. Now there's a thing."

"No one listens to ol' 'Al."

"I beg your pardon, Hal?" asked Sir Andrew.

"I said that we had a madman in the town preyin' on women - I still think it."

"Three women and one man, dead."

Hal's eyebrows rose as if to quiz me. "Can you count, sir?"

"My falconer Hawkes has a different killer, and I think I know who that is now," I said with a very slight shake of my head. "But Master Harbrook's murderer is still unknown."

"You gonna tell us?"

"No, not yet."

I walked round the dripping corpse. A stagnant riverine smell assailed my nose, along with that of putrefaction.

"When was the girl reported missing?" asked Andrew.

"Three weeks ago, I think," I said.

"Family?"

"None. Andrew, can you have the pinter fetched? He knew the girl. I'd as soon as not ask friends to identify her."

"I'll go," said Hal, turning to the door.

"Hal, don't tell him why I want him here. Just bring him."

"Right you are, sir."

A little while later, Dr Johannes of Salerno came squeezing in through the narrow doorway.

"I'm sorry, Aumary, I was away in St Martin's at the Widow Partridge, and Gabriel isn't well, so I stopped off there."

"Oh? I...I hope..."

"No, he's got a lung congestion. Coughing like an old cart horse." He was smiling, so the man was not dangerously ill, I thought.

Gabriel Gallipot was the town apothecary, an esteemed town councillor and a friend to us all.

"Something he could not cure himself?"

"Two heads were better than one." Johannes' eye strayed to the corpse on the trestle. "Oh dear."

"Been in the moat quite a while, we think."

"Looks like it."

His eye took in the whole body. He shrugged his pack from his shoulder and began to examine the girl. Andrew and I melted into the shadows.

"If this is Mabel, the missing girl," I whispered, "then how do we connect her death to that of Alysoun? What did she know? Did she, too, know the secret that Alysoun was about to tell Cedric?"

"Did she know Harbrook, do you think?" asked Andrew.

I shrugged. "I have no idea. There are so many unknowns in all this."

"Many people involved did know each other, Hal told me."

"Doesn't make them murderers, though, Andrew. There doesn't seem to be any motive."

We stood in silence for a while and watched.

"Ah…" At last, I heard Johannes exhale sadly.

"What, Johannes?"

"As far as I can tell, she was strangled. There are still visible contusions on the neck. And the shield bone is broken. No other wounds on the body which might have killed her."

I smiled. "Good ol' Hal. He said that was what he thought."

"Well, I believe he was right. It's very hard to tell with such a decomposed body. A woman about thirteen or fourteen perhaps, small, scrawny, not well developed. See how her breasts aren't all that proud and her body hair sparse?"

We peered in the gloom.

"More a girl than a woman, then?"

We drew back, and Andrew crossed himself.

At that moment, Hal came back in the door.

"Nope. No Pinter. He's away somewhere. In town, they think, but they aren't sure."

"Did you leave a message?"

"Aye, I did."

"Then it will have to wait."

"I saw that Burridge fella in the street. He's looking for you."

"For me? What does he want?"

"I dunno."

"Where is he now?"

Hal shrugged. "Last I saw, he was leaving the pinter's house. I told him you were here."

I nodded.

I drew Johannes away and spoke quietly. "Our missing girl, this Mabel, the friend of Cedric's dead love Alysoun; we think she's been missing for about three weeks. Might this be a three-week-old corpse, Johannes?"

He looked back towards the body. "If she has been in the water the whole time, perhaps not. If she was eased in after a while, maybe. It's really hard to say with watery deaths."

"A not very well-developed girl, strangled. Did young Alysoun see what happened…? No, she would have come straight to the authorities. Did she suspect someone, and if so, how might she have known it was them?"

Johannes shrugged. "Because she'd been seen in their company perhaps?"

"By Alysoun?"

"Was it the pinter, perhaps?"

"I have had him sent for to see if I can get him to identify the body. I'll watch him carefully when he first sees her. Any guilt might show on his face, though sangfroid is his other name, I think."

Johannes shook his head. "Good luck with that. I can't see him giving himself away."

"Anyone else? She hadn't been in the town long. Not much of a chance to form many acquaintances with too many people. She was a relatively new friend of Alysoun."

"People come and go all the time to the pinter's house. She worked there as a maidservant. Perhaps she knew someone from there?"

"I shall ask," I said.

Andrew touched me on the shoulder. "Aumary...the pinter." He nodded his head towards the door hole.

I went out into the light of the bailey.

Pinter was standing in front of my office door, and Bunce, one of the gate guards, was standing chatting with him.

They both stepped back to let a cart loaded high with sacks trundle through the gate, pass the gate house door and turn into the space by the kitchen.

The town pinter saw me and waved an arm. "My Lord Belvoir, I am here at your request. What is it you wish of me?"

Bunce looked left and right and waddled over the space by the gate. He gestured towards me, and then Pinter followed him.

"M'lord?"

"Here, Pinter. Thank you for coming. I have someone for you to look at," and I beckoned him closer.

"Jesus Christ in Heaven!" said Joscelin Pinter when he faced the decaying corpse. He put his hand across his mouth. His body was stiff; his face was white, and his eyes were huge in that white face. He took an involuntary step backwards. Andrew held up a candle, for there was little light in that place.

"Tell me, Pinter, might this be your missing servant?"

His eyes slowly rose from the abomination upon which he stared in horrid fascination.

"I don't know. The body is so..."

"Please, take another look."

After a while, he said, "Aye...It has her look. The hair is the same colour. She was small...had a small frame."

He swallowed and looked again. "Her face was dainty and oval-shaped. She was quite a pretty thing. Who could do such a wicked thing?"

"What's that?"

"Kill her so? Drown her?"

"Drown? You believe she was killed? Drowned? What makes you think it was murder?"

"Well, she has been in water for certain, and I'm sure you would not be interested, sir, if she had merely fallen in."

"She was in the moat, weighted down by stones."

"Christ!"

"But she was, we think, strangled first."

The town pinter looked up quickly. "Aye, it would be easy. She was small and had little strength - like a child. It might be easy to...to..."

"Put yer 'ands around 'er throat and squeeze?" asked Hal.

"Aye, strangle her."

"Thank you, Pinter. We suspected this was Mabel, your housemaid. Do you know if she was seen with anyone in particular about the town?"

The man chewed the side of his mouth. "A man, you mean?"

"We know she was friendly with the girl killed in the grain barn."

Pinter shook his head. "I cannot recall."

"Think on it. Anything you may remember, let Sir Andrew Merriman here know."

"Yes, sir. Of course, I didn't know the other girl at all. I told you that."

"Alysoun? So you say."

I guided him to the door with my hand on his back.

"Anything I can do to help, sir. You only have to ask."

I saw Pearson shifting on his spear just outside the gate. Bunce was standing in front of my office door again. I noticed Castleman leaning on the wall, looking up at the masons repairing the western parapet. Two more guards were at the beginning of the drawbridge. It was a quiet afternoon.

I walked to the dark space under the gate tower when I heard Pinter take in a breath to speak, "Of course… No. No. It's not of any import. It can't be…" The echo in the tunnel was disturbing.

"What's that?"

"Nothing, m'lord."

I turned away and began to walk back to the small building by the stable where I had left Johannes, Andrew and Hal. I had gone about twenty paces when the pinter called me back.

"Sir, m'lord Belvoir?"

"Hmm?"

He had not moved and was standing in the darkness of the gatehouse tunnel. I could not see him well, but I thought he looked shocked and worried.

"Pinter?"

"I cannot say with any certainty, sir, but…"

I started back towards him slowly. "Yes?"

"There was one who…spent time with the girl…"

"There was?"

"I thought that they were perhaps related…you know… I used to see them together now and again when she left work…being friendly, in a way…"

"Who?"

I was now a few feet from the blackness of the tunnel. Pinter was simply a dark shape against the brightness of the day beyond and the tumult of the busy road across the drawbridge.

"It cannot be anything, for he's a well-respected man, and…" he was shaking his head.

Suddenly, there were two deep 'thwacks'. It was a heavy sound like someone had released a large arbalest. I must have looked puzzled, for Bunce straightened up and stared at me with confusion on his rubicund face. I looked around. Then came a thrumming twang.

There was a clanking sound as feet of chain dislodged itself. I realised at once what was happening and foolishly, and with no thought for my own safety, threw myself at the pinter.

He staggered, unaware of the danger and righted himself, pushing me away in one movement, which caused me to stumble and fall to my knees some feet away.

"What are you…?" he cried.

All at once, in realisation, he looked up as tons of heavy iron-tipped oak came crashing down upon him, knocking him to the ground. The castle portcullis had been released.

Pinter made an almighty scream, then a bubbling series of high-pitched moans.

I picked myself up and staggered the few feet to the man on the floor. He was writhing and crying, gasping for breath.

Bunce ran up behind me, cursing. I went down on my knees.

"Raise the bloody thing somehow. Quick!" I yelled as Castleman also ran into the dark gatehouse tunnel. He immediately turned around and disappeared through the guardroom tower door. Bunce followed.

"Yessir."

I cradled the prone man's head. Blood trickled from his mouth. He gurgled.

"Doctor!" I yelled frantically.

Pearson ran through the door to the tower stair after Castleman. I looked up at the meurtrière which punctuated the stonework of the gateway above my head and saw Castleman's face peering down at me.

"Mechanism's gone, sir. Take some time to raise it." Then his face disappeared.

"Castleman! Who's up there?"

"No one, sir," came his muted voice. "Just me. And Pearson, now."

Johannes was running around the corner.

Joscelin Pinter grabbed my sleeve, "I…"

"Gently, "I said, more for want of something to say than anything else.

"I…man," gurgled Pinter, and then his head flopped to one side.

I left him to Johannes and took the stairs to the portcullis room at a lope.

I heard a sudden banging but ignored it even though I discerned Hal's voice yelling amongst others.

Castleman and Pearson were trying to lift the heavy portcullis to no avail.

"Leave it, lads. It will need more than your strength. He is past all saving now."

Castleman sighed. "How, sir? How did anyone get in here unseen?"

"We were all distracted somehow. No one expected…" I rubbed my forehead. "We don't man this room in times of peace…"

"But we can get up here quickly if we need to, m'lord," said Castleman, "in two blinks of an eye, we can be here.

And we partly lower the portcullis every evening."

"You passed no one on the stair, Ed?"

I heard the banging and yelling again.

"No, sir."

Looking down through the meurtrière, I saw Johannes was looking up at me, and he shook his head sadly.

I went back down the stairs with Hal's voice yelling, "Wait a while! We'll get the door open!"

"What, Hal?"

"Someone is locked in the guardroom."

"The key is missing?"

"Yes, m'lord."

"It was open a moment ago."

"Aye, sir…it was."

"Then force the door."

"Have you ever tried to force…?" Hal saw my face and sighed. "Oh, all right then," and he turned to Bunce, who had been trying to batter his way through the door with his body. "Get a sturdy log and a couple of big men, ol' Bunce. We shall knock it down."

The banging and muted yelling began again on the inside of the guardroom door.

"All right…all right," said Hal testily. "We're goin' as fast as we can."

"Who is it, Hal?"

"Dunno, sir."

"Find out."

Andrew came up behind me. "Dead then?"

"As a futted flame, Sir Andrew," answered Hal.

"Skewered through the middle like a lump o' bread over the fire," said Bunce, who was marshalling two men who held a large post from the building works into position close by.

"Bunce!"

"Sorry, sir."

Johannes came up to the door. His cotte was blood-splattered.

"No chance, Aumary. Pierced lungs, pierced liver...well, pierced everything ..."

I nodded. "Get some strong men up to that bloody wheelroom and raise that portcullis."

"Aye, sir," said Pearson.

"And, Pearson,"

"Yessir?"

"Did you pass anyone on the stairs? Like Castleman, you were quick up there."

"No, sir. No one."

"Right. No one at all?"

"Nosir!" He grimaced. "Sir...I did notice..."

"Yes?"

"The rope which held the chain was sliced through - clean through."

"I noticed that too, Pearson."

"A sharp sword, sir. No sawing, two blows perhaps and whack!"

"We would normally use the chain mechanism if we wished to lower it?"

"We do that every night, sir. Half lower it."

"So, a man with a sharp sword might be able to sever the rope?"

"Maybe, sir."

"Thank you, Pearson. Can you make a search for a discarded weapon in the machinery room? I have a feeling it will no longer be with the person who did this."

"Yessir."

"As I said, get more men and raise the portcullis however you can. And thank you for your quick thinking, you and Ed."

He smiled shyly and was gone.

Two more soldiers now appeared and, taking hold of the large ramming post, proceeded to run at the guard room door. Five knocks with the wood and the door shattered, but the lock held. A crowbar was needed to prise it open, and eventually, out fell a breathless and pink-faced Master John Burridge.

He was sweating profusely and shaking.

"Jesus Christ! I thought I'd be in there forever!"

"What are you doing there, Burridge?"

"I am come from my mistress, sir. She wants to…" he wiped a sleeve across his forehead.

As he moved, he caught sight of the body pinned by the sharp spikes of the portcullis.

"Holy…" He retched, " Holy…"

He turned away and took in some deep breaths.

After a short while, he turned back to me.

"That the pinter?"

"What do you want, Burridge?"

"God!" He crossed himself, "That might'a bin me."

"I said, what do you want?"

"I came in through the gate, and there was no one here save a guard at the edge of the drawbridge. He told me to find the man in the guardroom and to go and ask him to look for you."

"And then?"

"Then I poked my nose into the guardroom as instructed. There was no one there, as I could see. Next I knew, I was shoved in the back, and I tumbled in there," he gestured to the guardroom. "A…a…a…and the key was turned in the lock."

I closed my eyes to picture the scene. I looked back to the ravaged door. No key.

"And then?"

"I yelled and yelled, but there was so much noise that it seemed no one could hear me."

"I 'eard yer," said Hal, "but you was makin' such a noise yerself you couldn't 'ear what I was sayin' to you, yer loon!"

The man shook. "I don't like small spaces. Small spaces that I don't know. They…make me…uncomfortable."

Hal's eyes rose to Heaven.

"And small spaces made of stone are…really bad."

Hal put his head on one side in a feigned gesture of sympathy and in a girlish voice said, "Aw, you poor thing. All those tons of stone bearing down on yer. Enough t' make yer scream."

"Scream I did, Master Hal," said Burridge.

"Good job I 'eard yer, then."

"Did you see who pushed you, Burridge?"

"No, sir. I had my back to him."

"No one going up the stairs passed you?"

"No, sir. Well, someone musta' done, but I didn't see him."

"What does your mistress want with me, Burridge?"

I heard the portcullis groan as they attempted to lift it.

Burridge righted his short cotte and pulled his belt tighter, trying not to look at the body pinned to the ground.

"She said, sir, she has an idea who might have killed Master Harbrook. And she wants to speak to you."

"If her theory still involves the town pinter, Burridge… too late." I nodded to our corpse.

"Ah yes, sir…yes. But I don't know what she was going to tell you."

I sighed.

The portcullis groaned and clanked again.

"Tomorrow…Burridge. Tomorrow. Today…I am…busy. Go home and look after your mistress."

And I sighed again.

Hal looked at me under his grey brows.

"Another one gone then?"

"Another one, Hal. I told you we didn't need to lose another witness."

"Tsooo…we're gettin' careless, sir. Very. Careless."

The coroner came and went, and the body of the maid servant was released for burial. I argued with Sir Hugo of Ramsbury—it seemed it was something we were fated to do nowadays—about the deodand for the death of the town pinter.

Sir Hugo wanted the castle portcullis. There was not a chance I would release it to him. It was staying where it was.

"Do you understand the impracticality of what you ask, Sir Hugo?"

"The law says that the thing which causes the death shall be confiscated and sold to…"

"You cannot have the castle's portcullis, man. It stays where it is."

"It's…"

"It's tons of metal-spiked oak, sir. How long do you think it would take to extricate it? If we wanted to do it at all."

"I am sure…"

"No! It is part of the castle and in the castle it stays." It was almost laughable. The man was an idiot.

Eventually, he saw that it was not a sensible thing to try to remove, and huffed and puffed his way back to his horse.

He had been told by the witnesses that the portcullis had been tampered with, but still he wished to blame me, as under constable of the castle, for, as he put it, 'sailing a holed ship'.

By that, I supposed he meant that the castle was poorly managed and the guardroom poorly equipped. He didn't seem to understand that a perfectly good rope securing the chain to the windlass had been sliced in two and had not frayed. Or he didn't want to comprehend. Nevertheless, the jury for the pinter brought in a verdict of murder, and the coroner had to grudgingly accept it. A verdict of unlawful killing was also obtained for our poor maid in the moat.

Bunce came to me in my office a short while later. I had sent him out to look for the weapon which had cut the rope holding the portcullis taut; Pearson had not found it in the portcullis tower.

"Sir…seems you were right."

"Bunce?"

The man dashed outside to the steps and came back holding a sword.

"Found on the bank of the moat."

"Ah…" I took the weapon from his hand.

"Someone cut the rope holding the chain to the portcullis, let go the stop, and wallop."

"It was well timed, Bunce."

"Someone must have been watchin' the pinter, sir. Through the murder 'oles."

"Does anyone know who the sword belongs to?"

Bunce fingered his ear. "Er, no, sir. I don't recognise it."

Hal peered around the edge of the door. "Sir, might we release the body of the pinter?"

"Aye, Hal"

"Bunce…where was the sword found?"

"By the small loop to the east, by the tower, sir."

"Now all we need to know is how the man got up the stairs in full view of the soldiers at the gate."

"And back down again," said Bunce.

"Let us go up to the portcullis room and see if there is anything we might have missed," I said.

Sure enough, shoved down the side of the two large wooden crates that held the rocks that would be used to rain down on anyone attacking the castle, we found a scabbard.

"Planned then, sir?"

"Oh no, not planned in the way we might think. That someone knew that the pinter would be here and had come here to kill him: no. Whoever did this used this God-given opportunity to deal out his death. They think on their feet, Hal. They followed him, waited to see what he'd say and then picked their moment."

"Devilish." Hal craned his neck to look at the sword. "So, 'oo's is it, sir?"

"If I am not mistaken, it belongs to Mansur Grover. It's one I have seen at his hip a few times."

"But 'e wasn't 'ere. Surely we'd 'ave seen 'im."

As I'd thought, it was the one I had seen secured to Mansur Grover's belt when I had last seen him.

"So, do we arrest him now, m'lord?"

"No. That is what our murderer wants us to do, Hal."

"It is?"

"It is."

Hal coughed… "Er…right."

He sniffed. "Oh yes, and sir…there's this."

He held out his hand.

I took a large iron key from him.

"The key to the guardroom?"

"Yessir. It was found outside on the bit of ground by the wall when I was scouting around for the sword."

That, too, had gone through the window. I looked down at the huge key. I pictured the scene:

The pinter below the portcullis. The murderer above

in the machinery room. The key was in his hand. In my mind, the man was slicing the rope. Wallop, as Bunce had so vividly put it. The sword was dropped from the window, and the scabbard dropped into concealment...but not too cleverly concealed. It needed to be found. Down the stairs comes the felon. He pushes the hapless Burridge into the guardroom, locks the door and... ah no.

"Hal. Where exactly was the key found? Was it anywhere near the sword?"

"Well...erm...no, not exactly." Hal stroked the twin peaks of his long, grey beard. "It was a bit away. Under the small loop in the guardroom."

"Was it indeed? Under the window? A matter of a few feet away?"

"I 'spect it travelled a bit."

"Hmmm. If the two had been dropped together, Hal, would you not expect to find them close together?"

"I see what you mean, m'lord."

"The guardroom window is a ten-feet distance from the tower, and what's more, the window is a whole stairturn lower."

"Yes, sir. It is." He looked at me in puzzlement. "And that means..."

""It was thrown from the guardroom window and not the portcullis chamber."

"But it couldn'a bin!"

"No. Not if the door was locked from the outside."

"No, sir. That's impossible."

Chapter Ten

"WHAT did the pinter say to you, Aumary?" asked Johannes a little while later when we were sitting in my office on the eastern wall of the castle.

"He seemed to intimate that the person who was seen with this friend of Alysoun, the girl Mabel, was the iron master, Mansur Grover. He said what sounded like 'iron man'."

"He said, 'Grover'?"

"He actually said, 'I…man.'"

"Hmmm. Is that likely?"

"Grover tells me that he rarely comes to Marlborough, and the murdered girl would not have gone to Ramsbury," I said. "How would they meet?" I turned the guardroom key over and over in my hand. "I suppose there's just a chance they might have met at Burbage, where the girl comes from, but then, how did Pinter then see them? He had no business there, as far as I know. "

"It must have been someone in the town."

"Or Pinter did not say what I thought he said at the moment of his death. Besides, Grover is so very recognisable with his height and colour. Hard to miss."

"And yet a man's final words are considered the utter truth, Aumary."

"Yes. I know."

"Nemo moriturus praesumitur mentire..." said Johannes seriously.

"No person at the point of death should be presumed to be lying."

We sat in silence for a moment.

"Tell me again what Pinter told you."

I put down the key and leant back in my chair, my hands behind my head. I stretched. "He called me back and said that he had seen the girl Mabel with a well respected man and thought that they might have been related because of the way they behaved with each other. He didn't imply that there was anything sinister or improper in it. But the words 'well respected' uttered about Grover by Pinter grates a little, I think."

"Hmm. By all accounts, 'e didn't like him much, did he? And someone thought he was about to upset the apple barrel, for that someone..." said Hal.

"Who must have been lying in wait..."

"Then took the opportunity to cut the rope and kill Pinter before he could tell you too much. Ergo...there most certainly was something sinister in it."

"I'll get Hal here to pay a visit to Master Caspar and ask if there were any other men in Mabel's family. Men still living, that is."

Johannes stood. "And I will ask around. See what's known about this poor girl, Mabel, if anything. Someone must know something."

I picked up the key and rose from behind my table.

"A murder that was no murder leads us to five murders which are most certainly connected."

"Cedric's girl, Alysoun, her grandma, Harbrook, this girl

Mabel, and now Pinter."

"Harbrook? Hal tells me you have an idea about him," said Johannes, staring down at his blood splattered clothes. "Ack! I must go home and change. It looks bad for a doctor to be so besmirched."

I smiled. "You tell me that either wound would have been fatal to Harbrook, but you cannot say which one was the first, the pig goring or the boar spear, and my witnesses are divided about what happened."

"It's ever so with folk. You will always get a hundred views of the same event. No two men ever tell the same tale."

"And yet they all saw the same thing. They saw Harbrook gored by a boar and pierced by a spear."

"They aren't lying; they just have different recollections."

I shook my head. "If I could find a reason why any of these people had to die, I might have a chance to find my murderer. As it is..."

"Aumary, are you absolutely convinced that Harbrook's death was murder?"

"You mean that it was purely accidental? The boar gored him, and someone accidentally threw the spear and, perhaps momentarily distracted by the horror of it, missed and struck Yves?"

"They'd be unlikely to own up."

"It wouldn't be murder."

"No...it wouldn't," said Johannes. "But they would still be wary of an admission."

I shook my head again. "I would think that if it weren't for the missing spear."

"Missing spear?"

"Let us think about what happened. Grover stuck the pig from horseback and the beast ran off. Then the men dismounted, thinking that the dogs would hold her. They didn't. Grover had wounded the pig on the shoulder. His spear was not found. It had become dislodged from the pig's body. Others were readying their spears. All eyes were on the pig. One moment of inattention and it could cost you your life."

"It did for Harbrook."

"Someone then stuck a spear into Yves Harbook. "

"No one saw that?"

I shook my head. "Because that was the spear which killed the boar."

Johannes sat back in his seat, "I don't follow you."

"The spear which killed the boar was Mansur Grover's original one. Little did he know that it had killed the boar because the beast did not fall immediately."

"So why was his spear not found embedded in the beast?"

"Because someone pulled it out and stuck it into Harbrook, knowing the beast was dying."

"And no one saw this? That's hard to believe."

"Think of the sequence of events. The boar is stuck by Grover. It runs off mortally wounded, and then, in a last valiant and angry attempt, it goes for Harbrook. He is pinned to the tree, and all the men come up. The murderer removes the spear - he's the first on the scene and has none of his own in his hand - and Harbrook is stuck with it. That is why there was no spear in the pig."

"It was used twice?"

"Correct."

"But no one," said Johannes, "remembers who took out the boar spear."

"Everyone, bar one man, had a spear of his own. We found a spear lodged up in a tree when we looked later. They were all so intent on the boar for that instant that they saw what they wanted to see...everyone trying to stick the pig. Only one was taking a spear OUT of the pig."

"They must have pushed it further in momentarily to kill it and then stabbed Yves Harbrook."

"Precisely"

"Who, Amaury?"

I sat down heavily on the edge of my table. "One of only very few men who were close but not too close."

"This man is a cool foe, my friend. He does not seem to mind taking the most extraordinary risks."

"No, he doesn't."

I closed my eyes and pictured that glade in Savernake once more.

"He thinks so very quickly on his feet: the boar hunt, the portcullis. He doesn't mind being seen in broad daylight doing what he's doing. He would have a perfectly good explanation, no doubt, were he questioned or distrusted."

"I can just about see how your man might manage to kill a pig and then get the spear into Harbrook, but how on earth does he disappear into thin air after killing Pinter?" asked Johannes.

I shook my head. "Again, Johannes, people tell you what they think they see."

"Even if what they see is impossible?"

"That too, old friend." I tapped him on the shoulder. "Come, the key needs to be returned to the guardroom door."

"Even if there is no longer a door to the room, for it to return to, Aumary?"

"I must get the carpenters onto it," I said irritably.

"Mistress Grover," I gritted my teeth. "Do you mean to tell me that I have ridden all the way from the town just to hear you say that you cannot...?"

We had ridden to Ramsbury early the next day, hard

on the heels of the news of the pinter's death at the Grover household.

"Excuse me, please, my Lord Belvoir, I cannot answer your questions. I am indisposed today. I... I...I am not well..."

"Madam, I don't care if you are at death's door...I..."

"My Lord Belvoir!" said her maid, Margaret Harbrook, "How can you? That is not a gentlemanly thing to say. You can see that my poor mistress is very upset. We both are," she added tremulously.

Richildis Grover wept openly into her hands.

"Mistress Grover, you seem to spend most of your time being upset lately." I sighed and sat down in front of her, "What is it this time?"

Margaret Harbrook tutted and fiddled, arranging her mistress's veil around her head and tucking in stray locks of hair.

"The news about the pinter, my lord. It has been such a shock to us both."

"For Heaven's sake, what was the man to you?"

I realised my voice had risen in volume. I moderated my tone. "I thought that you, Richildis, could not stand Joscelin Pinter?"

Richildis wept all the louder.

"Sir. It's the shock. First, her father, then my brother and now the pinter. I am sure Richildis is frightened that Master Mansur will be next."

I threw off my cloak and folded it over the back of a bench. "Some water for your mistress, Margaret, now, I think."

"Oh...yes, sir...right away." She scurried off into another room.

I whispered. "Quickly - while she is away...Richildis. These tears? Tell me and do not dissemble, are they for a man you loved? A man who perhaps rejected you?"

The young woman slowly lifted her tear-filled eyes to my face. "Please, sir, you won't tell. Please. I…it…was… hard to…I did love him…yes…" It wasn't easy to hear the words through the sobbing and snuffling. "Once upon a time, we were to be married. But he decided that I wasn't good enough, and so…"

"Ah…right. So your assertions that he was guilty of murder were to punish him in some way for your rejection?"

"I did not mean that he would…be… killed, sir."

"No, I am sure you didn't."

Hal fiddled with the points of his beard. He always did this when embarrassed, puzzled or upset. "The poor man wasn't a murderer, gel. He's become a victim himself."

Richildis sobbed into her hands again. "I know…o.o.ow."

Margaret returned with the water; Mistress Grover sipped, and her eyes pleaded with me to say no more about Pinter.

"Master John of Burridge came to me yesterday to tell me that you, madam, had a message for me. He told me that he was unaware of the content of this message but that you had some idea about the death of Master Harbrook. Might you find the strength, please, to tell me exactly what you meant us to know?"

Suddenly, Richildis Grover, in an in-breath, ceased to cry. "A…A message?"

"And, please…no more nonsense about Master Pinter being the murderer."

"No, no, sir." Richildis rose and walked to a chest where a small piece of cloth rested on the oak. She dabbed her nose and eyes with it.

Those dark eyes slid to Margaret and back again to me. "I know now that it was not him. He was completely innocent, and I am sorry I ever led you to believe in his guilt."

"Good. So now, I repeat. What did you want to see me about?"

Richildis pulled and smoothed down her cherry red gown. I saw that the tablet weaving, attached to the post in the corner of the room, begun when I first met the woman, was almost complete.

"But, sir, I never asked you to call on me. I have no further information."

"Mistress - if this is another of your sillinesses. I will..."

"No, sir."

"Master Burridge sought me out yesterday at the castle. I have to say I do not think he would ride the distance from Ramsbury to Marlborough just to pay his respects to me there. Why did you send him?"

"I repeat, I did not send him." Her face was genuinely puzzled. "Perhaps you misheard, and it was from my husband that Master Burridge was sent."

I reiterated, "Burridge said that you wanted to see me and that you had further information about the death of Master Harbrook."

Her face took on a steely glare. "I am not a liar, sir. No, I did not send him."

"Not a liar...?" said Hal under his breath. "No, and I'm a nun, I am. A nun as pure as the driven..."

"Hal."

"Sorry, sir."

"I warn you, Richildis, if this is one of your silly games, well, I will not forget. Your husband will be informed that you have been wasting my time."

"No, sir. Please, I beg you, do not tell...but you must believe me, I didn't send him."

There was a small silence as I considered this.

"Very well." I turned to the maid. "Margaret, send one of your servants to the yard and ask Master Burridge to come here now, please."

Margaret tutted her displeasure and trotted out of the door.

"The Pinter…let's at least have the truth on that before she returns."

"It's as I told you, sir. He and I were to be married. I liked him. I liked him a lot and I thought he liked me. But then one day, he came to my father and said that he no longer wanted to marry me."

"You have no idea why?"

"No, sir. I thought, perhaps, he'd found another with a larger dowry."

'Yes…that's probably it,' I said to myself.

"Was your father angry?"

"No, not really, sir…Well, yes. Well, no, not angry, but he seemed… disappointed. He just said that there would be other folk who would want to marry me and that was that."

"And to punish your father for not pushing it further, for giving up so easily on a man to whom you were attracted, and to make it seem as if you had rejected the town pinter, and not the other way round, you married the iron master? To save face?"

"Yes, sir. I thought it was a good idea because he has much more money than the pinter and…and…was older and so…might…"

"Might…what?"

"Die one day soon?" asked Hal, his mouth open in disbelief.

She threw her hands to her face again and gabbled, "Oh, that was wicked, wasn't it? Wicked even to think of it. Wicked! But he is old, sir, oh so old."

Hal smirked. "Pinter was right, wa'n't he, m'lord?"

"Indeed, he was Hal. As was Johannes."

Richildis looked blankly at us, “And I thought when Mansur was gone…gone to God…”

“You weren’t thinkin’ o’ helpin’ ‘im along a little, were you, lass?” asked Hal in a shocked voice.

“Certainly not.” She dabbed her nose, “But, I thought the pinter would marry me when I was a wealthy widow.”

Hal and I exchanged glances.

“Why I ain’t never bin married, see, sir.” His eyes rose to Heaven.

“But then I heard the wretched man was going to marry the arrow maker’s daughter. It was all arranged.”

“Aye, he dropped you and picked up with this other girl as soon as blink,” said Hal.

“I was so angry…I…”

“Tried to make out that he was the murderer of your father and…”

“I know that was wrong. I know it.”

“You’re too right it was,” said Hal in a disgusted tone, “quite apart from leading the constable astray, you…”

“I am so sorry, sir.” She folded her hands in front of her and looked down.

“Nothing to be done now. We know how your father died and I am sure your brother will tell you when you see him next.”

“Ralph knows, sir?” She put her head on one side like a little bird.

“He does.”

“Oh.”

“But there is the matter of Master Harbrook’s death.”

“Poor Yves.”

“I am going to ask you a question, Richildis, and I want a truthful answer. Was there ever anything between you and Master Harbrook?”

“No, sir. I have never…” Richildis looked defiant.

"Not even before the pinter and Master Grover?"

"No, sir. Never."

"And have you heard any gossip about Master Harbrook and any other women of the locality?"

Richildis Grover sat down abruptly on her chair. "Yves was a charming man. Kind and gentle. Many women thought him so, I am sure, but apart from the usual silly gossip you hear in a town like this, I heard nothing about any particular woman or women, sir. Ask his wife. Ask Mistress Rousalie. She will tell you that they had eyes only for each other. Yves would never be false to her."

So now, I had two very conflicting views about the man.

Richildis' face turned away. "But I have heard…"

"Yes?"

"And I am sure it is just unkind tittle-tattle, because he was so gentle and sweet, that he was very much admired by a…a person…in Ramsbury…"

"A person?" said Hal. "Aw, c'mon. First, you say that he wasn't playing around with anyone's wife, and then you say…."

"No, Hal, I think Mistress Grover means something entirely different. Don't you, Richildis?"

"What…the girls…?"

"No, Hal, not girls at all."

Hal fell silent, and I watched as Richildis bit her lip and drew up her nose to look at me.

"He was a lovely man, and I'll not say anything… against him."

"But he did not have relationships with women?"

"I don't know. It's only what I have heard. It's gossip. He does have a lovely wife to whom he was devoted, so it cannot be true, can it? I told you, he was the kindest, sweetest man and I will not believe him such a…sinner, sir. Never!"

"Beezulbubs boobies!" said Hal looking away. "What a squirmy pile o' eels."

"From whom have you heard this?"

"Oh…I cannot remember."

At that moment, there was a scratch at the door, and Master Burridge's head came round the edge.

"You want to see me, sir?"

"Ah, Burridge, come in and shut the door."

The man squeezed through the gap. Richildis stood and faced him.

"What is all this nonsense about you…"

I interrupted. "Thank you, Richildis, I will ask the questions."

The girl pouted and looked down again. Margaret came into the room once more and laid out a tray of ale for us.

"Burridge, yesterday when I saw you at the castle…"

"Yessir."

"You told me that your mistress had sent you to Marlborough to give me a message. That I was to come and visit her here, for she wanted to speak to me."

"Yessir." He smiled broadly, "And here you are. Devil of a long way and me not a good rider. But she would have me go there and no one else…"

"I most certainly did not…"

"Me, who was her husband's right-hand man, she said."

"I did not say anything of the kind!"

"And coming on that awful scene with the pinter…aw…I wished myself anywhere other than there, sir."

"I did not send you, John, and you know I didn't!" piped up Richildis at full volume.

John Burridge's face sucked into itself. "Not send me?" He grimaced. "But…but…but…you asked me…"

"I most certainly did not."

Richildis turned to Margaret. "Did I ask you yesterday to

go to him at the yard and bring him back to me, Margaret?"

"No, madam."

"No, it wasn't that ol' harrid...it was Richard, I think, or was it Niccolo...? You know how hard it is to tell the brothers apart. Anyway, I got a message - come to the house and you would speak to me. I came, and you said..."

"I didn't speak to you yesterday, Burridge," squeaked Richildis."Or Richard or Niccolo."

"I beg to differ, madam. You asked me to go and find the constable because you had something really important to tell him about the Durnfords' man." Burridge was going pink in the face. "You did...yesterday. And out I went on Goldspur...and..."

"You, sir, are a liar!"

"Margaret, did you see Master Burridge?" I asked.

"No, sir...I was out supervising the..."

"But if you are saying you didn't say it, why did you send me to Marlborough."

"I didn't."

I interrupted their quarrel. "The young man you sent to fetch Burridge, this Niccolo or Richard, can we find them, mistress?"

Burridge sniffed. "Not today. They have gone to Seend with Master Mansur and won't be back till tomorrow."

"Then, when they are back, and you recall which one of them delivered your mistress's summons, send him to me."

"Aye, sir, I will," said Burridge in annoyance. "All that way for nothing," he continued under his breath.

Richildis screwed up her hands and stamped her foot. "He is lying. I didn't send anyone to Marlborough. I didn't call for Niccolo or Richard."

"Now, now, mistress. You haven't been yourself of late, we know that. Maybe you just forgot and can't remember what it is you said," said Burridge.

"I am not a liar, and I am not an imbecile that I forget things!" shouted Richildis bitterly.

"No… but…you have been…"

"Not a liar, pah!" said Hal in a whisper.

Margaret took Richildis' shoulders in her two hands. "Now, now, we can sort this out tomorrow when the lads return."

Richildis gave Burridge a deadly stare.

"He - is - lying," and she began to cry again.

"Why would I…what earthly reason would I have? I didn't want to ride all that way to Marlborough. I hate riding."

"Well, whatever happened, whatever misunderstanding we have had, there is no more to be said if there's no news. We shall take our leave."

Burridge smiled apologetically, "Goodbye, m'lord. I am so sorry about this."

He picked up an ale cup from the tray Margaret had brought in and downed it in one.

We left without ale.

Chapter Eleven

AS WE REACHED THE PATH, Hal said, scratching his beard, "What's goin' on in there with Mistress Richildis and that man Burridge, then?"

"A great deal of being economical with the truth, Hal."

"She lyin', or is he?"

"We need to know why either of them would lie about…?" I stopped. A thought occurred to me. "We need to go back to the beginning and look at this again, Hal."

"What? From the first murder? The falconer?"

"Ah, no, the first murder wasn't the first murder," I said enigmatically.

Hal snatched off his coif, "What? Aw c'mon!"

"The first murder was the killing of the young maid, Mabel, Alysoun's friend. She had been in the moat for at least three weeks. Everything else stems from this one death."

"You think, then, that Alysoun's death was because of Mabel's death?"

"I think so, yes. But then, the murderer started to get too clever and thought that he'd frame someone else for his ill-considered deed."

"But this Mabel girl wasn't meant to be found, ever, was she?"

"No, she was meant to stay weighted down at the bottom of the moat forever."

"But she didn't."

"No, she got dredged up by Perkin Fisher."

We retrieved our horses from the stable and walked them through the churchyard.

"I have a feeling that the murderer heard that a body had been found…somehow and wanted to see for himself if we'd found the girl he'd killed."

"And if it were anyone else, then he wouldn't be worried?" asked Hal.

"Nothing could connect him to a different corpse. Seeing the pinter come into the castle, well, he panicked. If the pinter could identify the girl, that would put our killer in danger."

"It would, Hal, it would. And so Joscelin Pinter had to die."

Before we reached Ramsbury the next day, we made a slight detour to Durley.

I hailed my young red-headed groom across the courtyard.

"Cedric!" He came running. "I have a task for you, should you wish to help me."

Cedric released my horse's bridle and ducked under his chin.

"Yessir. You know that I'll do anything to help you."

"I need you to come to Bedwyn and Ramsbury with me."

"Bedwyn, sir? Are there no grooms at Bedwyn who can help you?"

"I don't need you as a groom, Cedric. I need you to help

me in this investigation."

"But Master Hal always..."

"He does. And he will be there too. But I need your help, for I believe our murderer knows ol' Hal and does not know you, and I am in need of someone to, shall we say, lure our killer out into the open."

"Oh, sir. The killer of my Alysoun?"

"Yes, Cedric."

"Then, sir, I will do anything you need me to do."

I lay awake that night pondering, hypothesising and piecing together the things people had said.

It was a warm night, and I lay with the windows open to the air, listening to the owls hooting in the forest. The terrible death of the pinter went round and round in my head. He had been so close to telling me who had been seen with the young girl Mabel. I was convinced that this man was our murderer and that the subsequent deaths were covering for his mistake in pursuing Mabel.

A girl, young, naive and alone, meets a man at the pinter's house, a visitor who pays her attention and compliments, perhaps. He walks out with her now and again, ensuring they are not too easily or too often overlooked. Perhaps she expected more than the man was willing to give, a young girl not far out of childhood, impressionable and fanciful. Perhaps she found herself falling for him, her young and inexperienced mind inventing scenes: the man proposing to her perhaps, telling her how much he loves her and that, if she consented, he would take her away from her humdrum existence as a house maid and make her a worthy wife with a good home and a husband who has standing in the community.

Poor girl. She falls for his blandishments—if she will

just give him one kiss; if she will consent to lie with him; if she will do as he asks... and then. Then what?

I watched as a shaft of moonlight eerily pierced the window and landed smack on the chest in which I kept Master Quimper's books.

With that moonlight, an idea lit up in my head. I could see how things might have been. Mabel had decided to go to her man. She would try to get a cart going out of the town to take her where she needed to go, and she would turn up - out of the blue - to surprise her lover and take up his offer. She would be his wife.

Only the man had not promised marriage. Oh no. That was not in his plan. He would dally with the girl, get her to do as he wished, then he'd dump her, for he'd have no need of her after that. In fact, he might have been planning a marriage of a far better kind.

Before she can put her plan into action, her lover finds her.

"Well...then you can take me back with you," I hear her say. "I will ride pillion on your fine horse."

The man stalls. "Let us walk," he says, "Let's think and talk about this. I don't want to jump into anything just yet."

She might have said something like, "But you have had my maidenhead...you say you love me, we could be married. What is the need for thinking?"

"Ah, no, marriage can never happen."

Now, the girl is panicking. Has she been led astray, told a pack of lies? Walking by the river, perhaps, the man tries to get poor Mabel to lie with him one more time...sweet words and soft caresses and when she struggles and says, "Ah, no, not if I cannot be your wife," his strong hands, so used to lovingly touching her soft skin, wrap easily around her throat and they tighten and push and squeeze. Mabel thrashes and resists and eventually suffocates, there by the banks of the Kennet and close by the castle's moat. The killer removes her clothes and throws them into the river, weighted with a boulder, perhaps. Then he takes her slight body and eases that too into the far side of the moat where few folk pass or will see. She, too, is weighted with stones. Only when her flesh begins to rot will she be free of her bonds and see the light of day again.

But one person does know that he has been courting Mabel: Alysoun. She knows this for sure because Mabel has proudly told her. She then tells her grandmother. When Alysoun realises Mabel is missing, they agree that they must tell the authorities what they know. Poor Alysoun also knows what Mabel discovered—probably overheard when the men met to plan their hunt at the pinter's home—that many of the men in the forest were going for the boar illegally. She knows this is something that Cedric might tell me, and I, Aumary Belvoir, warden of Savernake, can catch them. Alysoun dies and takes the knowledge to her grave. The boar hunt takes place, and Harbrook is murdered.

'Now let me see,' I said to myself, 'who benefits from this intricate plan? Who might gain from this situation? Gain money, prestige and perhaps in the end the woman he has coveted for a while?'

I closed my eyes. But why? Why did the killer hate Grover so?

My wife Lydia stirred in her sleep and flung out a hand that landed on me. I gently tucked it back under the sheet. How lucky I was in my spouse, I thought. She had been the wife of another before me. I had had another wife before Lydia. Only I had had a child, and Lydia had taken to Hawise from the first, as a mallard duck sometimes takes to other orphaned ducklings. Lydia had had no children with her first husband. How lucky we were that there was no jealousy or difficulty with Simon and Phillip, our natural children, and Hawise, Lydia's stepchild. With that thought, I realised that I was very close to the heart of the problem surrounding the man Grover and the death of Harbrook. I locked that thought away in my head.

A little owl sitting on the roof of the kitchen building close by started his midnight barking and he was immediately answered by another not too far off. The sounds were similar, but I could tell one was the male and the other the female. Ah, our usual pair had nested that summer, I thought, in the hole in the wall to the rear of the manor. They had been there perhaps three years. Maybe this was not our original pair. The male might have found himself a new wife or she a new husband. However, I'd heard that they sometimes paired until the bond was broken by the death of one.

I began to muse upon the fidelity of some animals and the fickleness of the human race. Yes, I now thought I knew what motivated our murderer. I had met this situation before.

And then there was the death of my falconer Hawkes.

Now, that one was unusual and upon reflection, I felt it did not have any connection to our other murders in the forest. I nodded mentally to myself. Yes, I think I had that one solved.

We need to be near to the heart of the problem. I needed to take myself off to be closer to the people involved. I needed to go back to Bedwyn.

With that thought, I fell asleep until dawn.

The next evening, on the dais in Bedwyn Manor, I watched my daughter playing cat's cradle with Hal after supper.

I had asked for Ralph Hawkes, the falconer, to attend

me and he came to the door and bowed, “My Lord, you sent for me?”

“Come in, Ralph. Yes, I’d like to talk to you.”

Ralph came slowly up the hall. Today, he wore a green woollen capuchon hood over his usual light-coloured Belvoir gambeson with the blazon of three red flowers surrounded by oak leaves. His hose was dark green, and his ankle boots were his usual old black pair.

He stood before me, bowed once more and parted his feet, his arms hanging stiffly by his side.

“Ralph, we really haven’t had a chance to speak at length since your father’s death. I am sorry about that.”

“Yessir.”

“I hear that you were out at the boar hunt the other day with Master du May?”

“Yessir. I wanted to go. I’m sorry. I know I shouldn’t have been there, that it was forbidden, but I only went to observe.”

“Hmm. Observe? You should have informed me, Ralph, that a breach of the law was about to take place. You are a forest man employed by me.”

“Yessir.” He hung his head.

“I heard that you wanted to take a look at Masters Grover and Harbrook.” I stepped down from the dais. “Why was that?”

“I have seen them before, sir, it’s true, but…I just wanted to take another closer look.”

“Why, Ralph…why these men in particular?”

The man shifted his stance but looked me straight in the eye. “One of them is my brother-in-law, sir, my sister’s husband, and the other was an old friend of my father’s… why should I not?”

I walked around him. I could see he was becoming uncomfortable.

"Did you speak to either of them, Ralph?"

"No, m'lord."

"One of them is now dead."

"Yessir. I didn't see what happened. I was too far off."

"Master du May tells me you were with him by the horses."

"Yessir. That's so. We two were the only Bedwyn Manor men there, sir."

I stood before him again. "You were with my steward all the time?"

"Most of the time, m'lord. I ran with the horses to help the grooms. Master Burridge paid us all to help him."

"Appear at the court, and you will be judged by your peers."

"But Henry, sir…"

"Aye, Henry is as guilty as you and will not preside. I will conduct the court, Ralph."

"Yessir."

I changed the subject and sat back in my chair. "Is everything alright, Ralph? How are you managing all alone in your little cott by the church?"

"I have everything I need, m'lord. My neighbours have been so very helpful."

"Good. You are not too lonely now your father has gone to God?"

Ralph looked away. "I manage m'lord."

"I hear that you are courting. Am I right?"

Ralph Hawkes flipped his head round suddenly to look at me, "How…?"

I chuckled. "Hard to keep village gossip quiet, Ralph."

"I walk out with Elias of Shawgrove's daughter, sir, Osanna. I suppose Master Steward told you?"

"Ah yes, Elias, the man who died a little while ago." I leant forward and lowered my voice. "Do you feel a little happier now that your father and the father of your beloved lie in earth which the priest has blessed, Ralph?"

Ralph ground his teeth. "Much better, thank you. I thought that might be your doing, my Lord Belvoir. The land at the back of…" He caught my eye and tailed off.

I lowered my voice even further. "The strange fruit upon the tree in the churchyard. I thought it might be your handiwork, Ralph."

The man shuffled his feet together, his confident stance now totally gone. He did not deny or affirm it, however.

"We'll say no more about that incident, shall we? Nor the fact you were present at an illegal hunting party, if…"

"Yessir?"

"If you answer me truthfully."

He looked wary, and his eyes rose to look under his lashes.

"What about, my lord?"

Hal was watching us very carefully from his perch by the door. He'd looked up from his playing, though he could hear very little. He knew something important was happening.

Hawise, giggling loudly into the ensuing silence, made Ralph turn abruptly to see what she had laughed at. The moment was gone.

"The truth."

"The truth, sir?"

"About your father."

"I do not know the truth as you call it, sir," answered my falconer with a steady stare.

I flipped up my hand. "Think on it, Ralph."

"On what, sir?"

"On how your father died."

"He was murdered, sir," he said, "Probably by one of those two men…"

"Grover or Harbrook?"

Hawkes just continued to stare at me.

"No, Master Hawkes…I do not think your father was killed by either of those men."

I saw the brown stare falter and the eyes widen.

"As you wish, sir," he nodded quickly. "Can I go now, sir?"

"For the moment, Ralph, I am finished with you."

The man bowed and was about to turn on his heel to march off down the hall.

"I have a wish to take out one of the birds tomorrow morning, Ralph." I said, forestalling his exit.

He turned back. "Yes, m'lord."

"Which bird do you suggest?"

"Your preferred bird, Gilda, is a little out of sorts, sir."

"Is she? Why's that?"

"She'll come round. She hasn't been quite herself since… since my father died, sir."

"Oh, why do you think that is, Ralph?"

"She was particularly used to him, sir."

"And he, fond of her, I think," I said. "Well then, we shall take Brownun out tomorrow., shall we?"

"As you wish, sir," he nodded quickly. "When would you like the bird to be ready, sir, tomorrow?"

I smiled. "Let us say, depending on the day, Ralph, as soon as the sun is high enough for warmth, eh?"

"A little after dawn then, sir?" The man bowed, swivelled on his heels and marched off out of the hall door.

Hal came up, chuckling, "Well, well. What's the matter with 'im? He's as stiff as a spear."

"There is something bothering him, Hal, and I have given him the opportunity to speak out, but… he won't just yet. Give it time, I think."

"Aw no…he's not one of yer ol' boilin' fowl, is he?"

I wandered over to my children, Simon, Philip and Hawise. "No, Hal, he's more of a...." I fingered my close-cropped, bearded chin, "pig at the autumn killing. He's unsure if he's to be next for the knife or if he'll be reprieved and saved for next year to be put in with the sow of his choice."

"Eh?"

I laughed. "Never mind ol' Hal. All will become clear soon enough, I think." Then I gave myself over to the playing of cat's cradle with Hawise.

The morning dawned misty and chilly, though the later day would be unseasonably warm again. I donned my woollen gambeson with its blazon of three small red flowers surrounded by oak leaves - the Belvoir arms. Over this, I wore a cotte of pale blue, split for ease of riding.

Hal and I wandered down to the mews. I had asked Cedric to come out with us, and he was already there, marching up and down outside the door and slapping his arms about his body. He, too, wore his Belvoir livery.

"Go and fetch your cloak, man," I said. "It may be warm later, but it's damned chilly now."

"It's all right, sir. Like you say, it will warm up soon enough."

I unlocked and pulled open the door. The birds shuffled on their perches.

Hal looked round swiftly,

"Ralph's not here yet."

"No, I told him to wait beyond the cool of dawn so that we could come and be undisturbed here for a short while."

We entered the gloom of the mews, and Hal opened one of the side windows to let in the light.

I stood in the middle of the shed. All was much as we'd

left it after the death of Roger Hawkes. I began to go over the facts again.

"Roger was lying here. His head and chest were drenched in blood. His face, head and chest were scored as if the birds had attacked him."

"That's about the right of it," said Hal, nodding.

"Gilda was hooded here."

"There wasn't a knife, the knife that killed Roger, anywhere. I looked all over," said Hal.

"We now know that Roger had been pacing about in the night. Ralph heard him. However, his son says that he didn't hear him leave the house in the early morning."

Hal's face came up at that, and his brow wrinkled. "In that 'ouse? Can that be believed? Oh, I know, it's no small 'ouse, but still..."

"Perhaps he sleeps deeply, sir?" offered Cedric.

"Hmmm. Roger was found wearing only his underclothes and a shirt. Had he been coming out to work, he would have been fully dressed. Are we agreed?" I asked.

"I would say so, yes," said Hal, tucking his thumbs into his belt.

Cedric nodded. "He would never have come out half-dressed. It would be disrespectful to you, sir."

"So what if Roger came out here for another purpose?"

"Another purpose, m'lord? What could he possibly do here that wasn't associated with the birds?" asked Cedric with puzzlement in his voice.

"If you were ill unto death, Cedric, in great pain and discomfort, if you knew, beyond doubt, that this illness was shortly going to take you off to God, would you, perhaps, like to go and say your good-byes to the horses you had so lovingly tended all your working life? Before perhaps you became bedridden."

Cedric looked along the line of birds; I guessed he was

picturing the horses back in the stables at Durley on that, hopefully never to happen, imaginary day.

"Wouldn't you want to, for example, say your special farewells to Bayard, whom you had looked after almost all your working life?"

"Aye, sir, I would," said Cedric with a catch in his voice.

"It is my thought that Roger, knowing that his life was drawing to a close, worried and fretted the night away. I do not think he went to his bed that night at all. Maybe the pain was too much. I think he stayed up all night, perhaps praying, searching his conscience, thinking deeply upon what he wanted to do."

I had their full attention now.

I took a glove from the peg behind the door and fitted my hand into it.

"I think he came out before dawn to the mews in the clothes he had worn that previous day, for a falconer usually wears the same clothes at his work every day so that the birds, creatures who like routine, are not discomfited. He took Gilda, the bird his son tells us was his favourite bird, from her perch and hooded her so that she might not see what he was about to do."

Cedric took in a small breath of realisation. I took Gilda up on my glove and, holding a tiny hood in my right hand, slid the leather over her head.

"I think he then replaced Gilda on her perch, crooning his goodbyes, lay down on the floor, took his knife and plunged it into the area of his upper chest where lies the great blood line going up the neck. He then watched his beloved birds as life began to ebb from him."

I eased Gilda back onto her perch and took off the hood.

"And that is why Gilda was hooded when we found the body."

Hal was shaking his head. "Nah, nah, sir. That can't 'ave

been it. Where was the knife…? I couldn't find it, and 'ow did the man become so defaced about the 'ead and neck?"

"Did his birds in a panic claw him then, sir, after all?" whispered Cedric, giving the falcons a strange look.

"No." I moved to the door and opened it fully.

"Come in, Ralph, and tell us the rest of the tale, will you?"

Ralph started. He had been standing just outside the door. He drew back a step at first and then reluctantly came into the mews. His face was red, and sweat started out on his forehead even though it was a cool morning, as I said.

"Tell us, Ralph. What happened then?"

Ralph Hawkes put his hands up into his hair and, in a gesture of absolute despair, cradled his skull with his two palms.

"Ah…I…I… it's…"

"Come on, man. I know what happened. Tell my friends here."

Ralph shook his head. "I can't. I CAN'T."

"Shall I tell it then? Carry on the tale?"

Ralph Hawkes, looking horrified, shook his head again. After a while, he reluctantly said, "No, sir…I…I will, I WILL tell it."

He breathed noisily through his nose, and it took him some time to gather himself to speak.

"I had no idea my father was so ill. None. I just thought that he was getting old and crotchety. I heard him walking about that night. I slept fitfully, and upon the last time I woke, he was gone. It was not even light. His Belvoir jerkin was still sitting on the bench. His boots were by the door. I thought it odd he'd gone out without getting dressed, in his stockinged feet, so I took a cloak and his boots and followed him to the mews."

"How did you know that's where he'd gone?" asked Hal.

"I heard him, heard him open the door to the shed. It squeaks."

He swallowed tears, over and over.

"When I got there, he…he had just done the deed. There was nothing I could do…I tried to stem the bleeding, but it…"

He covered his face with his hands. "I couldn't do anything. I panicked. I lifted him and sat him by the door. He was fading fast then."

"Was it then that he told you about his illness and…?"

"Yes, m'lord. He wanted to die, he said. He wanted to be with his beloved birds when he drew his last breath. He wanted them to be the last thing he saw."

"And when he was finally unconscious?"

"I took the knife and scored him about the head and body to make it seem as if…I didn't know m'lord that you would come and find him. I didn't know that you would realise that it was not possible that his birds would hurt him…I just panicked. I did not want my father, my beloved father, to be buried in unconsecrated ground because he had killed himself. I took the knife…his knife, the knife he had used to kill himself and threw it into the river."

"And so you tried to make it seem as if either the birds had killed him or that a felon had done so."

Ralph wept openly now. "Yessir. He did not feel it, for he was almost dead. I do not know what I thought. I know it was wrong. Very wrong. I was so affeared and upset. It did not even occur to me at that point, that father couldn't lie in consecrated ground anyway because of the prohibition."

"So it wasn't murder after all?" said Hal, aghast.

"It was felo de se, Hal. Self-murder."

Ralph was sobbing into his hands now and leaning on the door post.

"I didn't know…I didn't know. I had no idea he was so ill."

"No one knew, Ralph." I patted his shoulder. "And no one shall know."

He looked up at me, his nose snotty, his eyes swollen and red.

"Sir?"

"We three will keep silent."

Hal cleared his throat, but I glared at him. Cedric nodded his head slightly, over and over.

"And you now admit that it was you who hung your father's coffin in the churchyard, Ralph?"

"Aye, sir. It was me, as you guessed. How did you know it, sir?"

I twisted my hands together before me.

"The knot you tied to secure the bodies to the trees, Ralph." I undid my hands. "They were the falconer's knot."

"What?" said Hal, scratching his cheek with a bristly rasping sound.

"The falconer's knot, Hal. A special knot known only by those who work with birds. Or fly them."

He still looked perplexed, so I enlightened him. "A knot which can be tied by one hand. Used to secure your bird to its perch when you only have one hand free..."

"Ah, I see... t'other is 'oldin' yer bird. Ah...right," he nodded.

Ralph, too, knotted his hands together. "I was so worried that God would not know...that he would be forgotten by God, and the devil would come and take his soul because he was a self-murderer, so I hung him up in the tree. In consecrated ground."

"And your beloved's father and her aunt, too, I think?"

"Aye, sir. They had all died recently." Ralph crossed himself. "It was a wicked, wicked deed, but..."

"I do understand why you did it, Ralph. I cannot condone it, however. When we are at last allowed to make confession again, you must tell Father Godfrey what you did."

"I cannot..."

"No, not what your father did but about your fear for his soul. That is all."

He nodded at me, unable to speak for grief and shame, his shoulders heaving with silent sobs.

I squeezed his arm as I passed him by and went out into the daylight.

"I would just like to know one thing, Ralph."

"Yes, sir, anything, sir."

"Why were you so keen to blame Grover or Harbrook for your father's death? You knew it could not have been either of them. You, of all people, knew the truth."

His sobbing ceased.

"Because I am sure that if that devil Grover had not stolen my sister away, sir, my father would have been longer in this world. It broke his heart."

"And Harbrook?"

Ralph wiped his hand over his snotty nose and took in a shaky breath. He seduced my aunt, sir. Oh, many years ago...but he did it. I saw them. I was young, but I saw them."

"Your aunt? Your mother's sister?"

He did not answer, and we left him to sob for a few moments. After a while, the crying ceased, and he ran his sleeve across his nose and eyes again.

"I'm sorry, sir. I have led you such a dance, I know."

"So it was revenge? Pure and simple...revenge?" asked Hal, folding his arms over his chest.

I looked down at the young man who had now backed and slid down against the outer wall of the mews. He sat with his knees up and his head bent forward, his arms protectively over it.

Cedric looked from one face to another. "Did Ralph kill Harbrook, sir? Did he kill my Alysoun?"

I hauled Ralph Hawkes up to his feet.

"Did you, Ralph? Answer Cedric."

The two young men faced each other over the grass outside the mews.

Ralph shook his head. "No, sir. No, Cedric. I didn't."

"No, Ced, Ralph isn't the culprit. He is foolish and misguided, but he isn't a murderer. No, we are up against a much cooler foe."

"So 'e didn't kill 'Arbrook out of revenge?" said Hal.

"No, Hal. He wanted so desperately to involve the bishop's man or the iron master in the pretended murder of his father, but he didn't kill anyone."

Ralph Hawkes stood straighter and took a deep breath, pulling down his jerkin and adjusting his belt.

"I'll make amends, sir. I will. Somehow..."

"We shall speak of it another time."

I caught him as he made to enter the bird shed.

"One more thing, Ralph."

"Yessir?" He wiped his nose on his sleeve.

"Your aunt? What was her name?"

"Sorry, sir?"

"Her name? Where did she live?"

"She lived in Ramsbury, sir. She was Alys Fulwood, sir, before she married."

"And when she married?"

"Alys Grover, sir."

I saw Hal's eyebrows leap up into his hair.

"Thank you."

Ralph looked at me earnestly, trying to work out why I had asked the question.

"Will you take out a bird, sir?"

I looked back into the shed.

"Aye...if you are up to it, Ralph. I shall."

"Alys Grover?" said Hal when we were out of earshot.

"Who is she?"

"If I'm not much mistaken, Hal—and I need to prove it—she was Old Man Grover's first wife."

"She's not the iron man's mother? She can't be."

"No, but she is part of that family. Or she was," I said.

We had hunted up towards the meadows near Chisbury Wood and Horse Copse and, early on, set up a fine heron from Bewley Pond. A morning out in the open and riding about the autumn countryside cleared the fog from my brain and, it seemed to me, gave Ralph some respite from his grief.

As we jogged home, Hal shook his head as if he was shaking out a fly from his ear.

"And the falconer killed himself."

"Poor man," I said, "how very desperate he must have been."

"He didn't know he had only a few days to live, did he? The thought of further torment for ...however long... must have turned his brain," said Hal. "But it's a mortal sin, whatever we think. It is."

"Who knows what any of us would do?" I said.

"Father Crispin would say that the church would tell us that the torment comes from God and that he gives us the strength to bear it," said Cedric, coming up behind us.

"What use is Johannes' job then," asked Hal with a slight scoff.

We were all silent with our own thoughts for a moment.

"At least this clears the muddy water a little, for we don't now need to add Hawkes' death to the others."

"But," said Hal, "what I can't see is this all started with the death of the falconer. All these folks were dragged out into the open because Roger was dead. Now we find it 'int nothin' to do with 'im. So what is it all about, eh?"

"I think the murderer took advantage of the death of Roger to set up these circumstances, Hal. Someone has gone to a lot of trouble to wind all the facts up into a ball."

"And toss it to us." He laughed out loud. "But gradually, the ball is unravellin'. We'll get to the core of it yet."

We clattered back into the manor yard at Bedwyn and wearily climbed down from our horses.

The grooms came to collect our beasts, but before they could be taken away, Henry du May came trotting down the manor steps.

"Sir, m'lord Belvoir. Oh, I am glad you're back."

"Thank you, Henry."

"Ah, no, sir. I mean, there's a message for you. You're to go to Ramsbury straight away."

"Oh?"

"There's been another death, sir."

Chapter Twelve

My HEART SANK as we approached the house by the church. I had tried to ascertain who'd been killed, but Henry Steward genuinely had no idea. A messenger had been searching for me much of the afternoon, all over the countryside, and had eventually found my Bedwyn steward, leaving the message with him.

We heard the weeping and wailing before we dismounted and made for the front door.

"Is that Mistress Grover, sir?" asked Hal. "Cryin'?"

"You think that our body is that of Master Grover, Hal?"

"Knowin' what we know, m'lord, is it likely that Mistress Grover would mourn the death of her husband so keenly?"

The nasty feeling grew more forceful in the pit of my stomach.

"I think she'd be shocked, but this sad wailing?"

The door was open, and I pushed it slowly. I could see no one, but the terrible keening went on and on.

Looking left into the hall, I could see a woman's shoes protruding from behind a large bench and a body slumped over it.

"Margaret?" I said. "What has happened here?"

The crying went on, and I understood not one word in five.

Hal came round the other end of the bench. "Mistress Grover, my lord," he said solemnly. "She's bin wurried."

Richildis lay on her back, her beautiful dark hair stretched out around her. I noticed her linen crown and barbette had fallen some way from her body. The pale oval of her face was serene and exquisite but for the terrible red weal which disfigured her throat and the series of black marks which discoloured her neck.

I leant over to grasp Margaret of Harbrook's arm. She screamed horribly and resisted my touch, but I pulled nevertheless, and eventually, she stood and went into the arms of Hal, who enveloped her in an embrace, crooning sweetly, and took her to sit down across the room.

The young mistress of the house bore the same sort of wound as Mabel, the housemaid, and the little bone in her neck had been broken, it seemed.

"What happened here, Margaret," I said quietly.

"I don't know. I don't know."

"You're saying you don't know who has done this?"

She shook her head, and her grey curls, dislodged from her head rail by her crying, fell free around her face.

"Hal, some water for Mistress Harbrook."

"Right you are, sir."

I turned the woman from the sight of the body on the floor and made her face me.

"Do you have any idea who might have done this to her?"

The woman stammered and continued to cry.

"Margaret, you want to help find the wicked person who killed Richildis, don't you?"

She nodded.

"So calm down and tell me what happened."

She took the water offered by Hal, and I whispered to

him that he should find something with which to cover the body of Richildis Grover.

"I..."I..."

"Yes, Margaret, I'm listening."

"I found her."

"When did you find her?"

"An hour or so after dinner."

"But that's three hours ago. Has no one been in here to comfort you? Be with you? I know that they took a long time to find me, but..."

"I could not believe she was dead, sir." She looked up at me with a face puffy and red with hours of weeping.

"I tried to revive her."

"Who did you send to let me know the girl was dead, Margaret?"

"I sent the first man I saw. Niccolo or his brother—they are so alike, I don't know which is which—and then I came back to be with her."

"You have been alone most of the afternoon with your dead mistress?"

"I couldn't leave her, sir."

"Did you call the hue and cry?"

She just looked at me dumbly.

"Margaret, have you told Master Grover about his wife's death?"

"No, sir. I couldn't. I'm sure that Niccolo or Richard will have found him and told him."

"And he hasn't been here to see you? To see for himself what has happened?"

"No, sir. Nobody's been," and she started to whimper again.

"Alright, Margaret. Master Hal here will find the iron master, and we shall tell him together."

I nodded to Hal. "Try the ironworks first, then,

depending on who has seen him and where, search for him at the last place he was seen."

"Right you are, sir."

"Margaret, where were you when your mistress was alone in the house?"

"Alone, sir? She wasn't alone."

"Oh?"

"Master Mansur was with her."

"When did he leave?"

"I don't know because I was supervising the linens to be washed and was talking to the laundress out the back."

"So Richildis was alone from the time he left to... when?"

"I came in after dinner, for I'd missed the meal, sir, and dear Richildis was just lying on the floor. I didn't see her at first, for she was hidden from view, but I was coming in here to tidy up and..." The woman gave a sharp cry, "I stumbled over her body."

"How long was she alone, do you think? Who was the last person to see her alive?"

"Me, sir...and her husband."

I walked about the room, taking in this and that. There had certainly been a struggle, for some stools had been overturned, and the cherry red weaving, which had been attached to the house post, had been pulled off and lay dangling forlornly. A lock of Richildis' dark hair had been pulled out at the root and was lying on the floor.

I also found a book on the floor, a small paternoster, which Margaret assured me had belonged to Richildis. A rosary, which I had previously seen attached to Richildis' belt, was lying on the boards, the beads broken from their string, and the cross lying flung away into a corner of the room.

"Did you hear an argument?"

"No, sir. I was out the back."

Another voice now broke into our conversation.

"No, sir. I don't suppose that Mistress Margaret did hear an argument. But I did."

Master Burridge stood in the doorway looking sadly down at the body of the beautiful Richildis.

"I could see this coming."

"You could see what coming, Burridge?" I asked, spreading my feet in a confident stance.

"Well, no...not this exactly, but I thought something would happen. Something...nasty."

"You knew that Mistress Grover was likely to be attacked, but you did not come to see that she was alright? You heard an argument? Who was arguing?"

"Mansur Grover and the mistress. I didn't do anything because I had work to do. And it wasn't the first time they'd argued. I left it alone."

"Why would you think that something nasty might happen?" I asked.

"The way the master has been behaving. He's an angry man, m'lord. Angry and...disappointed and very, very jealous."

"And in your opinion, did he have anything to be jealous about?" I asked.

"Why ask me, sir? What do I know?"

"You must know something, for haven't you said you could see...something coming?"

Burridge sighed. "The master has of late been bad-tempered, oh not just with his wife but with all of us."

This was what we'd heard from Rousalie Harbrook, I recalled.

"And what do you think had happened to make Mansur so angry and bad-tempered?"

Burridge took a filthy hand to his forehead, leaving black smudges across his skin.

"He'd recently found out that his wife had been unfaithful, I think. I don't know the details, but I think that is what happened."

"You believe that Mansur has killed his wife in a fit of jealous rage?"

"He is my master, sir, and I am loath to speak ill of him. He is a friend of many years, a good employer, and a good man, but he does allow his emotions to get the better of him. Lately, he cannot keep them in check, it seems."

"Tell me, Master Burridge, with whom is Mistress Richildis supposed to have had an adulterous relationship?"

"I'm unsure. But I do know that Master Pinter from Marlborough town was involved with her before she married my master. Perhaps it was him."

"Only Pinter?"

"I think I told you, sir, that Master Harbrook was known to Mistress Grover for many years. And we all know what he was like."

"Ah…yes…free with his affections, eh, Burridge?" I said with a smile.

"Just so, my lord. It's widely known. I wouldn't be surprised if…no, no. I've said too much."

I nodded. "We do know that she was most distressed to hear about his death."

Margaret, who had been looking on aghast, rose quickly at my utterance.

"She was, my lord, but it was not because she was unfaithful with my brother."

"She told me it was because she was upset for you. Isn't that right, mistress?"

"She had known my brother all her life…"

Burridge scoffed, "All the more reason to think that something had been going on, eh?"

"My brother, Yves, was a good man, and you have no right..."

I interrupted their quarrelling, "We need to find Master Grover. We need to hear his side of the story."

"You'll not get at the truth, sir. You know he'll wriggle from the hook," said Burridge.

"You have no right to besmirch the reputation of a man who is unable to fight back!" Margaret took no notice of me and launched a verbal attack on Burridge. "My brother was a good man, and what is more, I have never ever known Master Grover lie, you disgusting little tittle-tattle," said Margaret suddenly really angry. Margaret's face was a furious grimace. "It's you who is the liar!"

"Me!" Burridge looked horrified. "I'm the one who keeps this place going. I'm the dogsbody everyone bosses around, including your silly mistress..."

"Pah, you...good for nothing...deceiver!"

"I'm the honest one here. I tell it like it is."

"And though you don't like to speak ill of your employer?" I said, "if it means telling the truth, you will?"

"No, sir, I don't."

"But..."

"But like I say, I've seen something like this coming. He's an angry, jealous man, sir. Who knew what he might do?"

"You are saying that Master Grover has killed his wife?" I said, wanting to set things absolutely straight and have it out in the open.

"I am saying he is angry and jealous, was angry and jealous. Now we cannot find him. Don't you think that is the behaviour of a guilty man who has fled from the scene of his crime?"

The body of Mistress Grover had been removed, and all relevant authorities had been informed at last. Master Burridge had gone back to the ironworks to oversee everything in the absence of its master.

Hal came back a short while later. "Mansur Grover's nowhere to be found, and no one has seen him all afternoon."

I could tell that he was upset. Yes, Richildis had been a naive, silly and emotional girl, but she did not deserve to be struck down in this way, and I knew that Hal felt pity for her, pity and anger at her death.

I slapped him on the back in a gesture of camaraderie. "Come, let's go home. We need to think about things."

We collected our horses and were about to ride for Durley when a young man with bright red hair rode into the ironworks.

He left his horse and strode confidently to the office where Burridge had just closed the door.

We followed and heard the man call out, "I need to make myself known to Master John of Burridge!" The young man was freckled of face and wore a bright green tunic, a shade which complemented his colouring perfectly. "Is he here, please?"

The door opened. "What is your business with him?" said Burridge, eyeing him up and down carefully.

Hal's eyebrows rose comically to his hair. "I wonder what his name is?"

"I expect we will find out in due course, Hal," I said with a chuckle.

"Especially if we listen in," said Hal with a cheeky grin.

"I seek Master Burridge to introduce myself. I have been appointed to the role of bailiff of the Lord Durnford's estate after the death of Master Yves of Harbrook. We will have business to discuss, I have no doubt."

As the door closed on them both, Hal and I ran over and quietly pressed our ears to the wood.

There were few people in the courtyard of the workings, but only one or two gave us strange looks as we loitered outside the door.

"My name is Geoffrey Grover. Have I the honour of speaking with the overseer here?"

"Aye, that's me. Grover, you say? Well, well, fancy that! I trust all is well at the manor of Durnford since the terrible death of its previous bailiff?"

"Things were somewhat in disarray, but we shall have everything working perfectly again soon."

"Well, Master Grover. You did say Grover?"

"I did. I am from a distant branch of the family from a place called Cadley. Do you know it? It sits in the forest not far from Marlborough. On the Salisbury road."

Hall chuckled quietly into his beard. "He's good at this, ain't he?"

"Shhh."

"No, I can't say I do. And are you related to our ironmaster, Mansur Grover, at all?" asked Burridge. I would have given anything to have seen his expression.

"Oh, I suppose I must be. Though without discussing the ancestry of Master Grover's father with him, I cannot say exactly. I do know that my father told me once that we were related to someone in this neck of the woods. A second cousin or something. It was through the first marriage of Master Mansur's father. But he was uncertain."

"As far as I know," said Burridge flatly, "Master Grover has no living family."

"No family? To whom does the ironworks pass on his demise, then?"

With a shrug in his voice, Burridge answered, "I can't say, but he had, just over a month ago, married a fine young filly, and there surely would have been some offspring from that union, but, sadly, she had just been found dead."

"Dead?" The man's voice faltered, and I wondered if he would give himself away, but he carried on bravely. "Oh, that is terrible news. I had, of course, heard about the marriage of Master Grover to his young bride, but this is grave news indeed."

"And Master Mansur cannot be found."

"He doesn't yet know of his wife's death?"

"No, not yet. Though..."

"Yes...?"

"There is a suspicion that he might be guilty of his wife's murder."

"Murder?"

"There is no doubt it was murder."

There was a little silence while drinks were procured and offered, and they sat down together. We heard the clinking of the cups and the rustling of fabric.

"The poor girl was murdered, you say?" said the red-headed man.

"Ay, strangled."

"Terrible, terrible. Who would wish to do such a thing to an innocent young girl?"

I thought the man's voice wobbled with his last utterance, but he recovered well.

"Perhaps, since I come at a very bad time, Master Burridge, we should postpone our business meeting until another less...inauspicious time."

"Cor!" whispered Hal, "I didn't know he knew such long words."

"Shhh."

"My timing is unfortunate."

"Ah no, Master Grover, my friend, I might call you my friend, might I? There is no time like the present."

"If you are sure."

"I am certain, Geoffrey. I presume upon you, but I am called John. May I call you Geoffrey? I had a good relationship with your predecessor. He and I were on first-name terms."

"Like Hell they were?" whispered Hal.

The red-headed man sipped his drink. "Of course you may."

"Maybe you'd like me to take you on a tour of the ironworks? I can show you what a tidy sort of business we have here."

"That would be a good idea."

"But first, we finish our drink."

"Your health, Master Burridge."

"And yours, Master Grover."

They drank.

"It is sad that Master Grover has no offspring to inherit. The business, as you say, is a tidy one. It would have been gratifying to see it pass to a son."

Burridge chuckled. "As the only living relative... perhaps...Geoffrey, you might put your name forward if..."

"If?"

"If Mansur Grover is convicted of murdering his wife."

"Ah no, I think not...I know nothing about iron-working," chuckled the man.

"Oh, but I beg to differ. You must have at least a little knowledge to have risen highly in the ranks at Durnford at such a young age. To have become the bailiff."

"Kind of you to say so...John."

I thought I detected a little hesitation in the manner of the bailiff, but I need not have worried.

"Managing an ironworks, I suppose, is akin to managing

an estate, with all its complexities. But the iron-working itself, naturally, would be left to those workers who are adept at producing the iron."

"I get my hands dirty when I need to," said Burridge with a smile, and he must have opened his palms for the bailiff to see, for he answered, "Oh yes, as I see," with a note of levity. "Ah… no, although it may transpire that I am one of the only living relatives, I have very little hope of inheriting the ironworks."

"Oh, why?"

"There is, apparently, or so I've heard, another son with a finer claim than mine."

Standing outside the door, we heard Burridge sigh heavily and clear his throat. "Another son? I have heard nothing of this…other son." Burridge quickly changed the subject."And now, Geoffrey, that tour of the works and perhaps we can discuss the needs of your masters at Durnford Manor?"

"By all means," said the bailiff.

We made for Durley at a pace.

What if Master Mansur is found?"

"Then there will be further character assassination and lies. I'm sure it's all set up nicely, Hal.

"Master Mansur Grover was indeed found, for as we entered the hall, the man himself rose from a bench by the fire and turned to face us.

"Well, I'll be buried in Burbage," said Hal under his breath

"Sir Aumary, my lord, I have come…" The man's cheeks were wet with tears, and he sniffed several times, "to confess to the murder of my wife."

Hal gave me a strange look under grey eyebrows. "You killed 'er?" he said.

"Aye. I…I did. I killed her."

I called for Henry to pour us wine, and I sat down on the bench and gestured for Grover to do the same.

We waited a while for the big man to collect himself, and then I asked, "I need to know at what hour you attacked and killed your wife, Mansur."

"It was around the dinner hour, sir. I had gone home for my meal…"

"Was this your usual habit? I asked.

"No, sir. I usually take food at work. But today, today, I wanted to speak to Richildis."

"What did you want to speak to her about…in particular?"

"I wanted once and for all to have it out with her."

"What did you need to clarify?"

He shifted on the bench, and it seemed to me as if he was a little embarrassed.

"I wanted to know if she really loved me. I needed to know that she had not simply married me because she had been jilted by the pinter. After his death, my lord, she was so… discomposed and upset. She was crying hysterically and became unreachable; I began to wonder if the relationship had not ended when she said it had."

"That they had carried on an affair?"

"I didn't want to believe it. But there had been rumours flying around."

"Where did you hear these rumours, Mansur?"

"My man, Burridge, had heard that they'd met secretly after we were married. He did not want to tell me and kept it to himself, but in the end, I got the secret from him. He is a man of absolute trustworthiness."

"Ahhh," said Hal, looking at me with a wink.

"I am almost certain, Mansur, that these rumours are untrue. Pinter himself told me the reasons why he passed over Richildis, and there were no grounds to disbelieve him. Neither do I think that he would be courting the Fletchier's daughter in the town and at the same time be involving himself with your wife. He was a most punctilious man."

"But..."

"I asked your wife, Mansur, not long ago, if she was having an affair and she was most adamant that it was untrue. Neither did she involve herself in an affair with Master Harbrook as the gossip has it."

I saw Hal look at me sideways to see if I would tell him what else I knew: the truth.

"She also said that she had married you almost without thinking after her jilting by the town pinter. However, once you were married, she was most ecstatically happy and had never been more glad that she had married you. Her words were sincere, I'm certain."

Hal had been holding his breath through my speech, and now he let it go with an enormous sigh.

"Do not doubt, Mansur, that she loved you," I added.

The man took in an immense breath and screamed in pain—an inarticulate cry which ended in a hoarse sob.

"And I killed her in my jealousy."

"Tell me everything that happened."

Again, we had to wait for him to collect his thoughts.

"I came into the house and found her sitting with one of my men."

"One of the brothers, Richard or Niccolo?"

"Yes, how...how did you know, sir?"

"Those two are in the pay of your enemy and have been helping all along to sow the seeds of discord."

"Niccolo had no need to be there, but there he was, and my wife was weeping and taking consolation from him."

"Were they embracing, touching?"

"No, my lord. But in my hard heart, I thought they most certainly had been."

"Go on."

"Niccolo excused himself promptly and left. I thought to tackle him later."

"And you asked Richildis why he was there?"

"Again, my lord, you seem to know..."

"I think she had called Niccolo to the house because she needed to know the answer to a question which I had posed to her the day before."

Oh?"

"Namely, did she speak to him or his brother to send Master Burridge to Marlborough to inform me she needed to see me the day the pinter died?"

"But she was alone...no chaperone."

"She would see Niccolo alone; she wanted as few witnesses as possible. I'm sure once she had the information I needed, she would have come to me with it. She suspected she was being lied to and used, Mansur."

The man's expression was one of complete confusion.

"As you are being lied to and used and framed for deeds for which you were not responsible."

Hal stood and faced him. Right from the beginning, you've been fed, groomed and pulled by the nose by someone who knew you well and knew that you would be likely to lose your temper."

"Tell me, how did you kill your wife?" I asked quickly, giving him no pause.

He stammered," I...I took her in my arms, laid her down, and I...I...crushed the life from her. I took a pillow and put it over her nose and mouth. I could not bring myself to spill her blood. I couldn't bear to desecrate her body with a wound. Her perfect skin, as white as alabaster."

"You didn't strangle her?" asked Hal.

No...no...I could not have done that for...she was so beautiful and I did not want to mark her beauty." He began to weep again.

"Then, if this is true, Mansur, and I have no reason to suspect it isn't true, then you did not kill your wife," I said.

"But she lies dead in my house. John Burridge was there shortly after, and he saw her dead body and said that I should flee."

"She is dead, but not by your hand."

He had not heard me and continued. "I was so distressed, my lord, I left, not thinking properly what I ought to do."

"So why are you here?"

"I rode out into the forest at a furious pace with no idea where to go, what to do. I was so thrown and agitated, but as I came to my senses and slowed in my flight, I realised that my mind had directed me close to your manor."

"And you came to confess?" asked Hal.

"I did. I realised that I could not outrun this horror, and I needed to speak to the constable, to confess my crime."

"Did you quarrel viciously with Richildis?"

"No, my lord, we were surprisingly calm."

"And did you rush about the place after her? Did she try to evade you? I noticed that some possessions had been broken and it looked as if there'd been a struggle."

"No, my lord. It was almost as if she knew what was coming and was resigned."

"Tell me, Mansur, for how long did you press the pillow to your wife's face?"

"It did not take long, sir. She was a small woman, delicate and powerless to resist me."

You will be surprised, Mansur, how long it takes to truly suffocate someone."

"But, my lord..."

"My friend, Doctor Johannes of Marlborough town,

tells me that to accomplish asphyxiation until someone is totally robbed of their breath and is not able to recover takes as long as the recitation of ten paternosters out loud. Imagine that. So long. Did you keep up the pressure for that long, Mansur?"

His face was a mask of horror. "No, no, I came to my senses quickly and pulled away. I knew what I'd done, and suddenly I…I…"

"Didn't wanna do it any longer?" said Hal.

"No. No, I realised what I was doing and stopped. My anger had utterly cooled. But I thought it was too late. I had killed her!"

Had you waited, your wife would have taken a breath and recovered, I'm sure."

"No…no…I did not wait. I fled, ashamed of what I had done."

"Then, I am telling you that you did not kill your wife, Mansur. Another did."

Chapter Thirteen

I FOUND MY red-headed groom in the stables when we returned to Durley.

"Well done, Cedric," I said, slapping him on the shoulders. "You have sown the seed."

"You were amazing, lad," said Hal. "I think you've missed yer calling."

"I admit I was nervous."

"Didn't sound like it from where we were standing," smiled Hal.

"I kept thinking of my poor Alysoun, and I must admit it crossed my mind once or twice that I could end his life there and then. But I trust your judgement, sir. You think he's the man. You think you can catch him?"

I nodded. "But you didn't end his life, Ced."

"You say that he's been trying to blame the ironmaster for everything that has happened?"

"I'm sure he has. He is a devious and clever man."

"Are you absolutely certain that this Burridge fellow is our culprit, Sir Aumary?"

"He showed you his dirty hands?"

"He did, sir, willingly, though I'm sure he had no idea

how significant it was to us."

"I suspect it was those hands which left the dirty marks on the throat of Richildis Grover when he strangled her."

Hal's brow rose. "Aye, there were marks. She were proper mucky."

"But we cannot prove that he is our killer, sir, with just a pair of dirty hands," said Cedric.

"No. That's true."

"There is something else though, sir."

"Yes, Ced?"

"Alysoun took a flask of ale from Master Barbflet's house on the day she… didn't she?"

"That's right. She was permitted, I'm told."

"I know what Master Nick's leather flasks are like, Sir Aumary. He has them embossed with the mill cypher."

"Yes, you're right, he does."

"I drank ale from one of his flasks today. At the office of Master Mansur Grover. Why was it there? It didn't belong there. It can't have been there long, for the ale was reasonably good. The flask wasn't found, they tell me, in the grain barn after Alysoun…"

"No, it wasn't," said Hal quickly. "The barn was searched."

"Thanks, Cedric," I said. "We now need things to unfold, and unfold they will, I'm certain. Tomorrow, we need to get you back to the Durnford estate. That's where our final act will be played out like a Greek tragedy."

"A what, sir?" said both Hal and Cedric together.

"Aw, never mind, boys," I said, smiling.

Our tragedy, as I'd called it, began to take form quite quickly.

Just one day after Cedric's visit to the ironworks, John

Burridge jogged into the yard at the manor of Durnford and dismounted, looking around him appreciatively.

"You have a superior place of work here, Master Grover," he said as Cedric came out to meet him. "Not at all like my own."

"Good morning, John, yes, it's a fine place to spend one's working day. But surely you have been here before."

"Ah, no. My master, Mansur Grover, was the one to do business here. I have never been to Durnford."

"Then you must allow me to respond in kind to your thoughtful action of the other day."

"Master Grover?"

"And take you on a tour of the property."

"Ah, I see."

"Shall we begin in the stables?"

"Have you many fine horses left here?" asked Burridge. "I know we supply you with much of the metal for their shoeing, amongst other things."

"Oh, we do. Under normal circumstances, we do, but at the moment, with the lord away at his manor at Netton, his horses are with him."

Hal and I were hiding by the manor steps as Cedric stepped out with John Burridge towards the stables. We followed quietly so we'd not be detected.

"And does the lord leave many servants here when he visits his other properties?" we heard Burridge say.

"Only a few. I am here, of course, to keep everything running for when he returns, but a mere handful of folk are in the house and kitchen. The miller naturally stays put, but he lives over there," Cedric waved his hand in the general direction of the river. "Close by the mill."

"It's a lonely place then, Geoffrey, for you, during the day."

"There are the villeins and the reeve, of course, out and

about the village."

Hal put his hand on my sleeve, "He's trying to work out if Cedric is alone here," he whispered.

"It seems like it."

"Shall we walk about, John, as we talk?"

They entered the stable buildings.

We slid up to the door and listened.

"Ah, yes. I heard that you lodged your cider press in the stables. I cannot remember who told me. This is a very fine device."

"It is famous in the locality," answered the bailiff. "It's very large, and we press many apples from the estate here. Our orchards are vast, and in the right season, the place is all hustle and bustle."

"But now, it's still."

"Indeed."

"I have always wanted to know how one of these presses works, Geoffrey."

"Oh?"

"Would it be possible for you to give me a demonstration? Show me how it's done?"

"Ah..." I could almost hear the uncertainty in Cedric's voice as he said. "It's not my job, I'm afraid, and we need more than a few people to operate it."

"Oh, of course. Another time, perhaps?"

"Phew!" said Hal in my ear. "I had visions of Cedric being squashed under those gert stones."

"He's too wily to be taken in like that, Hal."

"So, you have cider and sheep, and I know that you breed dogs and..."

"We have lymers and alaunts in the main. But that was poor Master Harbrook's special pleasure."

"We are so sad to lose him. He was a fine fellow. Not that we aren't glad that you have taken over, of course, Geoffrey."

"Pah!" said Hal.

"Very kind of you to say so, John."

"Do you know if the constable has found out anything further about the poor man's terrible death?"

"I do happen to know that Sir Aumary is close to an arrest for that murder. My cousin is a groom in his stable."

"Ah. It was murder, then?"

"Oh yes. Sir Aumary Belvoir is certain he was unlawfully killed. It was not an accident as was first thought."

Burridge was shaking his head. I could see him through the gap at the door's edge.

"Does he suspect my master, Mansur Grover, at all?"

I held my breath. How would Cedric answer?

"I am not privy to that sort of information, Master Burridge. I'm sorry."

"John, please."

"John." There was a smile in Cedric's voice, but it somehow didn't ring true.

"Very fine stables, very fine. It's just that, well, Mansur has been present when many of the deaths…certainly the recent deaths, have been accomplished."

"Oh?"

We had to scurry around the corner quickly, for the two men were exiting the stables.

"I did wonder to myself…if, for some warped reason of his own, he had been involved in the deaths."

"What reason do you think that would be…John?"

"Oh, it's well known he is a jealous and angry man. That is why it did not surprise me when he fled the scene of his wife's murder. I came in shortly afterwards to find her strangled and the man weeping and kneeling over her body."

"You found her? That must have been distressing for you."

"He said not a word, pushed past me and was gone. I have no idea where."

"If he's found and arrested, he'll no doubt hang for his many crimes," said Cedric more sharply than he needed.

"And the ironworks will be left masterless."

"Shall we look at our new barn, John?"

The two men sauntered off to the large grain barn at the edge of the enclave.

"And yet you tell me that there is another son," said Burridge. "He will no doubt inherit. Eventually."

Then, Cedric delivered the one major piece of information which Master Burridge had come to hear. He turned to him, "Ah, John, I am sorry. I was not entirely honest with you when we last spoke about this. Please accept my apology, but I was unsure if I could trust you, not knowing you well."

"Not honest, Geoffrey?"

"Now I know you are an honest man, I can confide in you. I told you that I had no chance of inheriting."

"You did."

"Because of this 'other son'."

"You did. You did, indeed. Do you have any idea where this other son might be?"

"Yes, yes, I do."

"Oh, I would truly love to know."

"I bet you would," whispered Hal in my left ear.

"Well…it's me, John. Me. I am the other son."

Chapter Fourteen

THERE WAS a long silence, and John Burridge quickly looked down at his boots.

"You are the other son?"

"I am."

"But how?"

"Ah, it's a sad tale of the death of a beloved wife and the grief which drove a man to leave England, his family and his business to seek solace in another country where, contrary to this man's expectation, he fell in love again."

Slowly, they exited the grain barn.

"Wait, wait. You go too fast!" Burridge put his hand on the bailiff's sleeve. The man was…?"

They stopped.

"My father and Mansur's father are one and the same. We are half brothers."

"Another mother?"

"A second wife. My mother died when I was very small, and my father, the senior Grover, in his mourning, felt he could not stay in England. He left Ramsbury and me, went off to the crusade and settled in Africa for a while."

"Where he met and married Mansur's mother?"

"That is correct."

"But, Geoffrey, no. You are far too young to be the first son. It cannot be."

Cedric laughed, "There is but eighteen months or so between Mansur and I. No, I am a lot older than I look."

Burridge's face was creased in puzzlement. Hal and I had now nipped into the barn, and were resting in the shadows listening. Again, I could see through the door panel, which was ill-fitting.

Burridge lifted his face to the barn roof. "It's not true. It's a lie. You lie."

"Why is it a lie?"

"You cannot be approaching thirty-six. I am thirty-nine and a first son. Mansur is thirty-five."

"I assure you…"

Burridge turned quickly. "What's your game, Master Grover, if that is indeed your name? Somehow, I doubt it."

"You wish me to bring you proof?"

"If you want to take over the ironworks, that's just what you'll have to do. Prove who you are."

"And I can."

"No. You are not who you say you are."

"You told me that you had never heard of a second son, and now you are ill at ease when you are confronted with the evidence. Why is that, sir?"

Burridge settled his hand on his knife hilt. Cedric noted his movement.

"It's a lie, I say."

"You must have a reason for thinking this."

"Because, Geoffrey, or whoever you are, I am the first son. I am Mansur's half-brother. My father left when I was young. I was farmed out to a couple in Burridge, thrown out as if I didn't matter. And, of course, I didn't matter because, when they eventually returned, Mansur was the be-all and end-all. The favourite son. The one who could do no wrong. It should have been me, as the eldest son, who inherited the works. But no, it was Mansur."

"How did you come to your position as Mansur's right hand-man?"

"That was easy - it's no difficult task to take in a man as naive as Mansur," he chuckled.

The bailiff shrugged his shoulders. "Then I am not the only son. Does he know he has another brother?"

"You are not Mansur's brother… No!" spat John Burridge. "He has not the first notion that I am his half-brother. And he will never know." This was definitely a threat.

Cedric stepped back.

"Well done, lad," said Hal at my side. "Keep space between you."

"And so, if Mansur Grover is convicted of the murder of his wife and…"

"And, of course, for the murder of the bailiff, your predecessor." Burridge's teeth were clenched.

"And the young girl in Marlborough?"

"Careful now, Cedric," said Hal at my side. "Don't let on too much."

"What about her?"

"Did he kill her too?"

Burridge laughed nastily. "Aw, come, Master Grover or whoever you are, we are skirting around each other, but we both know that Mansur hasn't killed anyone."

"Then take the credit for what you have done. You have planned this so meticulously. All except for the girl in the barn."

Hal and I looked at each other in the half-light of the large stone building. Would Burridge confess to Alysoun's murder?

"That was an accident. She shouldn't have been there. It

was Harbrook I was after there."

"You killed Master Harbrook…eventually?"

"I failed to get him at the barn, so it had to be at the hunt, and it was remarkably easy. And, naturally, I planned to frame Mansur Grover."

Cedric backed away. "I think you'll find that the county constable, Sir Aumary Belvoir, is aware of your transgressions, Burridge, and how you accomplished them."

"Well, he isn't going to be able to prove a thing? You won't be saying anything."

Burridge followed Cedric as he backed away, keeping him within a few feet.

"Who are you? You are certainly not who you say you are. I know that. And you know too much."

"Don't turn yer back, lad," said Hal.

Cedric laughed a terrible cackle with no humour in it at all. "Who am I? Only the man whose life you ruined. You took away my beloved. Killed her, murdered her in cold blood, like you would a pig at the slaughter." Cedric's face was pink and angry.

"Careful," said Hal. "Careful, don't lose your temper."

Burridge looked surprised. "Mabel?"

"Ah, so you admit to killing Mabel too?" Cedric folded his arms across his breast. "No, Alysoun was my girl. The girl in the grain barn. You are a piece of work, Burridge."

"Grover, my name is John Grover!"

"And the pinter. He could identify you, couldn't he? You, the man who was over-familiar with Pinter's little housemaid, Mabel. That's how all this began."

"How do you know so much?"

Again, Cedric laughed. "I told you, the constable is perfectly aware of what you have done, your crimes. I work for him. And you have just admitted in front of witnesses to almost every single murder you have committed."

Burridge looked around. "I see no witnesses."

Cedric shrugged.

With a flick of his wrist, Burridge grabbed his knife and launched himself at Cedric. "And there will be no witnesses because you are going the same way as all the rest!" he yelled.

Cedric parried his thrust with a strong arm. Burridge went in for another strike.

"NO! He isn't going anywhere!" cried a voice, a deep, rich, smooth sound.

"Deal with me first."

Burridge turned on his heel. "YOU!" He spat at his feet.

Mansur Grover stood there in the sunshine, his face furious.

"You!" said Burridge, "You should have been miles away by now. Or rotting in some gaol somewhere." He looked down his nose at Mansur. "You killed your wife!"

"Well, I am sorry to disappoint you, John, but the constable tells me that I did not kill my wife. I've killed no one. I am guilty, yes. I am guilty of believing every word you said. Guilty of trusting you too much. I believed you to be a worthy man. A man who hates the evil words that others spew and who keeps his counsel until pushed and then tells the truth no matter how it hurts, eh? But I know you now; you're not what you seem. You have never been what you seemed."

Burridge chuckled low in his throat, "Imbecile!"

"Yes, I am an imbecile. My jealousy, willingness to believe, and stupid, stupid pride have brought me to this terrible moment."

Burridge was now laughing. "It was so easy to get into your febrile mind, to manipulate your brooding anxieties. It was so easy to influence you...I didn't think it would be so simple." He stepped back, giving himself space to think and maybe to run. "But I have killed no one. You have no idea what it is you have done in your…strange fits of temper, Mansur."

"I am not guilty, and you know it."

Burridge chuckled. "You'll find it hard to prove. I have left no trace."

"You killed my love!" Mansur howled to the sky.

"And he also killed my love, Master Mansur, with no more thought than he'd give to stepping on an insect," said Cedric with a wobble to his voice.

Mansur took out a long-bladed knife. "Then perhaps, we can be avenged, young man, by working together."

Burridge licked his lips. "You might do it…but this mewling boy here, no, He hasn't the guts."

Cedric slowly and deliberately removed the knife from the scabbard at his side. His eyes never left Burridge's face.

"Haven't I? What is my life now without my Alysoun? Empty. We were to be married soon, and now my life is ruined. No, I'll run my knife across your throat and laugh while I do it."

"But you won't, Cedric," I said quietly, stepping out from the darkness of the barn into the light. "You won't kill him, either of you. You'll let the law deal with him."

Burridge gave a rapid glance around the area. "My Lord Belvoir, what are you doing here? Ah, yes, you have come to apprehend the murderer. Well, there he is - the wife killer."

"And still you bluff," I said. "Now who is wriggling on the hook, Master Burridge?"

Hal was not far behind me. "Well done, Cedric. It took some courage to face him like you did."

"Is it enough, Master Hal?" said my young groom, his eyes filling with tears.

"Aye. It's enough."

Mansur Grover drew himself up to spring at Burridge,

but I put my body between them and grasped Mansur's shoulders.

"Put away your knife, Mansur. If you kill him now, you will never know the whole story."

It was just as well Hal was watching my back, for Burridge grasped his own knife and raised his arm to give me a death blow, but the blow did not land, and the knife spun out of his hand and landed on the earth. John Burridge was suddenly leaning back in Hal's grasp, cursing and swearing,. as much as he could curse and swear with Hal's arm pinning him by the neck.

"I know the story. How can I not know it?" said Mansur sadly. He, too, had tears in his eyes.

"He will hang, and you'll be there to watch him suffer."

Burridge sneered,

"You had no idea, did you, that I was just waiting? Waiting for the right moment, brother," said the strangulated voice of John Burridge.

"You are no brother of mine. We share no blood."

"We have all heard your confession, John, all of us. There is no escape for you now. I'll take your knife." I stepped forward and picked it up from the floor.

Hal was fiddling with a set of manacles which he had brought with him.

Burridge chose his moment and tossed Hal away, kicking him for good measure, but he was too slow, and Hal was too prepared. However, Cedric chose his moment and spun on the balls of his feet. With a wonderful slice to the jaw, he punched the man full on the chin, and John Burridge went down in a daze and didn't get up. Hal quickly recovered and snapped the manacles on the man's hands behind his back.

"You'll come with us to the castle in Marlborough," he said angrily. "No nonsense now, or, make no mistake, I'll do what Cedric wanted to do and wipe my knife across your ruddy throat and smile whilst I do it. I'll have no worry over it. I'm going to get you thrown into the deepest gaol, and I'm going to get them to forget all about you."

I saw Cedric smirk. He sheathed his knife.

"Oh, Hal..." he said with a weak smile. Please can I be the one to turn the key on him?"

There, Paul, my scribe. That is the end of the tale of the ironmaster and his murderous half-brother.

Yes, it is a sad story. Sad for my young groom, Cedric, who never recovered from the death of his love, Alysoun.

Pardon? Has he ever married? Ah, no, he never did, not to this day. It was also sad for Mansur Grover, who lost his true love on that terrible day. He did remarry, though, and has two fine children now.

It was sad for the little maid Mabel, who was so taken in by the charm and lies of John Burridge, a snake, a snake akin to that which tempted Eve in that perfect and wonderful garden of Eden: plausible, clever, inventive and thoroughly evil.

What's that? You want to know how clever he was, how he did it. I haven't told you how I worked it out.

Well then, we haven't finished our tale after all, have we? Let's lay it all out, eh?

We did get the man to the gaol at Marlborough Castle, and for quite some time, he said nothing about his terrible crimes.

I prepared my case for the justices, and once I had it all sorted in my mind, I went down to the gaol and faced John Burridge with his felonies.

He had already admitted, in front of us all, to killing Alysoun and we'd realised that it was Yves Harbrook at whom he was truly aiming his boar spear, as we'd surmised. Or rather the boar spear of his master, Mansur Grover. Burridge had been the man who, as the pigman had said, 'didn't like his backside to come into contact with the saddle'. He hated riding. We'd had this admission from him when he'd ridden to Marlborough to see the pinter and eventually taken the opportunity to kill him. And once the pigman was taken to see the miscreant in the gaol, he confirmed that it was he who had encouraged him to hide the boar spear in his cart out on Forest Hill. The fact that he also repeatedly called this man his 'friend' was another nail in his coffin. He'd done the same thing to Hal.

Poor, poor Alysoun. She had opened the door of the barn expecting to see her beloved, Cedric. Instead, she had been spitted by a boar spear. She had not needed to die there, but Burridge, as we'd thought, expecting Harbrook and blinded by the sun in the doorway, had let fly without knowing exactly who was in the path of the spear.

"You show no remorse, Burridge?" I'd said to him as he sat in the cold and dark of the castle gaol, his manacles and gyves clanking at every movement of his body, every breath.

He sniffed. "I am not sorry she died. But that was genuinely an accident. She shouldn't have been there, plain and simple."

"Ah no, Burridge, you meant to kill her at some point because you knew she knew about you and poor Mabel. As did her Grannie. They would, both of them, have given you away eventually."

"They got what they deserved, I suppose. But Mabel?

Ah, I should have been more careful there."

"In what way?"

"Poor Mabel, she was such a sweet thing. I allowed myself to become obsessed with her, which was foolish, I know, but she wanted more than I could give. I wasn't able to resist her. If I hadn't been so lustful of her...then this whole story might have been different."

So, I had been right. Mabel was nothing more than a dalliance for him. It had been lust which drove him on.

"The girl was barely out of childhood," I said in disgust.

"What can I say? I like them young," he cackled. "It runs in the family, you see."

Ah, yes, a dig at Mansur Grover and his young bride. I folded my arms over my chest as if the action would protect me from the depravity of the man.

"Tell me how you managed the death of Harbrook."

Burridge laughed. "You all believed me when I said I was a useless spearman."

"We now know that wasn't true. You hit Alysoun with a perfectly aimed throw."

"And I hit the boar too, except no one saw me do it."

"You killed the boar, pulled out the spear, and used it on Harbrook?"

"If you know, why ask?" derided the man.

"Why Harbrook?"

"He was a thoroughly disgusting man."

"Ah...yes. The seduction of your mother. We know about that. Alice Grover, the aunt of my falconer. It's amazing how so many are related in this forest, Burridge. You told me that yourself."

"Like I say...if you know, why ask?"

"Let's talk about the pinter."

Burridge gave a raucous chuckle, and it echoed around the stony cell like the call of a demented goose.

"People see what they expect to see."

"They take for granted that a man who says he has been locked in a room has actually been locked in," I said.

"Oh, I was locked in."

"You just weren't locked in by this mysterious man who ran up the steps and took a sword to the portcullis mechanism."

Burridge beamed from ear to ear. "My finest moment."

"In you come to the castle, following the pinter, wondering what I wanted with him, hoping against hope that little Mabel hasn't been found. You came on a spurious pretext about your mistress needing to speak to me. An untruth," I said. "Another untruth in a list of untruths."

"I took the opportunity to duck behind the cart coming into the castle through the gateway and hooked myself onto the side as it passed the guardroom. I then let go and nipped up the stairs. Clever, eh? I then heard you talking to Pinter. It had to be done there and then. I'd taken Mansur's sword in case I could use it."

"And you did. You found a perfect use for it."

"Pinter was about to tell you that I was the man who'd been seen with Mabel. I couldn't have that."

"You severed the rope and the portcullis came crashing down."

"And I came back down as quick as lightning after throwing the sword out of the window."

"And the key...the key to the guardroom? Now, I must say, and it pains me to do so, that was sheer genius."

"Why thank you, my Lord Belvoir."

"You run into the guardroom, lock yourself in from the inside, and drop the key out of the arrow loop. You cannot be connected, for you are locked away!" I chuckled. "Naturally, we all thought the killer had pushed you in and locked the door from the outside."

"It took something for me to do that, for I wasn't lying when I said I don't like small confined spaces of stone."

"Ah well, Burridge! You are here until the justices come for you. That could be some time. Small enough and stony enough for you, is it?"

"I've had better accommodation."

"And it's going to be very difficult while you are in here to spread gossip as you have been doing. I must say, you are a master at it."

"Why, that's kind of you to say, my lord."

I shook my head. "Why did you have to kill young Richildis?"

"Oh, come, come, sir. You know that she had fathomed my little lie about my being sent to the town. I needed to go to see the pinter. I knew you'd get to the truth of that soon enough, so I couldn't let Richildis work out what I was doing there. Yes, I lied about her sending me, and she knew it."

"So you killed her."

"Not only for that reason."

"Oh?"

"Mansur attacked her…you know about that."

"I do."

"But he didn't finish the job. I needed him to be taken up for her death…"

"And so you completed what he began."

"She fought me, but I managed it in the end."

"You scattered her book and toppled stools as you pursued her around the room and tore out her hair as you held her down, broke her rosary and her throat."

"Like I say, if you know…why ask me?"

"As my groom, Cedric, said, you are a piece of work, Burridge."

"That was underhand, sir."

"What was?"

"Getting that lad to pretend to be me. Underhand."

"I knew you'd never stand for it. I knew you'd have to admit that you were Grover's half-brother."

The man shrugged, and his manacles rattled.

I looked down at him with disgust.

"It should have been me. I am the eldest son. It should have been me who inherited the ironworks."

"Perhaps your father realised just what a nasty bastard you are and decided against you."

"I am no bastard."

I walked around the small cell. "Oh yes, you are. "I had a bastard half-brother once," I said. "Strangely, his mind was deranged too."

The man did not seem to notice that I'd called him deranged.

"Oh, what happened to him?"

"He died in Rouen a few years ago."

"Did you kill him?"

Now it was my turn to laugh. "No, I didn't kill him. I'm not like you."

"More fool you then."

"He died, but it wasn't me who exacted revenge. Someone else did it for me," and with a last look of distaste at John Grover, who was Burridge, I turned tail and took the gaol steps two at a time, banging the door after me. It was the last time I ever spoke to him.

I felt a ton lighter. It was a relief to come out into the open, feel the September sun on my face, and leave all that evil down in the base of the keep.

I trotted down the steep steps, and a loud voice hailed me as I stood halfway down, echoing around the stone.

"My lord!"

"Ah, Andrew!"

I located him across the bailey.

He brandished a flask of ale in his hand.

"Fancy a cup of Mistress Brewster's best?"

"Don't mind if I do," I said and I jogged down the remaining steps with a light heart.

Author's Note

Contrary to general belief, there were some black people in early Medieval England. Many of them had come over in the wake of the Crusades and had settled here. Naturally, they were viewed with great suspicion, and I try to convey the difficulties these people had in their daily life in the early 13th century in this book.

This book is my Othello, Desdemona and Iago story, with a twist. I hope Shakespeare will forgive me for my little liberties with his ideas.

There really was iron ore at Seend, near Devizes in Wiltshire, which was extracted from peat dug from bogs - hence bog iron.

Girls were considered adults at twelve, boys at fourteen at the time about which I write. Marriage was permissible at a very young age but was rarely consummated until fifteen or sixteen. A girl might be kidnapped, though, and forced into marriage - known as a rape marriage. This was perfectly legal. Once consummated, the marriage could only be annulled by the intervention of the church.

In the days before newspapers, television, radio and the internet, information was gleaned by word of mouth.

There were few letters and documents circulating giving information. Most people could not read. Gossip, hearsay and rumour were rife. It would be quite easy to blacken someone's name or spread tittle-tattle, scandal and indulge in idle talk when there were very few means of corroboration available to people.

This was a time when town councils were beginning to be formed and more organisation was evolving to make the business of the town more free flowing. Weights and measures were not, as they are now, regulated centrally, and there was more freedom within the environment of the towns of England. Nevertheless, businesses were regulated and the pinter (originating from the word pint) was one of the officers paid to make sure that things ran smoothly.

Glossary

Alaunt - an ancient mastiff-like dog now extinct.
Barbette and crown - headdress worn by ladies. It consisted of a linen band stretched under the chin, and a stiff gathered crown of linen.
Bliaut - a t-shaped dress of wool or silk caught at the waist by a long belt.
Bothy - a small (usually round) house of wattle and daub with a beaten earth floor.
Braies - a man's underclothes.
Carding - a process whereby raw wool (or flax) is teased out on carding combs into long strands.
Deodand - a thing forfeited or given to God, specifically, in law, an object or instrument that becomes forfeited because it has caused a person's death.
Dock Fever - diphtheria, a terrible disease mostly affecting children. So-called because they believed it was introduced at the docks.
Felo de se - suicide.

Gazehound - Sighthounds are a type of hound that hunt primarily by sight and speed rather than by scent and endurance as scent hounds do.

Gyves - Leg irons

Interdict - The Papal Interdict of 1208 was a prohibition laid on England and Wales by Pope Innocent III, which enforced the closure of the churches, forbade the administration of the Catholic sacraments and prohibited the use of churchyards for burials. Issued on 23 March 1208, the interdict lasted for more than six years until it was lifted on 2 July 1214.

Loop - a small window in a castle wall which facilitates the loosing of arrows.

Lymer - a scenthound used on a leash in Medieval times to find large game before it was hunted down by the pack.

Manacles - handcuffs

Melee - a disorganised hand-to-hand combat in battles with little central control once it starts.

Meurtrières - murder holes - holes in the roof of the gateway or passageway in a fortification through which the defenders could shoot, throw or pour boiling water, hot sand or boulders.

Pattens - wooden overshoes for walking outside in bad weather.

Pinter - the man responsible for weights and measures in a town.

Pobbies - a mixture of bread and milk.

Splinter-new - A phrase used in the Medieval at a time when everything was made of wood. Brand new.

Tarriwags - a male animal's genitalia.

Town reeve - mayor

If you have enjoyed
ALYSOUN
(book 15 in the
Savernake series)…

read on for a snippet of

MAIDEN
IN THE MOR!

Maiden in the mor lay,
In the mor lay,
Sevenight fulle,
Sevenight fulle.
Maiden in the mor lay,
In the mor lay,
Sevenight fulle and a day.

Where was hire mete?
Wher what was hire mete?
The primerole and,
The primerole and,
Wher was hire mete?
Wher wat was hire mete?
The primerole and the violet.

Where was hire dring?
What was hire dring?
The chelde water of,
The chelde water of,
Where was hire dring?
What was hire dring?
The chelde water of the welle-spring.

Where was hire bowr?
Where what was hire bowr?
The rede rose and,
The rede rose and,
What was hire bowr?
What was hire bowr?
The rede rose and the lilye flour.

Maiden in the mor lay,
In the mor lay,
Sevenight fulle,
Sevenight fulle.
Maiden in the mor lay,
In the mor lay,
Sevenight fulle and a day.

Maiden in the moor lay,
In the moor lay,
Seven nights full,
Seven nights full.
Maiden in the moor lay,
In the moor lay,
Seven nights full and a day.

Where was her meat?
What was her meat?
The primerole and,
The primerole and,
Where was her meat?
What was her meat?
The primerole and the violet.

Where was her drink?
What was her drink?
The chilled water of,
The chilled water of,
Where was her drink?
What was her drink?
The chilled water of the well-spring.

Where was her bower?
What was her bower?
The red rose and,
The red rose and,
Where was her bower?
What was her bower?
The red rose and the lily flower.

Maiden in the moor lay,
In the moor lay,
Seven nights full,
Seven nights full,
Maiden in the moor lay,
In the morr lay,
Seven nights full and a day.

English song, possibly 13th century

Chapter One

MY NINE-YEAR-OLD-DAUGHTER Hawise had finished rolling the rags into a ball and, as I watched, knotted the last one tightly. She spun it between her hands to squash it down, looked at it carefully, and gave it a tentative push on the wooden floor of the solar.

She took it back, squashed it some more and, with a couple more pushes, declared herself satisfied. She sprang up from the floor, dusted off her kirtle and was off down the solar steps, leaving the rest of the rags lying on the boards.

I had been ill with a head cold over the last few days and was feeling somewhat fragile.

I looked over at my wife, Lydia. “What’s that for?”

“The ball? It’s for Cleaver. He likes to chase balls, and she has made him a soft one with old rags so that they can play indoors safely. The old wooden one Hal made is too heavy, and he just chews it.”

“Hal does?”

“No, don’t be silly.”

Cleaver was my daughter’s six-month-old gazehound, a creature who was all legs, sharp teeth and speed.

“Ah, clever.” I lay back on the bed, my hands locked

behind my head. “I can’t believe how the time has flown since we got him. Three months, and they have whisked by like three weeks!”

Lydia guffawed. “They say it’s a sign of getting old, Aumary, the time flying.”

“Is it?”

She put down her sewing in her lap. “You have little to do at this season. The forest work takes care of itself in December. It will be Christmas soon; you have no real reason to be at the castle… and…”

“No, not until John comes for Christmas,” I said.

“*If* John the King comes for Christmas. Admit it, you’re bored,” she said.

“I am not bored….merely….”

“You’re bored, and if you really want something to do, I can find you some…”

“Ah, no, I’m not that bored,” I said, leaping off the bed and pulling on my boots.

“You need a good murder to get your teeth into. That would suit you,” chuckled my wife.

I had to admit that I did find my role as constable of North Wiltshire diverting and interesting. The king had given me the special role in 1204, for he had been concerned that justice was not being achieved to his complete satisfaction, that felons were not being apprehended for their crimes and that too many innocents were unjustly fined or were going to the gallows because proper evidence was not sought by the sheriffs, whose job it ultimately was.

It was now *my* job, amongst others, to seek for that evidence, pursue the true felons and bring them to justice. Oh, I didn’t mete out that justice. That was ultimately the job of the judges and the sheriff. I just collected the information and apprehended the felon, and I had been doing it successfully for four years. My last true crime had been in September. I had my own manor courts for small misdemeanours and forest offences, but my wife was right; I was bored, although I was not going to admit it, and I had no wish for there to be a murder just to please me and keep me occupied.

> *However, there is a saying, isn't there, Paul, my scribe? 'One must be careful what one wishes for.'*

I sailed down the solar steps and into the hall.

Hal of Potterne, my senior man-at-arms, was there by the fire, whittling a stick into some shape or other. He looked up. "Why I'm sitting by this fire, I 'ave no idea," he said, grinning inanely. "It's not cold today; in fact, it's damned warm." He wiped his wrist across his forehead.

The weather *was* very unseasonable for December. I thought back to the winter of 1204/05 when the little town of Marlborough had gained its charter from the king and I had been made constable. That winter had cut us off from the world here in Durley village, deep in the Forest of Savernake, and the snow and ice had locked us into a white desert for months. Many had died, and we all came close to starvation.

"Better this unseasonable warmth, Hal, than the winter of 1204."

He threw his whittling on the table and preened the twin points of his grey beard, worn long in imitation of his Viking ancestors.

"Aye, that's true enough…I 'ope I never see the like of *that* again in my lifetime."

Into the ensuing silence came the pattering of small feet and harsh breathing.

"Sir…sir…m'lord!"

I turned to the outer door, frowning.

PREVIEW OF THE NEXT BOOK

MAIDEN IN THE MOR

One of my woodwarden's little girls, I'd forgotten her name, came running up to the door hole. She wouldn't come over the threshold but sought my face with huge, frightened eyes.

"Sir, m'lord," She bounced a curtsey. "Come quick."

"What's the matter, Jeanne?" said Hal rising. He knew all the children of the demesne.

"It's the Lady Hawise, sir. She's fallen in the river."

I beamed at her, "Don't worry too much, Jeanne," I said, "she can swim."

"No, sir...I know, but..."

"Yes?"

"I think she's banged her head."

Hal and I flew down the manor's outer steps, across the courtyard, out of the gate and sped towards the willow trees, which leaned out over the river just before the area we called the Salley Gardens.

We knew exactly where Hawise had fallen, for little Cleaver was running up and down the bank barking. We both splashed through the shallows and into the deeper part of the river. The weather was warm, but the water was cold, and it was quite a shock on the legs, belly and loins.

Hal grabbed Hawise's copper hair and quickly turned her over onto her back. I swam around her and lifted her middle. Together, we got my daughter to the bank. Even before we reached it, she was coughing and spluttering, moaning and crying out.

"There...there..." Hal crooned to her as he pushed back her lustrous copper curls, now soaked and darkened. "'Ow did you manage to fall in then?"

Jeanne was hopping from foot to foot on the bank but dared not approach us too closely.

"Thank you, Jeanne. You're a good girl for being so vigilant," I said breathlessly. I rooted in my now sodden purse and fished out a quarter penny. "Here, this is for you."

Her eyes stood out in her head, and she came forward cautiously. "Thank you, m'lord."

"Tell your father what it was you did and why you have the coin."

"Yessir." She skipped off happily.

I turned back to Hawise. We wrung out her clothes, her favourite green bliaut and an under kirtle of palest pink, and then I took her up in my arms and we all sloshed back to the manor.

After a while, Hawise, still coughing, grinned up at me and put her arms around my neck.

Hal followed with the bouncing Cleaver behind him. I pushed back my daughter's hair carefully. There on her forehead was a huge pink abrasion. We got her up the solar stairs, and her mother, her face blanched and shocked, leapt up from her sewing. "Oh, Hawise Belvoir, what have you done now?"

"I fell in the river and banged my head, madam; it's nothing."

Hawise was taken into her room by Lydia and Felice, the childrens' nurse, and all was quiet again.

Hal and I looked at one another.

"I said it was warm," said my man-at-arms, shivering. "I take it back."

The full story emerged a little while later when Hawise, mended, dried and in clean clothes, was sitting up in her bed drinking some warm posset. Hal and I, too, had changed our clothes.

"So, how did you fall in?" I asked. "And how did you

manage to hit your head? There's nothing there in the river upon which to hit it."

Hawise squirmed a little. "Well, you see…"

"This means, my lord, she was doing something she was not supposed to be doing," said her mother sternly.

"Well, no, it's just that…" began my daughter.

"Yes, you were, own up."

"I…I…"

"I don't know why we bothered having boys when we have you, Hawise Belvoir. You are more trouble than both…."

"Lydia," I put out my hand to quell her. She had been very worried, and her concern always came out in a series of accusatory questions.

"Tell us." I sat forward to listen.

"I made the ball, you know, for Cleaver."

"Yes, I watched you do it."

We took it down to the grass by the river, and I threw it for him. He loved it. But I threw it a bit too high, and it got stuck in a tree branch."

I leaned back in my seat. "So you climbed the tree to retrieve it?"

"Yes, and the branch broke and tipped me into the river, and I hit my head on it." She put a shaky hand up to her forehead. The bruise was now quite a lump, and her mother had slathered some kind of green, sweet-smelling ointment onto it. No doubt tomorrow, it would be much less of a bump.

Lydia and I looked at each other. "Hawise, you should have asked someone to get it for you," said her mother intently.

"There was no one about."

"Hal was in the hall; he would have got it for you."

Hal shuffled his feet. "Aye, better that I end up in the

drink than you, my little lady."

Hawise giggled at the thought.

I slapped my knees and stood. "Well, no real harm done."

"Did you get the ball?" asked Hal, "or is it still in the tree?"

"I did get it, but I suppose I dropped it when I fell," said Hawise. "It'll be in the river."

"Then I'll go and look for it."

"Oh no, it's alright, Hal," said my daughter. "I can make Cleaver another one."

"Nah! No trouble. I can fish it out with a stick, I'm sure."

A little while later, Hal was back with the small fabric ball, which was heavy and dripping. He squeezed it out again, as best he could, on the top step of the manor stairs and then brought it into the hall to lay it beside the fire to dry.

"You found it?"

"I did. It weren't all I found, mind."

"Oh…?"

"Aye," He ran the back of his hand over his nose. "I think you'd better come and take a look."

My brow furrowed. "What's the matter?"

"I think your idea of a restful Christmas is about to be given a shake," he said.

Earlier, I had been talking about having a peaceful time, eating, drinking, making merry with my family and friends, and generally resting, for the autumn had been a busy and fraught time.

King John had been stockpiling coin at Marlborough castle and other places that autumn, and it had caused us not a little headache, for we had to store it, guard it and move it about at John's will, and often at short notice. It was known by all, of course, that large amounts of money were travelling the roads to and from Wiltshire, and the trouble it gave us, the biting of our nails, the fretting of our fingers and the tapping of our feet, were symptoms of the nervousness we all felt.

> *Yes, Paul, my scribe, you are quite right; that was the beginning of the trouble John stored up for us all with his stockpiling of money, though it was years before we really understood what had been happening and how it had beggared the country.*

"What…?" I yelled.

Hal jammed his coif on his grey locks. "C'mon. You won't want another dunkin' mind, so we'll take several folks who can get wet instead, shall we, sir?"

We called for Richard Marshall, my head groom, who was, at that moment, standing in the stable doorway talking to Hubert, our farrier. Both turned at the call and downed tools to join us.

We loped at a pace along the road to the village green and turned into the trees at the water's edge. This was a little way downstream from where my daughter had fallen into the water.

Hal squirmed his way under the salleys, the old willows that had jestingly given the place its name, the salley gardens, and that leaned over the river here and almost touched those on the other bank. Our little river was about fourteen feet wide at that place, and there had been enough rain this autumn to ensure it was deep.

I am tall, a full six feet, so I stooped almost bent double to navigate the pathway by the river. Hubert, too, was a big man, a little taller than me and the tallest man in the village, so he, too, had to stoop.

The bank was slippery, and we slithered along until we

reached the largest tree, one that had fallen in the gales of 1203. It had not completely fallen to the ground; it merely leaned out a little more over the river, perching on its companions, upending its roots to the elements. Many of those roots, those not desiccated by the wind, were now swaying gently in the river as it passed, the water gouging a hole under the bank. It would not be long before this tree fell altogether and even though its fellows held it up, we should have to remove it for it would become a danger and a nuisance and probably dam the river.

"There, look." Hal pointed to the other side of the water.

"What? I can't see anything, Master Hal," said Hubert, screwing up his eyes.

"There, see, a little bit o' blue."

"I see it," said Richard.

"Best one of us go over the stones at the washing place and see if we can come upon it from the other bank," I said.

Richard was the last in the line, so he returned the way we'd come and ran up the lane a little. After a while, he re-appeared on the other side of the river, making his way along the other bank.

His boots were wet to the ankles. The stones the women used to rub the laundry were slightly under water further up, and he'd crossed the river there. Richard Marshall came fully into view.

"Here, sir?"

"A little further that way, Rich!" I gesticulated.

Richard slid along the bank, holding on to the branches arching out in graceful curves over the flood.

"Oh, Almighty God. Woe Sakes, sir."

"That's what I thought," said Hal, crossing himself and looking up at me. "It's a body, m'lord."

PREVIEW OF THE NEXT BOOK

MAIDEN IN THE MOR

And so begins the tale I shall dictate to you, Paul, my scribe, from the winter of 1208 and into the spring of 1209 when I, Aumary Belvoir, warden of the forest of Savernake, Lord of Durley, hard by the town of Marlborough in the county of Wiltshire, constable to the King, was severely tried by a series of murders right on my doorstep. Another tale of murder for you to write down for me, for I can't even scribble my name nowadays. Hard to believe when you look at me now, an old man of seventy-three, that I was once a strong young man whose arm could wield a sword with deadly accuracy and ply a pen with veracity and clarity. Everything that happened in the forest and its environs was my business. And sometimes that business was murder.

You ask how exercised I was. For a very long time, I could not piece together this mystery; ingenuity is a mild word for the work of this murderer, and the truth behind this fantastic series of killings was elusive in the extreme. However, with the help of my friend, the doctor of Marlborough town, Johannes of Salerno, and my faithful man-at-arms, Hal of Potterne, I solved it, and justice was seen to be done.

You want to know why I seem so serious, Paul? Well, I have my reasons for seriousness. Take up your pen, and you will see why this tale in particular, is one which makes me sad. I think of all the murders I investigated - this one is very special to me....and you will see why....

It took us some time to get the body from the river, and we were all wet again by the time we had the woman—for woman it was—on the bank.

Hal turned her over. The fish had nibbled and pecked at her face. We stared down.

"Do any of us know her?"

"I hate to state the obvious, but I'd say she's floated down from the Burbage end," said Hubert. "I don't think she's one of ours."

Hal put his hands onto his knees and bent double for a proper look.

"Nah!" he shook his head. "Not one of ours." He knew every village inhabitant and many of the wider forest too.

"She's only a girl," said Rich, wringing out the hem of his tunic. "No more than thirteen, I'd say."

"Sometimes these girls from the outlying villages look older than they really are," said Hal authoritatively. "I bet she's only about eleven or twelve, maybe younger."

"Anyone missing, Hal, that we know about?"

Hal shook his head. "No one. At least no one who's reported missing."

"Yet," added Hubert.

"She's been in the river a while, I'd say," said Hal, looking with practised eyes at the girl again. "A couple of days or more, maybe. Dr Johannes will know."

"Perhaps she, like Hawise, fell in, Hal," I said. "But the doctor will look for suspicious wounds." I turned to Richard. "Can you send Bill to Marlborough town, Rich? We shall send for the coroner once we know what Johannes has found."

"Aye, sir," he sniffed, then turned into the trees.

"I'll fetch a blanket, sir, shall I?" said Hubert, then he was gone through the salleys.

Hal shook his head. "She might not 'a bin found if the little Lady Hawise 'adn't fallen. She mighta' bin halfway to the River Og."

"Perhaps that's what someone wanted, Hal."

MAIDEN IN THE MOR

I searched the immediate area but found nothing unusual.

I hunkered down in front of the small body.

"Not good clothes. Worn but serviceable."

"'Er shoes are the sort the lesser villeins wear," said Hal, lifting an ankle.

"Those that mould around the foot - yes, turnshoes." I picked up a hand. "Rough hands. She works outside, this girl, and she bites her nails."

"Very long hair," said Hal. "She's a bit thin."

"Hmm, that too." I turned her body a little. "Ah, a purse."

Hal offered me his knife, and I cut her purse from the belt around her waist. The small bag was made of thick felted wool.

The purse and everything in it was sodden. We found a bone comb, a quarter of a silver penny, a needle case made of beechwood but no needles, a small wooden spoon, a pretty stone and, strangely, a soggy acorn.

"Why would she keep that?"

"I dunno."

"What's this?"

From a very small piece of folded and oiled cloth, I teased out a fragment of parchment.

My fingers were wet, and I dried them on the back of my cotte so as not to smudge the ink, for the parchment and what was written on it was perfect and dry. I smoothed it out. It was a tiny drawing, a picture showing a man, a rather skeletal figure, in a sort of loincloth, bending over a river. In his hand, he had a large jar, and he was pouring water into the stream.

Hal looked over my shoulder.

"Why's 'e pouring water *into* water and not taking it *out*?"

"I don't know, Hal."

"Why would she 'ave such a thing in 'er purse."

"I don't know that either, Hal."

"She won't be doin' drawin', will she?"

"I doubt she could afford the ink and parchment."

"Why's she got that then?"

I stood up and looked over the river, hearing Hubert coming back with the blanket.

"I have a strange feeling about this, Hal."

"Oh?"

"I can't say why, but I do."

Hubert came up now wearing dry clothes. "Shall I, sir?" He gestured to our body with the blanket.

"Yes, Hubert. We'd also better get someone to wait here for a while until Dr Johannes gets here."

"I'll do it, sir. I don't mind. It's Sunday. I'm not doing anything in particular."

"I'll send James to you for company, shall I?" James was Hubert's apprentice.

My farrier guffawed. "Aw, no, sir, send Tom, he's much better company!"

"All right, I'll ask Tom Potter."

We turned to leave. I took up the sodden purse and held onto the parchment drawing.

By the time we had reached the manor steps, I thought I knew what it was I held in my hand.

"I'll go down to my room and change again," said Hal from across the courtyard. "Shall I meet you in the 'all, sir?"

"Yes, Hal. And I hope to have something to show you when you come back."

I ran up the steps to the solar, changed again and hung my muddy and soggy cotte on a peg to dry. I left my boots by the hearth and donned my indoor felt shoes. Then I took a key, turned it in the lock and rummaged in one of the chests which lay by the door to the back room on the upper floor where the children had their own sleeping place.

Searching through the contents, I found what I was looking for right at the bottom. I did not possess many books, but I had a few which had been left to me by a very learned man, my half-brother's tutor, many years ago. These were very valuable, so I kept them locked away from prying eyes and sticky little fingers.

Master Quimper had owned five books, and it was one of them I was looking for now. Amongst his possessions, he had a book on medicine. I pulled out the large, heavy volume and locked the chest again.

"Here, Hal," I said as my man-at-arms came back in through the hall door, buckling on a belt.

"What's that then?"

"I knew that I had seen that little drawing before...or something very like it."

Hal screwed up his eyes and scrutinised the drawing in the book I'd laid out on the hall table.

"Ah...It *is* like it, i'n't it?" He blinked. "What is it?"

"Your natal day is very close to mine, Hal."

"Aye, March 28th, as I remember me ol' mam sayin'."

"We are both born under the sign of Aries, the ram."

"Aye, we are. You on the 25th, the Feast of the Annunciation, and me three days later."

I took the little folded drawing and smoothed it out on top of the page in the book.

"This is Aquarius, Hal."

"Aye, it is, the water man."

"The water *bearer*."

Hal sat down on the bench beside me.

"What's that doin' in the purse of a woman that couldn't read, write, or draw?"

"It puzzles me, Hal."

"An' more 'an that, a woman that's drowndid in water?"
I shrugged.
"Are yer thumbs prickin'?"
"Yes, Ol' Hal, they most certainly are."
"Well, I'll be bugg...buried in Burbage!" he exclaimed.

S

The Savernake Forest Series
Susanna M. Newstead

Belvoir's Promise
She Moved Through the Fair
Down By the Salley Gardens
I Will Give My Love an Apple
Black is the Colour of My True Love's Hair
Long Lankyn
One Misty Moisty Morning
The Unquiet Grave
The Lark in the Morning
A Parcel of Rogues
Bushes & Briars
Though I Live Not Where I Love
Wynter Wakeneth
Worldes Blis
Alysoun
Maiden in the Mor

Other Historical Fiction

I Am Henry - **Jan Hendrik Verstraten & Massimo Barbato**
The Sebastian Foxley Series - **Toni Mount**
The Death Collector - **Toni Mount**
The Falcon's Rise & The Falcon's Flight - **Natalia Richards**
The Reversible Mask - **Loretta Goldberg**

History Colouring Books

The Mary, Queen of Scots Colouring Book - **Roland Hui**
The Life of Anne Boleyn Colouring Book - **Claire Ridgway**
The Wars of the Roses Colouring Book - **Debra Bayani**
The Tudor Colouring Book - **Ainhoa Modenes**

PLEASE LEAVE A REVIEW

If you enjoyed this book, *please* leave a review at the book seller where you purchased it. There is no better way to thank the author and it really does make a huge difference!
Thank you in advance.